The Unoriginal Sinner and the ICE-CREAM GOD

John R. Powers

cbi Contemporary Books, Inc.
Chicago

Library of Congress Cataloging in Publication Data

Powers, John R.
    The unoriginal sinner & the ice-cream God.

    I. Title.
PZ4.P8893Un   [PS3566.087]   813'.5'4   77-75850
ISBN 0-8092-7929-0

Published by Contemporary Books, Inc.
180 North Michigan Avenue, Chicago, Illinois 60601
Manufactured in the United States of America
Library of Congress Catalog Card Number: 77-75850
International Standard Book Number: 0-8092-7929-0

Published simultaneously in Canada by
Beaverbooks
953 Dillingham Road
Pickering, Ontario L1W 1Z7
Canada

To Once Upon A Time,
The People and the Places of Mt. Greenwood

Time is like a handful of sand. The tighter you grasp it, the faster it runs through your fingers. But if you caress it, as a mother does a child in her arms, it will leave in its wake memories of its gentle flow rather than the roughness of its stones.

ACKNOWLEDGMENTS

Just call me Hardrock. Randy. Mary, Margo Powers for that night at the roller rink. John F. and June R. Powers. Gay and Dr. Joseph V. Gioioso for their contributions. Joey, Randy Marie, Danielle. Dr. Martin J. Maloney of Northwestern University and Bill Wright for both their professional and personal assistance. Dan Bardy, Mary Gutekanst, Blair Kaplan and Fran Kotre for their interest and help in my work.

ONE

Alone.

Sitting in Parlor Number Three of Collier's Funeral Home. Remembering the first time I was in this room.

Thirteen years old. My parents and all of us older kids in the family were attending my Great Uncle Elmer's funeral. He wasn't great. My mother, whose uncle he really was, didn't like him. The rest of my family barely knew him. No matter. There is a magnetic force between the Irish and open coffins.

I had only a flashing memory of the man from when I was three or four years old. Hats and coats already on, my parents were standing at Uncle Elmer's door saying their good-byes. My Uncle Elmer picked me up and began playfully tossing me high into the air. Each time, as I hung momentarily suspended just before the downfall, I scanned my choices: going higher and smashing into the ceiling or falling back down to Uncle Elmer's bad breath and dirty hands. Discovering at an early age that gravity makes all the important decisions.

As they were getting ready to close Uncle Elmer's casket, the funeral director stood beside it and gestured towards the hallway as he talked. "Will everyone please come up and take a last look at Mr. Elmer Keegan and then pass out."

Giggles began gurgling in my throat. My father, sitting in the next chair, turned and threw his most ferocious frown at me. Despite my father's glare, and even my own feeble attempt to move it along, my mind remained riveted on the moment that was continuing to combust my laughter. I didn't realize it then, but I was a victim of my age. The younger ones didn't get it and the older ones didn't care to.

Still attempting to suppress a smirk, I whispered to my father that I had to go to the washroom. He gave me one of his patented pathetic nods.

Fully clothed, sitting in the only stall, laughing hysterically. When the laughter began subsiding, I would re-ignite it by thinking of the situation again, like an addict reaching for the needle to postpone that drop to ground level.

I heard the washroom door open. Silence, as I held my breath to choke off the laughter. He turned on the faucet. A geyser of pent-up laughs erupted out of me. The faucet was turned off. Still laughing, I began furiously flushing the toilet. It was a hydraulic flushing system so it gave off quite a whoosh.

"Are you all right in there?" he asked.

"Oh, yes sir, I'm fine, fine." Still laughing and flushing. I wondered if he thought I was hysterical with grief over losing old Uncle Elmer the tosser.

"You sure?"

"Yes sir, I'm sure."

The water was turned on again. A few seconds later, I heard the washroom door open and close.

I came out of the stall and went over to the mirror. My eyes were red and glistening with tears. When I walked back into Parlor Number Three, everyone, including Uncle Elmer, was gone. I imagined my parents and my brothers and sisters sitting in the car waiting for me, my mother's lecture already loaded and ready to be fired. "Now you've really fixed yourself. This is the last funeral you'll be going to for a long, long time."

An old lady toddled back into the parlor and picked up a pair of black gloves that she had apparently forgotten on the folding chair. She scowled at me, "I hope someone laughs at your funeral." As she spoke, a slight but sharp sneer slid across her wrinkled, riddled face. I thought it but I didn't say it. I hope everyone laughs at my funeral.

Later that afternoon, I went over to Caepan's apartment and, using the key he gave me, opened his mailbox and put in a note:

> *Dear God:*
>
> *Why do people die?*
>
> *Signed: Conroy*

I wasn't sure myself if it was a silly question or a serious one.

Early the next morning, I went back to Caepan's mailbox and retrieved the reply:

> *Conroy:*
>
> *Most people do not die. They cease to exist. In order to die, you first have to live. Don't forget, you owe me for two Cokes including deposits if you don't bring the bottles back.*
>
> *Signed: God*

I glance at my watch. Only five o'clock. Still a few hours to wait. Why not? No hurry.

Listening to the pattern of rush hour traffic outside the walls of Parlor Number Three. Every few moments, the purr of motors permeates the darkened room with a slight grumble and quickly swells into a muffled roar. Shortly, the shouts of traffic are turned off by the traffic light at the corner.

I remember reading somewhere that the song "Moon River" was written in twelve minutes. The next time the traffic is forced to hold its breath, I watch the second hand on my watch. Thirty seconds. Catching the red twenty-four times. Not that many. Wondering how many "Moon Rivers" have been lost at traffic lights.

Almost everyone in the neighborhood stops at Collier's Funeral Home for two or three days before leaving for good.

I look around Parlor Number Three and imagine the pockets of laughter and sorrow that inevitably fester in such places. Hearing the litany of unfinished sentences. "I'm sorry..." The last few words not being verbalized perhaps because even the speakers are unaware of them. "I'm sorry I had to come."

When I was an altar boy, funerals were supposed to be a good deal. They got you out of at least an hour and a half of school. But in all the years I was an altar boy, I only got four funerals and two of them were on Saturdays. How rotten can a guy be that he'd allow himself to be buried on a Saturday. Not only do none of his friends get the day off, but he ruins the weekend for them besides.

The last time I was in this room was eight years ago, just before I started college. A neighbor, Mr. Kearney, had died. He had a cute niece. I was talking to her when I saw Father Kepp, one of the parish priests, walk in. I knew what was coming next; a request for everyone to drop to their knees for a half dozen "Our Fathers," "Hail Marys," and "Glory Be's." I wanted to get the niece out to the lobby so that I could talk to her for a few more minutes.

"We can go this way," I said to her. Although my body had already turned around to head for the lobby, my eyes were still looking at the niece when I felt myself doing a somersault over somebody's shoulder. When I got up, I realized that I had flattened some neighborhood woman as she was kneeling to pray along with Father Kepp. They almost had to pry the rosary out of her chest. It was very embarrassing. The niece told me to do what her uncle had just done. Almost everybody in the place stoned me with dirty looks, but a few people thought it was funny.

Tonight, no laughs.

TWO

Mine was a family of practicing Catholics and though I practiced constantly I never got any better. When I got older, much older, people would sometimes ask me, "Are you still a Catholic?" Like asking a black person, "Well, I know you were raised Black, but what are you today?"

Straight lines of bulky bungalows and square shouldered apartment buildings ran through my neighborhood on Chicago's South Side. Often, their march was capped at the corner by a ma and pa food store, a gas station, or a "You can pick it up next Tuesday" twenty-four hour cleaner. It was the kind of neighborhood where fathers never went to stores to buy bikes for their children. Your father would always know somebody who knew somebody who knew somebody. Or maybe he'd find it in the alley, with a kid on it. In my neighborhood, if you left the house in the morning without a lunch pail, then you couldn't be going to work.

For the first part of my life, I served the sentence of childhood for the crime of growing up. Never was I able to discover any advantages to being little. My parents told me when to eat and sleep and what I couldn't do, which was everything I wanted to do. Teachers told me what to learn and when to learn it. Every kid in the neighborhood had enough muscle to tell me where to go.

Each afternoon after school, I was allowed to play outside for two hours. I was a small weak child with a big strong mouth. Where other children had tongues, I had a razor and where they had fists, I had wet palms.

I did a lot of running, mostly in a state of terror. When you're scared you run hard. I could wear out a pair of gym shoes in a block.

During a science class, the nun told us that over ninety percent of our body weight was liquids. I wasn't surprised. She had merely confirmed what I already knew; I was mostly adrenaline and sweat.

One afternoon, I went to a neighborhood barber shop, to my favorite barber, Mario, to get a haircut. Mario could not only cut hair, he also played a great second base for a local park team. A true renaissance man. Some kids came to my house after I left and asked my mother if I could come out and play. She was delighted that I had finally found some friends and told them where I was. Those kids were out to get me. I had to run home from the barber shop. As I ran by a neighbor who was holding a struggling baby, she smiled and said, "You sure are lucky to be a kid."

My father was from a family of fifteen children. He fought World War II and won. My mother came from a family of eleven. There were seven children in mine. When I was very young, there was a cartoon character on a lunch time television show named "Uncle Danny Duck." One of my older sisters convinced me that Uncle Danny Duck was really one of my uncles that I just hadn't met yet.

Throughout my growing up years, I was often accused of having a "smart mouth." But apparently, my intelligence went no further than the roof of it. I did rotten in school. For twelve straight years, my teachers told my parents that I wasn't applying myself. The first time I heard that, I thought they were talking about a paint brush.

I went to a Catholic school where we were taught that our

bodies lived in a democracy but our souls lived in a kingdom. Nobody elected God.

The school was extremely overcrowded. There were at least eighty-five kids in a classroom. We often had to share textbooks. The nuns were tyrants. A former graduate of my grammar school, who happened to end up in the state prison a few years later, told kids in the neighborhood that the prison was easier.

Many of the nuns had no more than two years of college. A state educator once came to the school and spent the day observing various classrooms. He told the principal that, of all the nuns he observed, not one of them used modern educational methods or had any idea of proper teaching techniques. If those nuns couldn't teach, they were very good at working miracles. We learned to read and write better than most.

In first grade, we were told that we were made in the image and likeness of God. I found it difficult to imagine a god that weighed thirty-seven pounds, had suspenders that wouldn't stay clamped to his pants, and had to force his feet into shoes already tied because he was afraid he wouldn't remember how to knot a bow.

We were also informed that we had, as infants, been baptized because we had come into this world with Original Sin, the sin of Adam and Eve eating the apple. The moment we were born, God was already ticked off at us.

I received my sex education from rumors, innuendos, paperback books that I was too young to buy, library books with titles that I couldn't pronounce, and observations of the most elementary kind.

Even when I was very young, it was common knowledge that women went to the hospital to have babies. But I had noticed they bloated up before they went. I was still at that age where ignorance blinded me to embarrassment so I asked my mother if there was any connection.

"Why do women get big before they go to a hospital for their babies?"

"You mean 'swell up'?"

"I guess."

"Oh," she said nonchalantly, "Everyone's stomach swells when they get nervous."

"Does mine?"

"Sure," she replied, "but only a little so you can't notice. But women who are going to get a baby worry a lot about whether the baby is going to be healthy."

When I was in second grade, and doing very badly at the blackboard, I waited for my navel to start pushing out over the top of my pants.

Wayne Leker was a good friend of mine. When he was a little kid, his mother told him that babies came from seeds. One day, Wayne's mother told him that there was soon going to be a new baby in the house. For the next few weeks, every morning, Wayne got up and checked to see if there was one growing in the back yard.

On a Monday afternoon, when we were both about thirteen years old, we went to the public library. Wayne was always interested in how things worked. His father had spent the entire weekend working on the furnace so Wayne was now looking for a book on furnaces. As his eyes skimmed along the shelves, they were grabbed by the title of a thin green book, *Female Anatomy*. Unlike the house furnace, Wayne's was just beginning to heat up.

We sat hunched over at a corner table as Wayne read in a whisper. "Among other sexual functions, the female breasts are used to offer security and comfort to the husband. . . . "

So that's what they're for, I thought to myself. The book read like the pamphlet the family had received with the new television set. "The dial on the upper right is for fine tuning and contrast while the lower dial is used to control volume. . . . "

In eighth grade, after the boys had been segregated from the girls, the priest told us that sports was an excellent way to burn up the "excess energy" that gave us impure thoughts. "No, no, Frank, you dribble the ball, you don't make love to it."

We were repeatedly told that sex belonged only in marriage and that, if we were lucky, we did not. The priests constantly told us to search our consciences to see if we had a "vocation." In other words, was God calling us to the priesthood? After all, Christ never married. He was the original Lone Ranger.

Like probably every other generation that has ever or will ever live, including the one that we have yet to raise, we young men were taught that women were to worship, despise, humiliate and fear. Millions of *me* grew up and made Hugh Hefner a rich man. And he never even bothered to send the Church a thank you note.

Life was a test, we were told, and God was the judge. If we played by His rules, the Church's rules actually, we would go to Heaven. They were kind of vague about what Heaven was. They did say we'd be able to look at God for eternity, which didn't sound too thrilling. But they were very specific about Hell. We would literally burn forever.

Like a test, life wasn't to be enjoyed but sweated out. And praying on your deathbed that the verdict was in your favor. For this kind of life we were expected to constantly give thanks to God for being alive. We were also supposed to love Him.

One day, in third grade, the nun had us discuss what we wanted to be when we grew up. No one showed any inclination to be an electrical engineer, a biochemist or anthropologist. Our dreams of the future were reasonable and easy to pronounce. Most of my classmates wanted to be priests, firemen, policemen, doctors, lawyers, nurses, teachers and mothers. Not me. I didn't know what else there was, but I knew I wanted it.

One of the nuns had told the class that you had to go to school for twenty years before you could be a doctor or a lawyer, so those two were out.

I had no desire to be a fireman. Even as a kid, I realized that running into burning buildings was not a very sane way to make a living.

I could never be a policeman. When I was younger and we used to play "cops and robbers," I was the only robber who always chose to plea bargain rather than shoot it out.

Before I was nine, I didn't want to be anything in particular. But that summer, my grandfather took me to a White Sox-Yankee doubleheader, and from that day I dreamed of becoming a major league baseball player.

Baseball was the perfect career for me. Not only did I love playing the game but I also figured that, since I could already count up to nine innings, I didn't need another day of education to be a major league ball player. For the rest of my grammar school years, and all of my high school years, I could fake it, which was exactly what I did. And had been doing.

I became convinced that when God thought up me, He created the perfect baseball player. Within my body, He had installed the confidence of Henry Aaron, the arrogance of Babe Ruth, the desire of Ty Cobb and the canniness of Casey Stengel. It took me years to discover the only thing that God had forgotten—talent.

In sixth grade, I read in a magazine that the chances of a kid eventually making it to the major leagues were one in ten thousand. At that age, I weighed less than the wind, had the complexion of a bed sheet and possessed eyes that looked like they lived at the end of a tunnel. I wondered what the other 9,999 were going to do for a living.

In many ways, my childhood was the same as a Jersey cow's. Whenever I got the chance, I stood in an empty field and waited for something to happen. I was a baseball fanatic and living proof that you don't have to be good to be obsessed.

When I managed to get into a neighborhood game, I would always be relegated to right field, the graveyard of baseball. Every few hours, a ground ball would plod towards me through the long grass. No matter how fast I ran, the ball would always have stopped by the time I got to it. Regardless, I would pick it up and heave it in the general direction of the infield to whichever kid was yelling loudest at me. Once or twice a week, a fly ball would float out to right field. On good days, I would almost catch it.

I spent most of my time in right field performing such traditional trivia as pounding my fist into my glove and chewing a huge wad of gum. Actually, I daydreamed a lot out there. I imagined myself racing deep into center field for a long fly ball. I would feel my spikes biting into the grass as I sprinted towards the wall. Glove outstretched, my head looking back over my shoulder to watch the flight of the ball, I would suddenly realize that my spikes were now digging into the dirt on the warning track. The wall was only a few feet away. Fearlessly, I would take one more long stride and leap high, my glove snaring the ball as I simultaneously slammed into the wall.

After collapsing to the ground, I would struggle to my feet and, although still dazed, I would throw the ball to second base, cutting down the runner who was trying to advance on the out. The rows of fans above the wall would madly cheer my efforts, but I'd ignore them.

I would walk around in a small circle, my glove hanging limply in my throwing hand while the other hand wiped the sweat from my brow and readjusted my cap. Coaches and players would come running out to me, but I'd wave them back. Quickly then I'd rub the crux of my neck and twist my head back and forth a few times so that the more astute fans would realize that I had, indeed, nearly broken my neck running into that wall.

Across the alley from my house, more specifically my garage, was the mammoth back wall of the Methodist Church. In the top center section of the wall was a large stained glass window, which contained an image of Jesus Christ.

Some Protestant friends of mine had told me that the stained glass Jesus overlooked their altar on the other side. Maybe. Being Catholic, I had to take their word for it. I wasn't allowed to go into churches other than my own. At that time, the Catholic Church felt that if you did something like that, you were admitting to the possibility that God actually had some use for Methodists or whatever.

I considered it a personal favor of God's that I had been born in a house that had such a huge wall in the alley for my private use. None of that bouncing the ball off the front steps stuff for me.

Although no one ever said so, I was sure that a lot of the neighborhood kids were jealous of my wall. And it was hardly the kind of thing you could ask your parents to get you for Christmas. Of course, any kid could have come along and used the wall, but no one ever did. Either you have a Methodist church wall behind your garage or you don't. It's not the same when you have to walk somewhere to use it.

Behind my garage and in my mind existed the entire National and American leagues. A major league game was played almost every night off the church wall. Rules, known only to me, were strictly enforced ("A ball caught as it bounces off the garage wall is a single. But if it hits the ground after bouncing off the garage then it's a double.") The box scores of one season would often fill three spiral notebooks. Periodically, I'd get bored with the whole scene and I'd throw all the spiral notebooks away. But within a few weeks, I'd be back in the alley with a new rubber ball and a new spiral notebook.

I could get all kinds of ground balls, line drives, and fly balls to bounce off that Methodist church wall. There was also just the right amount of alley between the church and my family's garage. If I threw the rubber ball through the telephone wires up to the bricks just above the stained glass Jesus' head, I would get a fly ball whose arc would carry it to the top part of the garage wall. Timing my leap perfectly, I would, most of the time, grab the ball just as it was about to bounce off the garage wall for extra bases. The fans loved it.

By the time I was eleven or twelve, playing with a rubber ball became so blasé that I switched to using a golf ball. I quickly discovered that a golf ball never comes off a brick wall the same way twice. Sometimes, the golf ball would crawl off the Methodist church wall with so little energy that the resulting ground ball would hardly reach me. Other times, the golf ball would careen off the wall with such force that it would rocket over the garage, the back yard and even the house, landing somewhere in the street.

Early one summer evening, right after supper, I went out to the alley to play a few games. Just warming up, I stood a few feet from the Methodist church wall and casually tossed the golf ball at the bricks. It hit and floated in a lazy lob over my head towards the garage wall. I turned and ran the few feet across the alley, hoping to catch the golf ball as it softly bounced off the wood of the garage. I was within a few feet of the wall when I noticed the protruding nail. The possibility had hardly formed in my mind when the golf ball hit the head of the nail and screamed back into my forehead.

Terror reigned inside my head. Everything was pushing to get out. For the first time in my life, I really thought I was dying. I could see my parents finding my body lying in the alley, a golf ball implanted in my forehead.

Struggling to open my eyes through the pain, I saw the stained glass Jesus, His colors alive with the rays of the setting sun, looking down at me. I began praying so intensely that the pain got even worse. Then I remembered that the stained glass Jesus was Methodist. My prayers would do no good. He was probably glad that His wall had nearly taken a Catholic's head off.

A few minutes later, propped up on my knees, I brushed the tear dampened gravel and dirt from my face and felt for the lump on my forehead. It felt larger than the golf ball that had caused it. Gradually, I got up and looked around for my glove. I found it sprawled behind a garbage can.

Opening the back gate and walking through the yard, I wondered what I'd be doing now if that golf ball had actually killed me. If I was unlucky and had gone to Hell, I'd be burning, that's all. In Heaven, according to the nuns, the Beatific Vision, seeing God, was a very big deal so that probably would have kept me busy for the night and the next couple of days. But what about after the novelty wore off?

Heaven was a totally spiritual world so there couldn't be any baseball. Then I realized that I wouldn't even be able to dream about baseball or anything at all. It wouldn't make sense for God to go through all the trouble of creating Heaven and then allowing people to dream about something else.

I was getting very worked up about all of this. It's a very bad habit of mine; worrying terrifically over something that I don't even know is true or not. Even while I'm doing the worrying, I know it's dumb because I know I don't have any control over what I'm worrying about anyway.

Dying and not being able to dream.

It wasn't until I graduated from college that I discovered that I really had something to worry about.

During eight years of grammar school and four years of high school, I learned almost nothing. As I've already mentioned, I did learn to read and write. I also knew my basic colors and could recognize most numbers. That was it.

Despite my less than brilliant academic record, my parents constantly informed me that I was going to college. I never gave much thought to it. Like most kids, even though I wanted to grow up, I ignored all the obvious evidence that surrounded me and refused to believe that if I was a kid long enough, I would unavoidably become an adult. Besides, I was going to play baseball when I grew up. You don't hit home runs with a diploma.

But as I grew older, I discovered that it took more than desire, a garage, an alley, and a Methodist church wall to become a major league baseball player.

During high school, I worked a number of part-time jobs and

realized that the only thing I liked less than school was work. Upon graduating from high school, I chose the lesser of two evils. Having graduated in the bottom twentieth of my high school class, yet still determined that I was not going to work for a living, I applied to and was rejected by over thirty-five colleges. Then someone told me to apply to Chicago's city college, Engrim University, because Engrim accepted just about anybody. I did. He was right. I was in.

THREE

Caepan owned a gas station, not a service station. There's a difference. A service station is a spiffy little structure that took about ten minutes to be snapped together. Both the attendants and the bathrooms perpetually flash hygienic smiles.

When you pull into a service station, besides getting gas, your oil is checked, your windows are cleaned and the attendant always says, "Thank you, sir, have a nice day." The mechanical ability of the average service station attendant extends to the point of putting air in your tires.

A gas station, at least Caepan's gas station, consisted of a large garage that seemed on the verge of swallowing up the small glass enclosed attached office that huddled meekly alongside it. The station, and the wide asphalt apron that surrounded it, were always crowded with cars in various stages of undress. A solid crust of grease covered everything in and around Caepan's gas station. You would no more sit on one of Caepan's toilets than you would sit on any other animal. People in the area lived in constant fear of someone dropping a match around Caepan's gas station. The explosion would have leveled the neighborhood.

Caepan owned a big dog named Butcher whose growl would send shivers through your stomach. Butcher was a gas station chameleon. He had been around Caepan's place so long that his fur had turned the same color as the grime that coated the gas station. When Butcher would lie down, it was almost impossible to see him. Walking around Caepan's gas station, you always had the fear that the patch of grease you were about to step on was Butcher.

Caepan was a massive man whose body was liberally, but solidly, spread over a six-and-a-half-foot frame. Although he never wore tight fitting clothes, you could still see his muscles rippling below the surface.

He was even stronger than he looked. The first year I knew him, Caepan decided to move the pop machine inside for the winter. It was one of those big upright kinds. I offered to get the two wheel truck for him. Caepan told me not to bother. He walked up to the side of the pop machine, put a flat hand on either side, pushed in, lifted it up and carried it inside the garage.

When it came to cars, Caepan was a messiah. He could put his hand on the hood and tell you what was wrong with the engine. Caepan loved working on cars and always had. He claimed that when he was a baby, he had a pacifier that was shaped like a steering wheel. Caepan wouldn't allow himself to put in more than twelve hours a day at his station because he believed that too much fun wasn't good for anybody.

Caepan kept gas pumps on the premises only because he was required to by the property lease. The only people who would pull into his station for gas were those whose tanks or heads were on empty.

When a car drove up and rang the bell at the gas pump, Caepan would come stomping out of the garage with all the patience of a brain surgeon who had just been called out of the operating room to take a collect call. He would say nothing as he filled up the tank and gruffly shoved his hand through the driver's window for the money. Butcher could be counted on to urinate on one of the fenders.

Caepan bought the gas station when I was in eighth grade. The place had been boarded up for years before that because there were at least four other gas stations within a few blocks of the site.

Part of his gas station was still boarded up the first day I stopped in to see Caepan. I was always anxious to meet new people in the neighborhood because anyone who knew me well didn't like me. Besides, it was a cold, snowy day and I wanted to warm up before I walked the rest of the way home.

That afternoon, I was worrying about whether I was losing my Catholic faith. During my morning religion class, Father Falkin, one of the parish priests, had told us the story of how Satan, the fallen angel, attempted to usurp the authority of God.

Satan, and all the angels that chose to follow him, tried to overthrow God. But St. Michael the Archangel, (it should be pointed out that he became a saint only after he won), defended God against His attackers. Not surprisingly, God's side won. Satan and all of his followers were sent to Hell, thereby becoming the devils for all eternity. But, apparently, just to make life interesting, God gave Satan the power to roam the world seeking the ruin of others.

It was a story we had all heard before. But this time, I found myself cheering for Satan. Who can hate a guy for trying to get ahead? Besides, I thought it was a cheap shot for God to send Satan to Hell. After all, God, being God, knew He couldn't lose. So what was the harm in Satan trying anyway? It was just another way for Father Falkin to drive home the same old line: "Don't mess with the big fellow."

Caepan was trying to get the bathroom door open when he heard me behind him. "Yeah? What can I do for you, kid?"

"Oh, nothing. I just stopped in to say 'hello.' My name's Tim Conroy. I live a couple of blocks from here."

Caepan noticed my school case. "You coming home from school?"

"Yeah. I'm in the eighth grade at St. Christina's, up on 111th Street."

Caepan glanced at his watch. "It's almost four-thirty. Kind of late to be coming home from school."

"I had to stay after."

Caepan finally got the door unjammed. He picked up a screwdriver and began tinkering with the lock. "What for?"

"I got caught holding some snow on the playground during the noon hour."

"And you were kept after school for that?"

"Yeah, because it looked like I was about to make a snowball."

"So what?"

"We're not allowed to make snowballs. The nuns told us that snowballs are very dangerous."

"You're kidding?"

"No. You can get suspended, even expelled, for throwing one."

"That's crazy," declared Caepan. He stuck the screwdriver in his back pocket and turned the bathroom doorknob back and forth a few times. "Seems all right now," he said to himself.

Caepan went over to the old wooden desk and began rummaging through the drawers, grabbing handfuls of debris and tossing them on the floor. He seemed to be forgetting I was there.

"I don't think it's so crazy," I said. I had a suspicion it was, but I felt an obligation to defend the nuns' craziness against Caepan.

"You don't, huh?"

"No. My nun told us how, a few years ago, some kid's eye got knocked out by a snowball."

Caepan was struggling to pull out a piece of paper that had become lodged behind one of the drawers. "You believe that story?"

"Sure, I do."

Caepan sat back in the swivel chair as he shoved all the drawers closed. "First of all, that story, most likely, isn't true. And even if it is, if all it took was a snowball to knock out that kid's eye, it was probably due to fall out anyway. Those teachers are handing you a line of shit, kid."

A line of shit! I was instantly stunned and fascinated. An adult actually saying that one of his own, a teacher at that, was handing me a line of shit. Of course, I had often suspected that teachers occasionally stretched the truth. But I would have never been capable of wording the accusation so elegantly.

"Are you an atheist?" I asked.

Caepan laughed as he got out of his chair and began sweeping up his office.

"I'll do that for you," I said as I reached for the broom.

"Thanks, kid." Caepan stood the broom up and let the handle fall towards me. He sat way back in his chair, forcing it completely onto its two hind legs. The heels of his feet strained to maintain an uneasy balance. "No, I'm not an atheist," said Caepan. "I just don't like God."

That sent my mind reeling. I had been warned about atheists and I had often been told that I had to love God. But no one had ever talked about liking Him.

"You don't like Him?"

"No, I think He's a jerk."

"A jerk!"

"Let's say there was a kid that sat next to you in school," said Caepan. "He never smiled and he never laughed. And every day you were expected to say hello to him and talk to him. But he would never talk to you. If he took you out and showed you a good time, you were supposed to thank him. But if he took you out and made sure that you had a lousy time, you were supposed to say, 'Well, that's okay because that's the way my friend wanted it.' What would you call that friend?"

I had no idea of what Caepan was talking about and he knew it.

Caepan sprung out of the chair, yawned and stretched his arms wide. Though he said nothing, I quickly translated the gesture, "Time to get lost, kid," and began moving towards the door.

"Well, I'll be seeing you," I said.

"You like to fool around with cars, kid? You know, work on them?"

"No, I'm too young." My age had nothing to do with it. I'm just not very mechanically inclined. My father once gave me a set of wrenches. The only time I touched them was seven years later when I threw them out. As I grew older, I didn't change. As long as a car continued to run for me, I wouldn't have looked under the hood even if there were a pair of legs sticking out from under it.

"Do you like to work on bikes?" asked Caepan.

"No."

"What do you like?"

"I play baseball a lot."

"Terrific," said Caepan blandly.

"Oh, you play, too?"

"No, no. Do you play very well?"

"Uh . . . some days I'm pretty good."

"Then why do you play it?"

"I like it."

I half opened the door to leave. "You really don't like God?"

"Nope."

"Why not?" I yelled defensively.

Caepan reached over my back and pointed to a spot. "Can you scratch there?"

"Yeah, easy." I stretched my arm behind me, but I couldn't reach the spot. Putting down my school case, I reached with the other arm but was still unsuccessful.

"See," said Caepan smugly, "sloppy work. He should have made your arms longer."

"That's silly," I said as I picked up my school case. I usually didn't speak so freely with an adult but I could sense that, with Caepan, the usual social protocol between kid and adult was unnecessary.

"You're right, it is silly," he said.

I had him on the run. "You think you could do a better job than God does?" The words were delivered almost with a shout.

"Yeah, I think so," Caepan drawled.

"You do?" My voice was flat now, his reply having punctured my confidence.

"Sure," he said.

"Prove it." Now I had him.

"Do you pray to God?"

"All the time."

"Do you get answers?"

"Sure."

"Let's see one of them."

"You don't get those kinds of answers," I said.

"What kind do you get?"

"I don't know. I mean, you get answers, you just don't get the kind you can show to somebody else."

"Yeah," said Caepan, "and when you're absolutely positive you didn't get an answer, some adult tells you, 'God heard your prayers. It's just that His answer was no.'"

This man had obviously been around.

"I tell you what," said Caepan. "The next time you have a question for God, you pray to Him for the answer. Then you ask me and I'll give you an answer. See which one you like best."

"Liking an answer doesn't make it the right answer," I said, suddenly aware that I had given a reasonably intelligent reply.

"Good point. Then you decide which one's the right answer."

"No ... I'd feel kind of goofy asking you questions as if you were God."

"That," said Caepan, "is your problem. All I can do is make the offer."

For the next few weeks, every couple of days, I'd stop in and talk to Caepan. We didn't talk about God again, though, just about things in general.

Report card day. Walking slowly to school, expecting the worst. I hadn't bothered praying to God. Long ago, the nuns had said that, in such matters as grades, God only helped those who helped themselves by studying. Of course, the nuns didn't bother mentioning that those students were just the ones who didn't need God's help. That was the trouble with praying to God. There was always a qualifying clause that made you ineligible for benefits. God would have done well in the insurance business.

As I walked by Caepan's gas station, I noticed that it wasn't open yet. I ripped a sheet of paper out of my spiral notebook, scribbled a request, folded the paper and stuck it under his door.

That afternoon, I got a report card that was even worse than I expected. On the way home from school, I walked a few blocks out of my way to avoid going by Caepan's gas station.

When I went by his place the next morning, I saw a piece of paper sticking out from beneath the door.

> *Conroy:*
>
> *I'm God, not a genie. I answer questions, I don't grant wishes. Since you didn't ask a question, I've decided to go a few up on you by giving you some answers anyway.*
>
> *First of all, just because someone works for me, you shouldn't believe everything they say. I've never been that fussy about who I hire.*

Now contrary to what some of these people might have said, I find being God a lot of fun. I'm very rich, you know. I own everything. I enjoy being alive and so I always have been.

I like to create things: Mountains, forests, oceans, people.

People are the toughest things of all to create. They're so minute and delicate. Just the wrong touch of this or that and you can ruin one of them.

Having people around makes me feel good. Mountains, forests, oceans and animals don't tell me how important I am. Well, they do, but not in as nice a way as people. Let's face it, you can't have a good time at a party when you're the only one there. I need you.

Signed: God

I saw Caepan the next day. He didn't say anything about the letter I had sent him or his reply. There would be other letters and other replies. But neither of us would ever mention them.

FOUR

A few weeks before I was due to start college, my Uncle Ted came over after supper to help me and my father get a few things down from the rafters in the garage. He was only about twenty years older than me. My Uncle Ted lived two blocks away in the "family" apartment building. My Aunt Millie, Uncle Bob and their two kids lived on the first floor. On the second floor lived Elizabeth, my grandmother's sister. My grandmother was dead. Uncle Ted lived in the basement apartment.

It was nearly dark by the time we finished the job. Sitting on the front porch with Uncle Ted, taking our time drinking our cans of beer. My father had gone to pick up one of my sisters from a dance.

"So when are you starting college?" my Uncle Ted asked. I was mildly surprised that he was aware of the fact that I was going to college. Although I had grown up around him, I had sometimes gotten the feeling that the details of my life were a blur to Uncle Ted. He once asked me why he didn't see me anymore walking by his building on the way home from St. Christina's Grammar School. I told him it was because I was now a junior in high school.

Uncle Ted put his can of beer down on the step beside him, pulled a cigarette from his shirt pocket and lit it. "You know," he said, "you're the first member of our family, the first one in the entire history of our family, to go to college."

I knew that Uncle Ted didn't know that for a fact. Our family tree had been traced no further back than to an apartment over a drugstore on the corner of 51st and Ashland.

"Do you realize that?" repeated Uncle Ted, "you're the first one in the entire history of our family to go to college."

"That must mean I'm the smartest."

He ignored the joke. "No, it means you're the luckiest. It's been quite a while since we've had a generation that hasn't had to flee a famine, fight a war or struggle through a depression. You've actually got the time to grow up."

I felt like saying it, but I didn't. "Gee, Uncle Ted, don't worry. Maybe I'll get lucky and there'll be another world war or a depression in the next few weeks." God, I hate that, when people try to make you feel bad for having it good. At least from their angle, you've got it good. Even if they're right, what are you supposed to do, poke your eyes out or something?

"Yeah, I guess you're right," I said.

The tone of the conversation was making me feel uneasy. Uncle Ted wasn't the kind of person who normally talked about such things. I had been expecting his usual serving of conversation: A main dish of the White Sox' chances for a pennant, side orders of what a bastard his foreman was and how Uncle Ted's car was running, topped off with dessert of dirty jokes.

"What do you want to become?" he asked.

"I don't know."

"You don't know?" Uncle Ted looked at me with a pained expression. "You mean you don't know whether you want to be a doctor or a lawyer or something like that?"

"I'm not quite sure what I want to be."

"Why not? Why are you going to spend all of that time and money going to college if you don't know what you want to do?"

"I figure that it'll help me decide." Uncle Ted was really beginning to get on my nerves. I was already aware of the fact that I didn't know what to do with my life. Pouncing up and down on the question wasn't going to make it go away.

The twilight lingering over the neighborhood had slowly ripened into complete darkness. I looked at the houses and apartment buildings that sat on my block. Only the blotches of yellow light pouring out of their windows defied the blackness of the night. I chose my words carefully, wanting to explain, not offend. "I don't think I'd want to spend the rest of my life living in one of these houses."

"Or in one of their basements?" my Uncle Ted asked quietly.

"I didn't mean it that way."

"That's all right," my Uncle Ted assured me, "I know what you mean. You want to do better than what you've already got. And that's the way it should be. Each generation has to grab for the rungs that are over their heads. I know it might seem hard for you to believe, but the way the family lives now is a hell of a lot better than the way we grew up. Your old man and me, the other nine kids . . ."

"I thought there were fifteen in the family?" I interrupted.

"There were," said Uncle Ted, "but some of them were already out and married."

"Oh."

"All nine of us kids and your grandmother," continued Uncle Ted, "lived in two rooms above a drugstore."

I already knew about the apartment over the drugstore. My mother had told me about it years ago. But my father, nor anyone else in the Conroy family had ever talked about it, until that night.

"It was crowded up there, but it was a great location." My Uncle Ted picked up his can of beer, but he didn't drink from it. "We couldn't afford it very often, but when we could, the soda fountain was only a flight of stairs away. I know those three rooms in my apartment don't seem like much to you, but they do to me. Just being able to walk through three rooms without bumping into somebody still gives me a damn good feeling."

"It's not so unusual," I said almost apologetically, "for someone my age not to know what he's going to do with his life. Lots of guys my age have no idea of what they want to make as a career. When you were my age, did you know what you wanted to do?"

"Yeah," said my Uncle Ted, "survive."

FIVE

Dear God:

I went to school with a kid named Norman Geltz. Norman had perfect handwriting, perfect workbook pages, perfect attendance and was a perfect pain. Most of us ignored Norman Geltz except on test days when we all wanted to be near him. Norman had, absolutely, all the answers.

Our homeroom teacher told us that if we wanted to do well in life, we should be more like Norman Geltz, and she made us feel guilty that we weren't.

Norman didn't enjoy life. I rarely saw him smile and I never saw him laugh. Norman Geltz reminds me a lot of you.

Signed: Conroy

Conroy:

Not surprising. All religions have worked hard to give you the impression that I'm a stiff; the kind of guy you'd never invite to a party.

Walk into a church with a friend and you find yourself using a tone of voice that you normally use only at a funeral home in front of an open casket. I could never understand why human silence is a sign of respect while the sound of a human voice, saying the usual things, is supposedly a sign of disrespect. And the most disrespectful thing that a person can do in a house of God, according to those who think they own them, is to laugh.

I like laughter and the people who do it; from the twitterers to the chucklers to those whose laughter roars out in a gallop of explosions. To me, laughter is taking a bite out of life and saying, "Just right."

It's no accident that most of you are stuck with a dismal image of me. According to the majority of organized religions, life is nothing more than a trial where, as your judge, I determine whether you go to Heaven or Hell. Where every day is a lump in the throat that's hard to swallow. Not exactly a laughable situation.

But maybe they're wrong. Maybe, just maybe, your life isn't a trial but a sample of what's to come. Maybe I'm giving you some Heaven and Hell right here just to see which one you really prefer. Letting you choose your own eternity.

If that's the case, then many of you are choosing a Hell of frowning faces, bad moods, constant complaining, uncomfortable suspicions and rainy weekends.

And Heaven? Ah, that'll be a lot of laughs.

Signed: God

SIX

She looked more like a whore than someone's alma mater. She wasn't one of those rosy cheeked, apple pie, girl-next-door types who lives in a small college town and whose catalog is full of dignified buildings resting on their laurels behind weeping willows.

Standing eighteen stories high, and leaning slightly to the right, the Engrim Hotel had, years ago, been one of Chicago's finest. But like most magnificent mistresses, she couldn't grow old graciously. Her once proud body, now sooted with age, had been sold to the city of Chicago, which converted her into a commuter college.

Commuter colleges have sprouted up in stranger places. A southern suburb of Chicago began its commuter college in a former supermarket. "Special Today, Social Sciences, Two For 49¢."

I once overheard a professor at Engrim University refer to all commuter schools as "paperback colleges": somewhat cheap, occasionally amusing, slightly educational and totally disposable.

People go to a commuter college for many reasons, I suppose.

Parents to support. Children to support. One's self to support. Some people are indecisive as to what out of town college they want to attend so they decide to spend a year at a commuter college while they make up their minds. Others have a good job in Chicago and want to keep it while going to school. Then there are those who choose to go to a commuter college for the same reason I did. They can't get in anywhere else.

Engrim University had no football team and a basketball team that was poorly supported by the student body. The coach considered it a full house if all of his players showed up.

The building that had formerly been the Engrim Hotel was located on Chicago's Near North Side in a neighborhood that was a kaleidoscope of contradictions. A half block north of the school was the city's night life district, which contained the usual conglomeration of topless joints, porno theatres, and singles bars. Glittering at Engrim from the east was the Gold Coast, one of Chicago's most affluent sections, while breathing stench on the back of her neck from the west was Clark Street, a skid row that was still skidding.

Go a block south of Engrim University and you were at Holy Name Cathedral, the Cardinal's church. Walk a block north of the university and you were at the Playboy Club, Hugh Hefner's church. Engrim University was in the middle of that patch of the city that made unwilling neighbors of priests, part-time poets, tourists, cops, pimps, company presidents, politicians and students.

My first day at Engrim, I sat in an auditorium with hundreds of other freshmen, listening to the Dean of Students. He warned us that the dropout rate was high. "Look at the person sitting to your left," he said. "Now look at the person sitting to your right. Four years from now, only one of you will be here.

"For the next four years," continued the dean, "you will spend most of your time studying. Occasionally, of course, you'll get a break from all that studying. The breaks will be called 'tests.' " He thought that was pretty funny.

"You are the privileged few," the dean continued somberly. "You are the scientists, teachers, and businessmen of the future. Because of the college degree you will earn in the next four years, you will become the leaders of tomorrow, the elite, the privileged few who will shape society."

It sounded terrific. How did we know that, across the country, the same promise was being made to hundreds of thousands of others.

Going to college was like walking through a blizzard. On Monday morning, I'd put my head down and relentlessly begin trudging through the week. I wouldn't be able to see it, but just the thought of it would keep me going; that clear sky and sunshine on the horizon called the weekend.

SEVEN

Dear God:

I didn't go to mass last Sunday morning.

Signed: Conroy

Conroy:

Don't worry about it. It was a nice day. I don't know who built the church but I made the sunshine.

Signed: God

EIGHT

Sitting across from Harvey Federstein, the world's largest hunk of arrogance, in a history class. He was writing furiously, taking down every word the professor said. As the teacher talked, he leaned over on his lectern. Suddenly, the base of the lectern cracked and the professor toppled forward onto the student in front of him. Both the student and the professor ended up on the floor beneath the overturned desk. Federstein looked up, totally serious, and said to no one in particular, "Are we responsible for that on the test?"

After class, I saw Federstein sitting alone in the cafeteria, pulling his lunch out of a brown bag. I sat down and introduced myself.

"You certainly seemed to be taking good notes in history class this morning," I commented.

"Thank you," said Federstein. "In fact, they're great notes. I was a straight A student in high school, you know. That's nothing to brag about, unless you happen to be stupid, which I am. Let me rephrase that, I'm not stupid, but I'm certainly not all that smart. My I.Q. is 110, which is ten points below the average college graduate's."

"If you're not smart," I asked, "then how come you're a straight A student?"

"Because," smiled Federstein, "I do something that the average student, whether he's smart or dumb, does not do. I, if you'll excuse the expression, think. I work very hard at my school work as do a lot of other students. But I also work very 'smart,' which makes me quite different from the rest. For instance, before I'll sign up for a course, I'll study the guy who's teaching it. I'll talk to other people who've already taken him for a course. . . ."

"That's nothing new," I interrupted, "I do the same thing myself."

"But," countered Federstein, "I'll bet the only thing you try to find out is whether or not he gives out many high grades."

"Well," I lied, "that's just one of the things I try to find out about him."

Both of Federstein's fists slammed down on either side of his lunch while his head and chest leered over his untouched sandwich. He looked like a rabbit sitting up at the table. His eyes became glassy and he was almost frothing at the mouth with enthusiasm.

"But you see," began Federstein, "the grades are the effect. You want the cause. There are only a few instructors in the entire school who give out a lot of high grades or a lot of low grades. Teachers are like us. They don't want the administration to notice them. Giving out too many high or low grades will do just that. You want to find out on what basis a teacher gives out a high grade. Talk to enough students who've taken those teachers, ask those students the right questions, listen carefully to their answers and you discover what teachers are virtually sure A's for you. Maybe not for someone else, but for you."

Federstein finally picked up the sandwich he had unwrapped, but he made no attempt to bring it up to his mouth.

"Some teachers tend to give higher grades to girls," said Federstein, "others favor guys. Quite a few teachers grade on personality. If they like you, you get a high grade. If they don't, you're dead. With my personality, I always avoid those kinds. I get high grades despite my personality, not because of it. As I've already told you," reminded Federstein, "I'm a very hard worker. If a teacher's grading system is a fair one, I'll get an A.

"Some teachers like extroverts," he continued. "Ask questions constantly and you get a good grade. I once got stuck with a teacher like that. When I went to him and asked him why I had gotten a C, he said that I hadn't participated enough in class. How can a teacher back up a statement like that? He can't. There's no test paper to show you or anything. It's just his opinion. In that particular class, I did participate quite a bit. The guy just didn't like me. If a teacher wants to label you with a bad grade, the best way to do it is to use that good old 'class participation' jazz."

Federstein finally snapped a bite out of his sandwich, chewed twice, and gulped it down. "That's another thing," said Federstein, "always look for a teacher who lays down the ground rules the very first day and then sticks to them. I mean, if something like class participation is really important to him, he should tell you on the first day.

"Another important factor is the time of day. There was this one teacher who taught two sections of Introduction to Sociology. One section was in the morning and the other was in the afternoon. This guy must have been tired in the afternoon, or maybe he was just bored with giving the material a second time, but he didn't do a very good job of lecturing in the afternoon class. Naturally, he put both classes on the same curve. The morning class got eight A's, the afternoon class only had one."

Federstein's mouth again jumped at the sandwich, ripping a bite out of it. The food bulged into his cheeks and went on "hold" as Federstein continued to talk.

"You know what that teacher's clever deduction was? He told the afternoon class they were loafing."

"Do you prefer teachers who grade on the curve?" I asked Federstein.

"Not particularly, but there are ways of psyching out your fellow students so that the curve dips in your favor. Walk into class on exam day and while everyone else is frantically cramming during those final seconds, you loudly slam your book closed and calmly announce, 'I'm ready for anything.' Or you can memorize a dozen trivial facts from the study material, the kinds of facts that are found in the footnotes to footnotes, and casually drop them into the conversation as you discuss the upcoming test. That particular maneuver is virtually guaranteed to pump panic into any potential competitor. After I've done that to some guys, they could have gone home through a straw.

"Time of the day is also very important to me," Federstein observed. "I do my best work in the morning so that's when I take the toughest courses.

"There's even one teacher," said Federstein, "who grades you on where you sit in his class. He directs his lectures to the people in the first two rows. He kids around with them and eventually gets to know them on a first name basis. Get in the first two rows with that guy and you'll never get anything lower than a B."

I was impressed. Halfway through Federstein's lecture, I had begun taking notes. But Federstein's only recognition of this extremely rare tribute to another student's words was when he glanced at my notebook and said, "I hope you don't write like that during an essay test."

"Why not?"

"Much too sloppy," said Federstein as he picked up my notebook from under my pen. "When you write that way on a test, a teacher thinks you're trying to hide your ignorance. When you write clearly and boldly, you show a sense of confidence. Even when you're wrong, sometimes, not always, but sometimes, a teacher will become convinced that you know what you're talking about. If you don't know the answer, at least be right in your delivery."

Annoyed, I grabbed my notebook out of Federstein's hands. "What do you think of the regurgitation method?" I asked, my voice trying to impart the dignity of an equal.

"Naturally," said Federstein disdainfully, "every teacher wants to get back on a test what he's been feeding you for the past few weeks. When a teacher looks at a test, he wants to see the smartest person in the world. The same guy he saw in the bathroom mirror this morning."

"Did you start working on the history term paper that's due next Friday?" I wanted to see if Federstein was capable of giving a normal answer to a normal question. He wasn't.

"I plan on writing those four pages over the weekend," said Federstein.

"But the paper has to be ten pages long."

"I've developed a twelve-page term paper with interchangeable parts," beamed Federstein. "By changing the first page, the last page and a few pages in the middle I can direct the paper to a variety of subjects such as History, Sociology, Psychology and Economics."

"What do you want to be when you get out of school?" The words had already slipped through my lips before I realized they made up the same question that had often tied my stomach in that knot of "I don't know."

Federstein, however, had a quick reply. As he shoved his barely eaten lunch back into the brown bag, he smiled and said, "Disgustingly rich. Many people say I'm already halfway there."

"I've got to get going," I said. "Have to study for a science quiz tomorrow morning."

"Multiple choice test?" asked Federstein.

"Yeah."

"Stay away from the option, 'E, None of the Above.' Percentage-wise, it's designed to sucker you away from the right answer."

Since that day I talked to Federstein, I've often wondered how he knew I was going to spend years on that one.

NINE

The Chicago Transit Authority, known more profanely to native Chicagoans as the CTA, has elevated tracks that stretch like strands of cancer through the neighborhoods of the city. Streets below the tracks, pinned down on both sides by the supports of the elevated structure, are locked into a perpetual twilight as they're harassed by the clatter of the train cars and the screech of their wheels. The darkness of the pavement is broken only by an occasional square of renegade sunlight that has managed to squeeze through the crossbeams of the tracks above. Blotched funnels of concrete for the dispossessed: tumbleweed newspapers, abandoned cars, abandoned children.

Approaching the downtown area, most of the tracks go underground, becoming Chicago's subway. The sudden drop in altitude is accompanied by the incessant belch of indigestion from the tunnel as trains heave and jostle along its walls.

It is a dirty world. Gum wrappers, with yellowing edges, lie crumpled on the floors of the trains. Obscenities fill the walls of the cars as well as some of the people. The windows are slick with slime, grease spots from heads that toppled over with sleepiness and smudges from young groping hands. Even the air is dirty, smelling as if each person had taken turns chewing it.

Many of the people, like the tunnels they travel through, are saved from being completely hollow only by the roars of their own anguish. "I wish the day was over. Didn't get enough sleep, had to watch the last part of that movie. Slept too late. Why did I lay there? I wish the day was over. No time for breakfast. Maybe I can grab a roll before I go into work. I wish the day was over. How could I have forgotten those papers at home? I had to have them ready by today. These slacks, they don't match anything I'm wearing. I wish the day was over. I think I forgot to use deodorant. I wish the day was over. God, is it only Tuesday? How I wish the day was over."

Each morning, they bobble alongside one another, earlobe to shoulder blade, hanging onto the overhead bars, newspapers and lives with little more for motivation than trying to live until the end of their day to see their morning wish come true. This is the commuter student's road to higher education.

Traveling on these trains to Engrim University was like joining a fraternity with a four-year initiation. Every week was hell week. Some train stations averaged a murder a month.

Bill Weatherly was a guy from a neighborhood a couple over from mine who also went to Engrim. He was a few years older than me. Weatherly was a professional student. One of those who took the minimum number of hours each semester and then dropped a few courses besides. The reason for his academic procrastination was, of course, the Vietnam War. He had a local draft board that was willing to extend student deferments beyond the usual four years. Weatherly had been at Engrim University so long by the time I met him that he claimed he was the only student with tenure. It would have taken a court hearing to get him out of school.

Weatherly was a rather strange fellow. He always had what appeared to be a three-day growth of beard, which meant that he must have gotten up every morning and shaved off one day's growth.

Weatherly had a currency conscience. He was against all wars, crime in the streets, welfare and fire departments because they cost him money. However, if an old lady dropped dead in front of him and he got to keep her bus fare, he might have considered that a moral good.

Sometimes, Weatherly and I traveled to Engrim together. I'd meet him on the bus that ran through our neighborhoods and stopped at the elevated station. One night, both of us had to stay late at school to work in the library. It was almost midnight by the time we were on our way home.

Since it was a cold autumn night, Weatherly had on three spring jackets. He didn't own a heavy coat. He just started out with one light jacket in the fall and kept adding on additional ones as the weather got colder.

As the train rumbled through the tunnel, I cautiously glanced at the five men who sat, scattered, throughout the car. All of them appeared to be killers looking for work.

I could already hear the judge going easy on them. "Well, after all, you did *ask* for the cigarette. And being a heavy smoker myself, I can understand how, when your request was refused, you overreacted and tore them apart. Two years, suspended sentence, and no cigarettes for thirty days."

Weatherly was leaning against the window, bouncing and pitching with the movements of the car, trying to sleep. One arm was propping up his head while the other wrapped tightly around his waist as if he were freezing. He had gone out and had a few drinks at a Rush Street bar while I had finished up studying at the library.

I started thinking about the article in the morning newspaper about the rising crime rate in the subways. Nudging Weatherly awake, I said to him, "Bill, if the crime rate's so high on these damn trains, why aren't there any cops around?"

Weatherly readjusted his fist, wedged lightly under his cheekbone, that he was using as a pillow and mumbled his reply. "There's no money in it."

"What do you mean?"

"Ever notice how many cops there are around writing traffic tickets?" said Weatherly with his eyes still shut. "When a parking meter expires, there's money to be made. The same cannot be said of a human being. Now for Christ's sake, let me get some sleep."

Nothing happened. Within minutes, the train climbed out of

the tunnel onto the elevated tracks. As the train ran along the dual strips of steel, its wheels spat out firecrackers of yellow static that glowed but for an instant in the night.

A few minutes later, I caught a glimpse of the White Sox' Comiskey Park sulking in the darkness. With the season over, I thought I'd relax for a few weeks and then maybe head south to play some winter ball.

TEN

Dear God:

Today, I went to Mr. Klakin's wake. He's a neighbor of mine. I didn't think that he led much of a life until I heard Mr. Challmers, another neighbor, talk about him.

Mr. Challmers said that Mr. Klakin never drank, ran around with other women or really made life unpleasant for anyone.

You know, I think most people are like Mr. Klakin. They lead pretty good lives. They don't do much of anything wrong.

Signed: Conroy

Conroy:

I also knew someone who died recently. He, too, never drank, ran around with other women or really made life unpleasant for anyone. Just like Mr. Klakin, he didn't do much of anything wrong either. He didn't do much of anything. He was a guppy.

Signed: God

ELEVEN

From what I've heard, others can recall the exact time in their lives when they lost their virginity. Not so with Catholics. Ours was wrapped beneath layers of guilt.

Cautiously, slowly, and hoping that God was too busy with other things to notice, our logic and lust would unravel quilts of Sunday morning sermons, catechism lessons, confessional admonitions and parental warnings.

Such apprehensive behavior would often overflow into other activities. A devout Catholic would never completely open his Christmas gifts until August. Catholics also did very well on bomb squads.

By the time we got through all the wrappings, we would often discover that our virginity had simply melted away. Ask a non-Catholic when they lost their virginity and they recall a specific moment. Ask a Catholic the same question and they begin counting the years on their fingers.

Sitting in the library trying to figure out mathematical equations for a statistics course. I looked up from my pad of scribblings to see Denise Meyers, a girl I vaguely knew from around school, straining to reach a book that was on one of the higher shelves. She was wearing a short skirt. Discovering a new mathematical equation: Arousal equals the distance of the short skirt above the knees times the shapeliness of the legs.

Denise Meyers was a reasonably attractive girl but, under the gaze of someone being affected by "Library Lunacy," she looked incredibly provocative. "Library Lunacy" was a state of mind reached by sitting in the library and concentrating on material so boring that, after a few minutes, even the seventy-year-old librarian begins looking good. One sure indication that your mind was slipping into "Library Lunacy" was when you were reading and the "B's" began looking sensuous.

I followed Denise out of the library and made a date with her as she was waiting for the elevator. I made sure there was no one around, though. In high school, at a dance, I made the mistake of asking a girl for a date in front of at least thirty people. She turned me down with a shocked stare and a "shove off" giggle.

A few minutes later, on my way to a class, I met Weatherly in the hall. "What are you doing this weekend?" I asked.

"Ah, nothing much. You?"

"Yeah, I'm going out with a girl named Denise Meyers on Saturday night."

"Is she kind of short, always wears glasses, good figure, reasonable face?"

"Well, I thought she had more than a reasonable face."

"She's in my philosophy class," said Weatherly. "You know, for high school, I heard that she went to a convent school. She should be a hot date."

"How do you figure?" I asked. "After all that purity indoctrination, she's probably a solid block of ice."

"That may be true of some girls who come out of convent schools, but with some of the others," said Weatherly, "it's like holding a spring down for four years. When you finally let up, look out."

"I'll keep that in mind."

"You know who I'd like to go out with?" said Weatherly. "That tall blond in our English class."

"The one who always wears white boots?"

"Yeah, yeah, that's the one," said Weatherly.

"I know her. She's from my neighborhood. Her name's Diane Kalton."

"Do you know why she always wears white boots?" Weatherly asked.

"She's a virgin from the knees down."

"Introduce me," said Weatherly enthusiastically.

"She has a nickname," I replied. "Thunderthighs."

"Introduce me, introduce me."

"She's got a boy friend," I said.

"Who cares?"

"There's a guy in Memorial Hospital with a broken leg and seventeen stitches in his face who was equally unimpressed with the fact."

Weatherly held up the two books he was carrying. "Who's got time for broads? I'll see you later, I gotta go study."

I didn't bother telling Weatherly but, during the summer after my junior year of high school, I had gone out with Thunderthighs. Who, at one time or another, hasn't gone by a candy store and wished they owned it?

She used to spend most of her afternoons then hanging around the Colonial Snack Shop, dancing in front of the jukebox. The rumor was they both cost a quarter.

It had taken my family, two schools and the Church a lot of years and tremendous amounts of time and energy to weld together my moral fiber. That night, when I went out with Thunderthighs, it took her a few seconds to leave it in shreds. But to no avail. You can't take someone who's been on a tricycle all his life, hand him the keys to a rocket ship and expect him to get very far.

I had asked Denise Meyers to a movie that was playing downtown. No more neighborhood shows for me. I was a college man now. Only later in the day did I realize that, by making that date with Denise, I had unintentionally challenged one of the more successful killers in the United States, the Dan Ryan Expressway.

The Dan Ryan Expressway is a huge tongue of concrete, fourteen lanes wide in some places, that sticks out of Chicago's downtown area and wags its way through the South Side of Chicago. The Dan Ryan averages more deaths per mile than any other expressway in the country. Supposedly, the Dan Ryan Expressway was claiming lives even while it was being poured. The syndicate allegedly used it as a dumping ground for some of its victims. "Vito always did like the fast life, bury him in the express lanes."

I had had my driver's license for only about six months when I started college. My father owned a stick shift car and it had taken me over a year to learn how to drive it. I had a left foot that stuttered. If my right foot had been as nervous, I would have been the world's greatest jitterbug dancer.

Even though he felt I still wasn't ready, I finally convinced my father to let me take the test for my driver's license.

The examiner sat clutching his clipboard as we crept around the test course. My left foot, with the clutch trapped beneath, jittered ferociously, which kept the car in a continuous spasm of hiccups. A few of the car's hiccups almost threw the examiner through the windshield.

Before the examiner had climbed into the car, he had hinted to my father that a bribe was a standard part of the procedure. My father, who never went for such things, acted like he didn't know what the examiner was suggesting. At the end of the course, the examiner hobbled out of the car, still flinching violently, and mumbled to my father, "I fixed you, buddy, I passed him."

On my way home from Engrim, I stopped in at Caepan's gas station to see if he could give me any suggestions on how to drive the Dan Ryan Expressway. I found Caepan sitting in the trunk of a car, working on the wiring.

"Funny you should ask," said Caepan. "I was on it last Tuesday morning. Had to go up to the North Side to pick up some parts." Caepan smiled to himself. "I was driving along and I noticed this school bus, crammed with kids, in the lane next to me. They were probably on their way to some field trip.

"Just as I'm about to accelerate past the bus, one little kid gave me the peace sign. Actually, it was half a peace sign, the taller half. Naturally, I returned the gesture. With that, every kid on the bus went wild and they all started giving me the finger. This went on from 79th to 31st Street. It got pretty boring just giving the finger so we started doing all sorts of things to amuse one another. You know, like sticking your thumb in your ear and wiggling all your fingers. By 31st Street, even the bus driver and a couple of the teachers had half joined in."

Caepan stopped working on the wiring for a moment. "What a nice way to start the day," he said wistfully. "Not even eight o'clock in the morning yet and already I had provided the high point of some class's field trip."

"That's swell, Caepan. I'm glad you had a good time. But all I want to know is can you give me any suggestions on how to drive it?"

"Sure, sure," Caepan said as he returned his attention to the wiring in the trunk. "The first thing is always drive faster than the posted speed limit. If you don't, you're begging to have somebody run right up your rear end. I'm talking about the car's, of course."

Caepan was a good teacher. He didn't presume anything.

"You should normally drive nine miles over the speed limit," continued Caepan. "Any faster and you might get picked up by radar. Any slower and you'll get picked up by an ambulance.

"Oh, yeah," said Caepan, "there's an electric sign along the Dan Ryan, at about 22nd Street, that flashes out messages to drivers as they go by. Don't look at it."

"Why not?"

"Because the messages are sent out so slowly, you have to cut down your speed to read them. That's a good way to get hit."

"Who would put up a stupid sign like that?" I asked.

"The Greater Chicago Body and Fender Shop."

Caepan climbed out of the trunk, slammed it shut and walked over to his workbench. "You going to be driving your parents' car?"

"Yeah."

"It's too expensive for the Dan Ryan Expressway," said Caepan.

"Too expensive? That car's only worth a few hundred bucks."

"I've had cigarette lighters that are worth more than some of the cars I've seen on the Dan Ryan Expressway," said Caepan.

"The cheaper the car, the better you can bluff with it. If you drive around in a machine that's worth less than a scratch it can put on another car, people are going to give you room."

Closing time. Caepan walked around the shop, turning off lights.

"Any other suggestions, Caepan?"

"Yeah. Don't open your eyes until you're on the exit ramp. No one does."

Sitting at a traffic light, with Denise Meyers beside me, waiting for the green. Looking out my window, I could see below me that raging river of headlights teeming with metallic piranha; the Dan Ryan Expressway.

As soon as we got to the bottom of the entrance ramp, I made a sharp turn and leaped into the first lane of traffic, right behind a bread truck and just in front of a pea-soup-colored Rambler. Caepan had told me that if I was going to cut somebody off, I should make it a Rambler. Rambler drivers are notoriously lax in seeking revenge.

Suddenly, a car came out of my right fender and squeezed in behind the bread truck. As I braked to slow down, I glanced up at the rear view mirror. The Rambler had been replaced by a station wagon that was following me so closely that I could barely see its headlights in the mirror.

WOWING WOWING WOWING WOWING WOWING. Then I heard it; an inferno of sound was roaring up from behind me. I glanced at the side view mirror but all that looked back was a large set of metal grill teeth.

The WOWING WOWING WOWING WOWING WOWING kept getting louder. I was convinced that within seconds, no matter what it was, the car, along with Denise and me, was going to become part of its digestive tract.

Omelettes of sweat sandwiched my eyes as they skittered from mirrors to the windshield. My hands clamped to the steering wheel as the toes wiggled in panic. The radio started playing "Teen Angel" and Denise kept asking, "Why are you so quiet?"

Just as the car was about to be engulfed by the WOWING WOWING WOWING, I saw it coming up the lane along my left side; the cab of a truck followed by a wall on wheels which, after it got past me, I realized was a semitrailer. The movie was half over by the time the WOWING subsided in my ears.

After the show and a snack, we began the drive back to Denise's house.

"You're going the wrong way to get back on the Dan Ryan," she said.

"I know, but I thought we'd take side streets on the way home. It's such a nice night for a drive."

"Are you kidding?" said Denise. "We'll have to go through the worst neighborhoods in the city to get back to my house."

"But we can drive along some very nice boulevards. Haven't you ever noticed all the beautiful trees on these streets. I love to look at trees."

"At night?"

Forty minutes and twenty miles of ghetto later, we were parking on Denise's street. We had been lucky. No one had bothered to destroy us.

I put my arms around Denise as she snuggled close to me. But as she did so, her glasses bumped into my shoulder. Denise quickly pushed her glasses back up against the bridge of her nose.

I'm very popular with women who can't see well. Almost every girl I've dated has either worn glasses sometimes or contact lenses all the time. But Denise was the first girl I had ever parked with who always wore her glasses.

I was debating how to get around her lensed obstacles when she whipped off her glasses and tossed them on the dashboard. "Now," she said, "we can get down to business."

Remembering Weatherly's words. He was right. The spring had sprung.

Denise and I dated regularly for about five months. Then something beautiful flowered in our relationship. Something that rarely happens to two people. We both got sick of each other at the same time.

On a Sunday night, over the telephone, Denise told me that she thought we were getting too serious and that we shouldn't see each other for a while. Her timing was miserable. I'm always depressed on Sunday night. It's even worse for me than Monday morning. On Sunday night, I am already worrying about Monday morning.

Even though it was a Sunday night, her words didn't upset me that much. As I've mentioned, I was getting pretty sick of her, too. But I didn't want to hurt her feelings, so I acted mildly hurt.

Actually, any kind of rejection bothers me. If a bum came up to me and said, "You look lousy," my immediate reaction would be to tell the bum to "shove off" and I'd tell myself, "What does that guy know? He's just a bum." But sooner or later, my mind would revive what that bum had said and I'd think, "Maybe that guy was right. Maybe I do look lousy." I have an incredibly delicate ego. I swear, a feather could dent it.

The following year, Denise Meyers was dating some senior. Three months later, she was pregnant and engaged, presumably in that order. I was sitting in the cafeteria one morning when Weatherly sat down at my table and informed me of Denise Meyers' new prominence.

"I saw your old girl friend, Denise Meyers, this morning."

"So?"

"She's pregnant."

"You sure?" I was offended. All she had taken off for me were her glasses.

"Most assuredly," replied Weatherly. "Ah, one cannot help but wonder," said Weatherly in a mocking tone of voice, "where that new life was conceived; that first ray of light that heralds the sunrise of a new generation."

"Cram it, Weatherly."

"Were they sitting in the back seat of a car surrounded by passion fogged windows or were they studying together and discovered their own battle of the bulge?

"By the way," Weatherly interrupted himself, "what's Denise majoring in?"

"Preschool education."

"That's it," said Weatherly, "it was an assignment."

TWELVE

Heading home from Engrim one afternoon with Bernie Servallion, a guy I had met during my first semester. We were walking out of the school when Bernie remembered that he had left his anthropology book in the student lounge.

When we went back to retrieve it, Brenda Sandling, who was in one of my classes, was sitting on the couch where Bernie had left his book. Servallion started a conversation with her. About ten minutes later, Brenda excused herself because she had a class to attend. Servallion watched her walk away and then turned to me and said, "I'm going to marry that girl."

"If it's this Saturday, and you want me to be 'best man,' you're going to have to make it in the late afternoon," I said. "I'm busy in the morning."

Servallion didn't answer me. He started talking about an English test that both of us had to take the following day.

Nearly an hour later, walking home from the bus stop, I stopped at Caepan's gas station and told him about Servallion meeting the girl and what he had said about marrying her. Caepan was standing under the hoist, working on the underbelly of a Buick.

"Luck's an interesting thing," said Caepan. "Because of a forgotten book, he may do something that will have a major effect upon his life as well as a number of lives around him. Every generation that descends from him will have been affected by that forgotten book."

"You don't think that kind of stuff is predetermined, huh?" I asked.

"Do you?"

"No, I don't think so. But luck isn't everything, either. People work hard for something and achieve it. That's simple cause and effect. If luck were everything, life would be nothing more than a series of accidents."

"Do you think I've gotten where I am today by hard work?" asked Caepan. "Have you ever heard of a piano player named Erroll Garner?"

"Vaguely," I replied.

"He's one of the greatest. Some reporter once asked him if he ever took music lessons. You know what he said?"

"What did he say?"

"He asked the reporter if a beaver had to have a degree in engineering before he built a dam."

"Very witty guy," I observed.

"Erroll Garner was born an artist, just like me. I may not be able to play 'Misty' on a dashboard, but when you drive a car I've worked on, you can just feel that natural rhythms of a machine that's been perfected by an artist. Erroll Garner's lucky. I'm lucky."

"Am I?" I asked. Feeling the pure pain and anguish of a thousand moments as I struggled to get the bat off my shoulders to hit a fast ball that was already past me.

"I don't know," said Caepan. "Maybe. I doubt it. You'd probably know it by now. That's the trouble with schools. They give their students the impression that they can be anything they want to be. Granted, most people don't push themselves to their full potential. But the really important things in life, being able to create beautiful music, beautiful engines, whether we can see in the morning when we open our eyes, whether our legs move when we tell them to, life itself, death, landing on a telephone wire . . ."

"Landing on a telephone wire?"

"Sure. A bird with a brain smaller than your fingernail can fly anywhere he wants. We can build things that fly, but that's just not the same. You could go to school for the rest of your life, but you'd never learn to flap your arms and land with both feet on a telephone wire. When it comes to flying, birds are just plain lucky. Everything important is left to luck, good or bad."

"I disagree," I said. "Each one of us determines our lives. Luck has very little to do with it."

Since I had entered the garage, Caepan had not bothered to turn away from the underside of the car as he talked to me. But now he looked up at me and slowly shook his head to show his disdain of my insistent ignorance. Then he returned his attention to his work.

Grunting as he yanked on his wrench, trying to turn a bolt. Between grunts, he said, "If you think you're the guy who's in control of your life, go home and ask your parents how they met."

THIRTEEN

Dear God:

What do people mean when they say that "It's God's will"?

Signed: Conroy

Conroy:

I don't know. I never felt the need to write one.

Signed: God

FOURTEEN

It was on a Saturday in late May. I was working a part-time job delivering packages. Driving around on the North Side of the city looking for an address, I turned a corner and spotted a neighborhood bakery. There aren't many of those left. Noticing the name as I walked in, "Betterman's Bakery."

I'm a "Chocoholic," especially chocolate chip cookies. Although I much prefer the homemade kind, the bakery ones run a respectful second.

The problem is that I'm allergic to chocolate. Sometimes, not always, but sometimes, I get violent headaches from it. When I was a kid, some neighborhood girl told me that people could die from eating too much chocolate. For the next few weeks, I had a nightmare where my parents found me dead at the kitchen table, slumped over a dish of chocolate ice cream. Years later, I mentioned the nightmare to Caepan. He told me if I ever o.d., he'd make sure that my ashes were scattered over Hershey, Pennsylvania.

Betterman's Bakery was really crowded. I had number twenty-seven, she had number twenty-six. She wasn't gorgeous or anything, but she was certainly a very attractive woman. And I could tell by looking at her that she had a sunshine and flowers personality, laced with just enough barbed wire to make it interesting. She was wearing a white uniform and standing right in front of me.

"You come here often?" I asked. A real original line.

She looked at me as if I was crazy. "I beg your pardon?"

"I said, do you come here often?"

"Here? The bakery? Oh, yes, I suppose so."

I had startled her, but she didn't want to talk to me anyway. Before I had said anything, she had had her back to me. When I began talking to her, she hadn't bothered turning around. Instead, she had tossed the words over her shoulder.

"Are you a nurse?"

"No, I'm not."

"You work in a bakery." She didn't bother answering that one but she did begin turning around.

"Waitress?"

"No, I'm studying to be a dental technician."

What an opportunity. I told her my Doctor Grossman story. When I was a kid, he was the only dentist in the neighborhood. The next nearest dentist was at least one busy street and two sets of railroad tracks away. In an area where ninety percent of the population was old people and kids, Dr. Grossman should have done all right. But he was a terrible dentist. His checkups were oral surgery. When you walked into his office and he said, "Hello," it hurt. The only people who would go to him were those who had never been to him before.

One day, Dr. Grossman got a break. A rabid dog attacked a woman and child right in front of his office. Dr. Grossman was dozing at the time. When he heard the screams, he woke up, automatically gazed at his chair, saw that no one was there, and ran out in front of his shop.

After wrestling with the rabid dog for a few minutes, Dr. Grossman managed to lock the dog up inside his shop. By then, the police had arrived. The front of Dr. Grossman's office was a large plate glass window with venetian blinds behind it. In order to kill the dog, the police shot thousands of rounds through Dr.

Grossman's front window. All of his equipment was ruined.

Naturally, Dr. Grossman became an instant hero. The city gave him a special hero award and everybody in the neighborhood started going back to him again. Within a few months, however, there was a rumor going around that someone was starting a fund to buy another rabid dog.

Sarah, that was her name, was only mildly amused. "None of that would have happened if the man had had a good dental assistant," she said.

"Who do you think the rabid dog was?"

"Number twenty-two," the woman behind the counter yelled. Sarah glanced at her plastic number card.

"They must have great chocolate chip cookies here," I said.

"Why?"

"Look how crowded the place is."

Sarah delivered her words very slowly as if she were adjusting her verbal speed to what she knew was a low I.Q.

"Did it ever dawn on you that people might come to this bakery for something other than chocolate chip cookies?"

"To be perfectly honest, no."

"It should have."

"I hope they don't have any chocolate chip cookies," I said.

"I thought that was what you came in here for?"

"They give me headaches."

"Then why are you buying them?"

"I like them."

"That's dumb."

"I know."

The woman behind the counter called out number twenty-six.

"I'd like to pick up a cake that was ordered last Wednesday," said Sarah. "The name is Faber."

"What's your first name?" I asked.

"Sarah Faber." She directed her reply to the woman behind the counter.

"Sarah Faber," I repeated, "is your number listed in the phone book?" I don't know why I just didn't ask her for the damn thing.

Sarah showed me her plastic number twenty-six card as she handed it to the woman. "My number's twenty-six." Then she put her money on the counter, picked up her cake and began moving through the crowd for the door.

"Clever, quite clever," I said.

Sarah looked over her shoulder. "Good-bye." She almost hummed it.

They were out of chocolate chip cookies.

I called her early that night.

"Hello?" The voice that answered the phone was dressed in the kind of work clothes that are found between a hard hat and steel tipped shoes.

"Hello. May I speak to Sarah, please?"

"Who's calling?"

"Tim Conroy."

"Just a minute."

"Hello?" Sarah's voice sounded as if it were peeking apprehensively around a corner. I hadn't noticed in the bakery that she had such a sensual voice, probably because I was too busy noticing her other sensuals.

"Hi, this is Tim Conroy."

"Who?"

"Tim Conroy. I met you at the bakery today."

"Oh, yes, how are you?"

"Fine. You?"

"I'm okay."

I asked her out for the following Saturday night. She was busy. She was also busy for the next Saturday night and the one after that. Friday nights were taken up with her part-time job as a nurse's aide at a local hospital.

"How about this Saturday afternoon?" I asked.

"Saturday, during the day?"

She sounded surprised. Just as I had suspected, she had no daytime excuses ready.

"Sure, why not?" I asked.

"What would we do?"

"We could go stand in Betterman's Bakery and I could tell you a great story about this dentist who used to live in my neighborhood."

"No thanks," she said. "I don't think I could stand the excitement again."

"We could play tennis."

"I don't play tennis," she said.

"Neither do I. We could just play games." Her silence sounded irritated. "We could take a ride. Something like that."

"What would I wear?"

"Riding clothes? I don't know. I'll pick you up at nine this Saturday morning." I said it quickly, hoping that the speed of my delivery would discourage any objections she might throw at me. The strategy didn't work.

"Nine in the morning? That early?"

"Nine fifteen?"

"How about eleven o'clock?"

"Nine thirty?"

For the rest of the night, I relived every word of that conversation time and time again. I agonized over moments where I could have been more clever. "What I should have said was ..." I wondered what she had thought when I had said something and I wondered what she had really meant when she had said something. I had this tremendous urge to call her back up and explain everything I had said to her during the first phone call. But I knew if I did that I'd spend all night calling her up to tell her what I really meant to say during the previous phone call.

FIFTEEN

Droplets of dew were still running down the cheeks of her front window when I pulled up to Sarah's house. Her father answered the door.

"Good morning, sir. My name's Tim Conroy and I'd like to see Sarah Faber." How do you meet a girl's father for the first time without feeling like an ass?

He turned around and bellowed, "Sarah, your school friend is here." He stood there and sort of stared at me.

A few moments later, she appeared in the door and I mumbled hello. She returned the mumble. Nothing like the presence of a father to muzzle a conversation.

After Sarah got in the car, I walked over to my side, opened the door, and jumped in behind the wheel. She reached into her shoulder bag and pulled out a small brown paper bag. Then she slid a chocolate chip cookie out of the bag and handed it to me. Smiling, Sarah said, "Here, have a headache."

Snapping the cookie in half, I offered her a piece. "Like to share the pain?"

Sarah smiled, slid across the seat and draped her arm over the back of the seat behind me. "Okay, I'll wait until later to give you a real headache."

"What do you mean by that?"

She just continued to smile as she held out her hand for her half of the cookie.

Driving through the streets of her neighborhood.

"Why did your father call me your 'school friend?' "

"He refers to all of my male acquaintances as 'school friends,' " explained Sarah. "He hates to admit that I'm no longer his 'little girl.' I mean," she quickly corrected herself, "I'll always be his 'little girl' in that sense, but he hates to realize that I've grown up. So he calls every male acquaintance I have a 'school friend' as if they were coming over for me to help them with their school work."

I had caught the "acquaintance" label. Not even a "friend" yet. "I could use a little help in my reading," I said.

"You're too big to sit on my lap."

"It's worth a try."

"No, it isn't."

Time to change the subject, I decided. "What would you like to do this fine morning?" It was a fine morning, too. A hard rain had scrubbed all night to come up with a clean, cool, shiny day.

"How about going to Riverview for a few hours?" Sarah replied.

"Riverview, the amusement park?"

"Do you know of any other Riverview?"

"No."

"If you don't like the idea, we don't have to do it," said Sarah.

"No, that's fine with me. You really like Riverview, huh?"

"When I was young, my father used to take the entire family at least once a summer. It's been a couple of years now since I've been there. But we don't have to go if you don't want to."

"No, Riverview's fine with me," I said. "How many in your family?"

"I have an older sister who's married and a younger brother. How many kids in your family?"

"Seven."

"That's quite a family," said Sarah. "But look, if you don't want to go to Riverview, we don't have to. If you don't have enough money, I have some."

Emphatically, "I have plenty of money." I didn't. Glancing at my watch, I said, "Riverview doesn't open for an hour yet. A friend of mine lives right near you and I have to pick up a book from him sometime this weekend. Why don't we drive over there and then go straight to Riverview?"

"Okay."

Forty-five minutes later, I pulled up in front of Weatherly's house. "My," said Sarah snidely, "he does live close to me."

"Wait here," I said as I got out of the car. "I'll be right back."

Weatherly came to the door in his underwear. He had a cup of coffee in one hand and a donut in the other. "What the hell are you doing here, and so early?"

"I got a date in the car and I'm a little short of money. I need ten bucks."

"Hey, a date on Saturday morning. This must be the big time. Where did you find her? At the park on a swing?"

"Just give me the money, will you, I'm late already." A lie.

Weatherly left the door and came back with his wallet. He pulled out a ten dollar bill and handed it to me. "I hope she has big tits. No girl's worth getting up this early in the morning for unless she has big tits. Unless, of course, you happen to wake up with her."

"You're a real romantic, you know that, Weatherly?" My remark was purely a defensive jab. On weekend mornings, for some reason, my tongue has all the sharpness of a blimp. I shoved the ten dollars in my pocket.

"Yeah, I know," he smiled. Pointing to his T-shirt sleeve, he said, "I wear my heart right here. You can't see it because it's a very small one. You want to know what I hang out when I don't wear my heart?"

"I suspect that's so small I wouldn't be able to see it either." A brilliant comeback for me, considering it was Saturday morning.

"Funny guy," said Weatherly as he held out his hand, "Give me back my ten bucks."

When I got back into the car, Sarah asked, "What kind of book fits into your wallet?"

I had forgotten about the damn book excuse. "A very small one."

Riverview was in a league of its own. At the time, it was the world's largest amusement park with over one hundred rides and concessions. It had a typical Chicago personality. Riverview was big, tough, mean and crazy.

Disneyland, successor to Riverview's title of "World's Largest," is designed to appeal only to young children, women who don't like getting their hair mussed and junior executives whose idea of living dangerously is taking the express elevator. Riverview, though, was for anyone who was willing to lay his life on the line for a few cheap thrills.

The rides at Disneyland are, quite naturally, strictly "Mickey Mouse." Most of them do little more than smile weakly at the law of gravity. The most impressive of the Disneyland rides glides you through darkened arenas filled with technological wonders: hundreds of dancing dolls cavort through the blackness. Ghostly images seem to float through the air while waves of animated color wistfully wrap around you. At the end of the ride, you feel like you're stepping out of a cartoon. The question you automatically ask yourself is, "How did they do it?" Oozing off a Riverview ride, the standard self-asked question was "Why?"

Riverview could have been cleaner. It was not a good idea, for instance, to buy a hot dog there. The sesame seeds on the bun tended to walk around.

Although Riverview was called an "amusement" park, many people thought of it more as a "terror" park. Most of Riverview's rides had been put in the park, not for purposes of enjoyment, but rather for purposes of testing one's manhood, even if one were a woman. Pepto-Bismol sales always skyrocketed during the Riverview season.

Every summer, rumors would circulate that someone had just been killed on one of the rides at Riverview but that the newspapers were hushing it up. On one of my visits to Riverview, a ride attendant told me that most of the rumors were started by employees of Riverview. It was good for business. The attendant told me that people did occasionally get hurt or killed at Riverview but that most of them did something really crazy, like riding one of the roller coasters.

When I was little, my Uncle Arnie would take all the kids in the family to Riverview every Fourth of July. The first attraction he would take us to would be Aladdin's Castle, Riverview's funhouse. Aladdin's Castle, with its rolling barrel that you had to try and walk or crawl through, the mirror maze, the tilted rooms, the twisting discs in the corridors and the seat that folded out from under you and dropped you down a slide, would dish out more injuries than any other Riverview attraction. Every kid in the family, myself included, would stagger out of Aladdin's Castle with some kind of bump or bruise. But Uncle Arnie would waltz through Aladdin's Castle, totally immune to all of its deceptions. Uncle Arnie was lucky. He was a drunk. As far as he was concerned, the whole world should have been in the same shape as Aladdin's Castle. Uncle Arnie spent the remainder of the day falling over the rest of the park.

Even the ducks who migrated to the park's lagoon every year weren't immune to the hazards of living in an amusement park. One of them waddled too close to a kiddie train and lost his leg. His spirit for the fun life, however, was not dampened. Every spring, the one-legged duck was one of the first birds to arrive back, although he now kept a respectful distance between himself and that kiddie train.

As Sarah and I entered the park, we noticed the long line in front of the freak show. "Why would a person want to see someone who looks weird?" I asked.

Sarah didn't even break stride as she said, "I'm sure my father's going to ask me the same question when I get home tonight."

Already, I was behind in a game I hadn't even known I was playing.

"I can see me filling out my next job application," I countered, "Previous employment, straight man for Sarah Faber."

Then I discovered that Sarah was a speed freak. We were walking by the Chute the Chutes, which consisted of a boat ride down a big slide into a small lagoon. On a terror meter, the ride would have hardly nudged the needle. The Chute the Chutes was one of the few rides in Riverview that didn't scare me. I have a "yellow belly" for a stomach.

When I was a kid and refused to get into a fight, wouldn't jump off the top of a garage or wouldn't leave my back yard for years at a time, kids would call me a yellow belly. When I was in sixth grade, I ended up in the hospital for a few days with stomach trouble. I lived in fear that the doctor was going to walk into my room and announce to my family and me, "Well, we've diagnosed the problem. You're a yellow belly." Of course, he never did. It took a couple of trips to Riverview to confirm the fact. Indeed, I did have a yellow belly for a stomach.

"How about a ride on the Chute the Chutes?" I suggested to Sarah.

She stopped walking and latched her hand onto her hip. "Why?"

"Why not? It's a very nice ride."

" 'Nice' is the word," said Sarah. "Let's go on the roller coaster."

"Which one?" Riverview had six roller coasters, but I already knew which one she was talking about.

"The Bobs."

"We'll see," I said.

" 'We'll see' means 'No,' " said Sarah defiantly. "My father used that routine on me when I was a child."

"I tell you what . . . ," I said to Sarah in a patronizing voice.

"Don't talk to me in a patronizing voice."

"All right," I said, my voice now straining not to sound patronizing, "we'll skip the Chute the Chutes. But why don't we ride all the other roller coasters and sort of work our way up to the Bobs?"

Sarah sighed. "It's going to be a very long day."

"Okay," I said, "the Greyhound's over this way."

"We're going to start with the Greyhound?"

"Yep, we sure are." I thought of grabbing for her hand, as if the only reason I was doing it was that I wanted to show her the way. But I decided against it. I was afraid I'd find her fingers wrapped into a fist.

Walking towards the Greyhound. "You know," I said, "you're making a mistake not riding the Chute the Chutes. They aren't as tame as they look."

"They aren't?" Sarah said disinterestedly.

"A friend of mine from Engrim, Carl Lagstrom, worked on

them one summer as a boatsman. Every morning, before Riverview opened, each guy working on the ride had to take a boat down on a test run. To make it interesting, they formed a betting pool, a quarter from each guy, and whoever glided farthest across the lagoon won the pot.

"Lagstrom came into work, his second day on the job, and the boss told him to grease the rails. You see, they grease the last four feet of rails so that the boats don't stick in the tracks just as they're about to hit the water. But nobody told Lagstrom that so he greased the tracks all the way up.

"He was the first guy to take a boat down that morning. His boat barely skimmed the water, bounced out of the lagoon, over a fence and slid halfway through the picnic grove before it slammed into a storage shed. Guess who . . . "

"And guess who won the pot that day?" interrupted Sarah in a singsong way. She was stealing my wrap-up line. "Carl . . . whatever his last name is."

"No, he didn't," I said. "The next boat that came down the tracks didn't stop until it hit the outskirts of Detroit."

But it was no use. Sarah's smugness had completely flattened the pinnacle of a good story. I was really beginning to like her.

The line in front of the Greyhound was a short one. Not surprising. A ride on the Greyhound lasted five minutes and fifteen seconds, all of it a waste of time for the true roller coaster connoisseur. The Greyhound looked like a roller coaster but rode like a baby carriage with shock absorbers. There were city streets with better dips. People who rode the Greyhound climbed out of its cars smiling and contented instead of leaning on their stomachs.

Our next stop in our climb toward the Bobs was the Comet. Although Sarah wasn't impressed by the Comet's jabs, I was. The Comet was a very underrated roller coaster. Not only did it have a number of extremely sharp dips, but they were squeezed together so that the Comet's tracks ran virtually up and down.

Like most felons, the Comet had operated under a number of aliases. It started out at Riverview as the Big Dipper and quickly established a reputation as the most dangerous ride in the park. The Big Dipper used its rapid-fire dips to spit people out of its cars. After a few such incidents, some of the dips were smoothed out and the ride was rechristened the Zephyr. Even though the roller coaster had a new name, it still retained its old habit. It was eventually remodeled a second time, given a third name, the Comet, and muzzled by tops that were built onto each one of its cars.

After riding the Greyhound, the Comet, and the Fireball, an extremely fast roller coaster but with few surprises, Sarah and I stood in that long, twisting line, which was slowly being bitten off and chewed up by that high altar of roller coaster terrorism, the Bobs.

I had never before been trapped into riding the Bobs. The obvious excuse was always there. "The line's too long." When I was a kid, I once tried to think if there were any advantages to going to Hell. About the only one I could come up with was that there wouldn't be a line waiting to try and get in. My first visit to Riverview and the Bobs blew that theory.

Carl Lagstrom, that friend of mine who had worked at Riverview, told me that during the week before the park opened in the spring, all the rides were tested by putting sandbags on them. The Bobs was the only ride where the sandbags had to be cut out.

Sarah and I didn't converse as the line crept forward. I've always found it difficult to talk and pray at the same time. Really, I was praying. I felt like a jerk doing it, but I did it anyway. As I've gotten older, the only time I bother to pray is when I'm scared. And the older I get, the more scared I have to be to do it. As I prayed, I couldn't help but think that if there was a God, He must have been amused. "Hey, Peter, you know who's calling me? Some guy who's afraid to go on a roller coaster. Can you imagine? Me, the Almighty, he's bothering for something like that. The kid must be a nut."

Standing at the front of the line. Two tickets were tossed at Sarah and me and a few seconds later we were stepping from the platform into one of the cars of the Bobs. As we sat down, the attendant locked the guard rail across us in the same curt manner, I'm sure, that the guard slaps the restraining strap across your chest after you've just plopped into the electric chair.

As the train began to inch forward, I giggled, "Hey, this is fun." I looked over at Sarah. She hadn't heard me. Both of her hands were wrapped around the guard rail and she was jiggling them as if they were reins, trying to get the train to work up more speed.

So slowly, the train began to climb up that first hill whose backside would send us swooshing around the tracks of the Bobs. Beneath the car, I could hear the chain clicking off the remaining seconds of my life. Somewhere, in one of those caves that peered through the tracks from deep within the Bobs, I could already see my death certificate being signed. Cause of death: Male ego.

Then, as I expected, my mind flung a blob of panic at me in the form of a question I had already heard three times that day, a question I always hear when I'm being dragged up the first hill of a roller coaster. "What am I doing here?" I don't need this, I said to myself. I don't have to prove anything to anybody. My mind always lapses into sanity when it will do me the least good.

As prongs of panic ripped through every nerve in my body, I could feel Sarah bouncing up and down on the seat.

"Isn't this neat? Isn't this terrific?" she said.

I stared straight ahead. "Yeah, neat. Neat."

We were almost at the top. The sky and eternity were waiting to meet us. Cautiously, the first car peered over the top of the hill and then began to ease down the track. The next three cars followed the calm example of their leader. Nearly half the cars had safely passed the top of the hill when the entire train paused momentarily as if to take a deep breath. Then the cars in the second half of the train, apparently in a rush to get it over with, all tried to scramble over the top together, sending the Bobs into a screaming plunge.

My yellow belly stomach shot through my chest and lodged in my throat as it struggled to get out of my body. We were already climbing a second, much smaller hill when I realized that, miraculously, my head had not been ripped off by the enragement of the first dive.

"Don't you just love this?" shouted Sarah as she slapped my hand.

"Love it, love it," I swooned.

Then it happened. I got a cramp in the back of my leg. There was only one way I could get rid of one of those; relax my leg by gently walking on it.

At the end of the ride, the attendant sliced me open and let the sand run out.

Hobbling down the exit ramp.

"You're limping," said Sarah. "What's wrong?"

"It's nothing," I said as I increased the limp. "It's the knee. An old football injury."

I didn't dare mention the word "cramp." When a girl hears that, she immediately thinks of her period. Hardly the kind of image you want to be associated with.

"I didn't know you played football."

"Not organized football, but, of course, I've played football." As if everyone in the world did.

"Is there anything I can do?"

Sex would help, I thought to myself. "No, why don't we just walk around for a few minutes?"

"Okay," she agreed.

Sarah was actually subdued. I was delighted and limped even more. Old football injury, my ass. I was three years old the first time I got a cramp in my leg. I had been sitting on my feet in the sandbox too long.

A few minutes later, Sarah pointed to a bench. "Why don't we rest here a while before we go on the parachute ride?"

"The parachute ride?" I began limping so much that my head was almost touching the ground. "You want to go on the parachute ride?"

"Who would come to Riverview without riding the parachutes?" asked Sarah.

"No one," I lied. "I just thought that you'd like to go on some other rides before we go on the parachutes."

"It's getting late," said Sarah. "We'd better go straight to the parachutes from here."

I knew lots of people who had come to Riverview and had never gone on the parachute ride. I knew families of them. In fact, I knew families who, for generations, had never ridden the parachutes. Actually, an excellent way to guarantee that you didn't have generations of families was to ride the parachutes.

Although it was a clear day, one corner of Riverview's sky, as usual, was covered with clouds; parachutes drifting down from the huge tower that stood in a corner of the park.

The customer end of the parachute ride consisted of one small flat board to sit on, another small one to lean on and a wooden rail that clamped across the front. Twenty-five feet above you hung the parachute. Six guide wires ran through its perimeter. A large magnetic disc, which actually pulled the parachute to the top of the tower, was attached to the center of the canvas.

There was no line at the parachute ride when Sarah and I arrived. There was never a line at the parachute ride. As we sat motionless on the seat, the attendant locked the guard rail in front of us and said, "Make sure you hold on. Otherwise, you might slip under the rail." Sarah disdainfully glared at him. I immediately welded my hands onto the rail.

As the cable slowly inched us and our parachute skyward, I refused to look down because I didn't want to know how high I was. Neither did I want to look up at the overhanging arm of the tower. If I did, I'd realize how high I was soon going to be. Nor did I want to close my eyes. I've never been too fond of the dark. I had no choice but to stare straight ahead at the Chicago downtown skyline that clustered on the horizon a few miles away and try to convince myself that I was looking at a postcard.

Halfway up, I realized that Sarah wasn't talking. She wasn't babbling on about how terrifically exciting all of this was. We both sat perfectly still and especially tried to keep our dangling legs from moving, fully aware that we were one slippery rear end away from oblivion. I decided to show Sarah that I was quite accustomed to hanging two hundred feet up in the air.

"This sure is a good view," I uttered. The words of an imbecile. What normal person would risk his life simply for a "good view?"

A few moments later, as we continued to be reeled away from the earth, I tried it again. "Gee, this isn't as bad as I thought it would be." My words didn't carry much conviction since, in the middle of them, my voice had jumped twelve octaves.

I found myself praying again. Soon, I had myself convinced that if the parachute went any higher, I'd be talking to God face to face.

Suddenly, the entire parachute bounced away from the overhanging arm of the tower and floated back down to earth. I glanced over at Sarah. Her face, like mine, was drenched in perspiration. Human beings went up on the parachute ride, but only dishrags came down.

Jumping out of the seat, squeezing each other's hands and almost skipping down the exit ramp. She told me how much fun she had on all the rides and would I buy her some cotton candy and wasn't the weather fantastic and could she have some popcorn, too, and how was my knee and why wasn't everyone else in the world at Riverview and did I have enough money for a large box of popcorn and did I really have a good time? I said yes, yes, yes, fine, I don't know, yes, yes, and I only got mildly depressed when I remembered that Sarah wouldn't be next to me forever. She wouldn't even be with me for the rest of the day.

As we walked towards the concession stand, I stopped and announced, "Not so fast. There's going to be a slight charge for all of these culinary delights."

Sarah smiled, stepped close to me, reached up and cupped her hand behind my neck and kissed me much harder than she had to.

"Keep the change," she whispered. "By the way, can I have butter on that popcorn?"

"You can have the world on that popcorn."

Two hours later, we were parked across the street from her parish church. A flat sheet of clouds was slowly choking off the blue sky.

"Do you always go to confession on Saturday afternoon?" I asked.

"When I can. Do you ever go to confession?"

"No, not in a long while. No."

"I see," said Sarah, "you don't sin any more."

"That's it," I quickly agreed. "I'm a very good person."

"At what? Going numb on roller coasters?"

We both noticed the front door of the church quiver and gradually give way to an old nun who toddled out from behind it. Her feet, shuffling mechanically, eased her gingerly towards the convent a few dozen yards away.

"That's Sister Mary Albert," said Sarah. "I had her in seventh grade. She could hardly walk even then. You know what she used to do? If kids were misbehaving in the back of the room, Sister Albert would walk up to Eddie O'Connor, who sat in the front of the room. She'd pick up the ruler from his desk and hold it high above her head. Then she'd say, 'If you people in the back of the room don't stop misbehaving, I'm going to come down there and snap you in half,' and she'd break Eddie O'Connor's ruler to show them exactly what she meant. According to Sister Albert's classroom regulations, we had to keep a ruler on our desks at all times, so Eddie O'Connor was constantly buying a new one."

"Maybe Sister Albert was getting a kickback from the school supplies store."

"I doubt that," said Sarah.

"Were you a brownnose?" I asked.

"What did you say?"

"You know. Were you one of the kids who the nuns were always asking to do things for them?"

"No, I wish I had been."

"Me, too," I said. "But being a boy, there was no chance. There was this one girl, Mary Gilbert, who always sat in a front seat and who was always running errands for the nun. I hated her. 'Mary Gilbert, will you please come up to my desk? I have a message to send to the Pope.' And when the nun left the room, Mary Gilbert was the one who stood up in front and took names. She would have made a great Nazi.

"I had this one nun in second grade, though," I continued, "who didn't bother putting anybody up in front of the room when she left. When she got back in the room, she'd ask the people who had talked while she was gone to stand up. If enough kids didn't stand, the nun would tell us this story about some kid, from a different school, of course, who had lied to a nun and how, just before three o'clock, his desk burst into flames. Man, after that, we'd come flying out of those desks."

"Remember," asked Sarah, "how, years ago, if you wanted to go to communion in the morning, you couldn't eat or drink anything after midnight?"

"Yeah," I replied, "all of that certainly has changed."

"Well, the night before my First Holy Communion," said

Sarah, "I got confused and I thought the rule was that you couldn't go to the washroom after midnight. It was a very tense Sunday morning," she laughed.

"I'll bet."

Sarah abruptly sobered up. "What time is it?"

"Almost four-thirty."

"I'd better get going. Confessions end at five."

"I forgot," I said, "big date, tonight."

"Don't be sarcastic."

I felt like a relay man in Sarah's Saturday marathon. Handing her off to a guy who'd get all the glory of finishing the day with her. At least, tonight, I thought, he was getting a girl with used lips.

"How about next Saturday night?" I asked.

"Okay."

I didn't remind her that she had previously told me she was busy that night.

Sarah didn't say another word. She simply got out of the car, gently closed the door and went and stood in front of the car to wait for a break in the traffic.

She didn't say "good-bye" or even look back at me. I liked that. As if all the hours that would pass before we talked again were going to be nothing more than a slight pause in our conversation.

Watching her cross the street. I mean, I really watched her cross the street. She did it superbly.

I waited until she entered the church. Speckles of rain began decorating the windshield. Pulling away from the curb, singing with a fast song on the radio, my hand pounding out the rhythm on the dashboard. When the lead singer went into falsetto, I did my best to go right along with him.

Laughing over nothing.

SIXTEEN

Sunday morning, on my way to the hardware store, I took a walk by Caepan's gas station, hoping that it would be open. He rarely worked on weekends, but that morning he was there.

When I walked into the garage, Caepan was standing beneath the hoist, unscrewing a metal plate from the bottom of a car.

"How come you're working this morning?"

"Got in so late last night," said Caepan, "I thought I'd come over here and get this job out of the way."

I didn't ask him where he had been the previous night. Caepan was an intensely private person. When I first knew him, I once asked him if he had ever been married or if he dated much. He said he couldn't remember. From different things he had said, I knew that Caepan saw a lot of women in a lot of ways. When he volunteered information, I listened. But no questions.

"This job's going to cost my friend Tony plenty," said Caepan.

"It's taking you quite a while, huh?"

"No, that's not how it's going to cost him. This is a stick shift car. The reverse gear was all screwed up. It was very tricky to pop in. What Tony would do is he'd stop at a traffic light and wait

81

for some guy to pull up behind him. Tony would then shift the car into reverse and hit him. Then he'd tell the guy he'd just smacked into that his car had no reverse so the guy must have hit him. For a few bucks, Tony wouldn't call the cops. If the guy decided to call the cops anyway, Tony would still come out ahead with the insurance because the cop wouldn't be able to get the car into reverse either."

"So why are you fixing it?"

"Last week, the cop who showed up had a family car with the same kind of transmission problem."

"Oh. By the way," I said, "I went out with a really sharp girl yesterday."

"Yeah? that's nice." said Caepan as he continued to work.

"You know," I said, "it seems that, sooner or later, most people get married."

"That they do."

I chose my words carefully so that the question would sound like one of philosophy rather than a personal inquiry. "Does that make sense to you?"

"A friend of mine once owned a race horse," said Caepan. "He warned me never to invest in anything I had to feed."

I looked at my watch and realized that I had already been gone from the house for nearly a half hour. I hadn't bothered telling my father that I was stopping at Caepan's. One reason was that I didn't think Caepan would be around. The other reason was that my father, like the rest of the neighborhood, didn't like him. I don't know why.

Caepan was always pleasant to people and he had more business than he could handle because he was good, fast and cheap. Regardless, people from the neighborhood always acted annoyed whenever I mentioned him. That, of course, had been years ago. I never talked about Caepan to anyone any more. Not anyone.

"I've got to get going, Caepan. Anyway, I'm really looking forward to going out with this girl again. She's something else."

Caepan walked over to his workbench and put down his tools. Then he took a clean rag out of his back pocket and wiped the grease off his face. "You like to buy girls flowers, don't you, Conroy?"

"I suppose so. What do you mean?"

"You really like to show them a good time. Wine 'em and dine 'em. Surprise them with little gifts. That sort of thing."

"What are you driving at?" He was beginning to get on my nerves. I could tell that he was setting me up for something. Not a joke, Caepan wasn't the joke telling kind.

"You don't have to answer me," said Caepan. "I've known it for quite a while. You've got a disease that's going to drive you, and quite a few people around you, nuts."

"Okay, I'll bite," I said. "What's the disease?"

"You're an incurable romantic."

"That's not funny."

"I know," said Caepan. "Believe me, I know."

SEVENTEEN

Sitting around on a Saturday morning, wondering what I was going to do with the rest of my life. As close as I could figure, after two more years of college, I had the next fifty years open. At least.

We were out of bread, so I decided to take a walk down to Cohen's Food Store. Rain had fallen the night before so when I got to the alley at the end of the block, I had to walk out in the street to get around the puddle.

Mrs. Vitoli, who lived closest to the puddle, was always calling the city about it. At least three times a year, a city crew would come out and dump an entire truckload of gravel onto the puddle. Two weeks later, the puddle would be bigger than ever. My father claimed that it was the biggest tax drain on the neighborhood. My Aunt Clare, who was married to my Uncle Arnie the drinker, lived a few houses away from the puddle. She said that it was just like her husband: never dry.

When I was a kid, I used to ice skate at the park. The custodian would spray water over the outfields of diamonds three and four. If the water was poured on a windy day, your skates would spend the next three months clunking over the tiny frozen waves.

At the beginning of the winter, I'd check the puddle on my way to school. If even its edges were beginning to freeze, then I knew that the water at the park had frozen solid. The puddle never completely froze over. I once asked my father about that. He said something about it freezing the day after Hell did.

I used to read that scouting magazine, *Boys' Life,* a lot, too. Each month, they ran a "true story" about how a scout had saved someone's life by either carrying them out of a burning building, dragging them away from an auto accident, rescuing them from a cliff or waterfall or saving them from drowning as the potential victim broke through the ice. Naturally, I hoped that someday I'd get lucky and save somebody's life and end up immortalized in a "true story" in *Boys' Life.*

What a fantastic way to impress girls. "Hey, have you read the recent issue of *Boys' Life*?" But I knew that the odds were against me.

My neighborhood had very little in common with the catastrophic atmosphere of "true stories." The only things that caught on fire in my neighborhood were garbage cans and outdoor grills. I was once sitting on the front porch when two cars collided at the intersection of my corner. I ran up to one of the cars and opened the door, looking for victims. The woman immediately screamed, grabbed her purse and slammed the door. There are no cliffs or waterfalls in Chicago. And with three inches of water at the park, even a Barbie doll couldn't get into trouble.

One night, I even dreamed that I saved someone from the puddle. Even if such a silly thing was possible, it was hardly the fare that *Boys' Life* would write about. "Scout saves mother of three from drowning in puddle, injured by flying gravel."

That's the trouble with growing up. When you're a kid, a puddle's a puddle. But when you're an adult, or close enough, it's just a spot of rainwater with nowhere to go.

Walking into Mr. Cohen's store. It was located on 111th Street, down the block and around the corner from my house. He and his wife, Dolores, his son, Leonard, when he was home from college, and Mr. Cohen's mother lived in an apartment in the back of the store. They also had an older married daughter.

Mr. Cohen treated every person who came into the store with

the same courtesy as if that person was in Mr. Cohen's living room. Actually, before the building was remodeled, that's exactly where the customer was.

Years ago, there had been four or five stores like Mr. Cohen's within walking distance of my house. But they had been snuffed out of existence by two supermarkets that opened up a mile away, across the street from one another.

Mr. Cohen, however, had managed to survive. Bread and milk still moved well. So did penny candy. Most of the pop, he sold a bottle at a time. The cigarettes went out by the pack rather than the carton. Now, the only ones who did all of their weekly shopping at the corner store were young housewives who didn't have the time, old ladies who didn't have the legs and young kids who didn't have permission to go any further.

When I was a kid, I'd go up to Mr. Cohen's store almost every evening for something the family needed. On cold winter nights, I'd hustle along the sidewalk, the note for the store wrapped tightly in my fist, which huddled deep in my coat pocket.

When I got inside Mr. Cohen's store, its warmth would glow around me and I'd feel so much cozier than in any other room I'd been in that day, if for no other reason than I knew I'd shortly be going back out into the cold again.

On hot summer days, there wasn't a screen door in the entire neighborhood that slammed as sweetly as the one on Mr. Cohen's store. Within a few feet of that slam were the coolest things around: ice cream, Popsicles, Fudgsicles, Push-ups, even frozen candy bars. Over in the bright red, waist high cooler, swarmed by cold water, were bottles of cola, root beer, orange pop, cherry, raspberry, and for the true gourmet, cream soda.

Even though the Cohens were one of the few Jewish families in the neighborhood, their store still drew the largest crowd on Sunday morning. After the usual church services, no matter what kind they were, most of the neighborhood people would pass through the corner store; picking up the Sunday papers, buying an extra gallon of milk for the company that was coming over for Sunday dinner, or simply coming in to mix with the crowd because everyone seemed to be there, and buying something to justify the visit.

When I walked into the store, Mrs. Fenns, a fat, stocky woman with Fig Newton legs, was standing at the counter stashing her day's supply of cola and potato chips into a large brown bag. She never liked the way Mr. Cohen packed them. He was standing on the other side of the counter, rearranging a display of pocket combs.

"Ours was a marriage made in Heaven," said Mrs. Fenns. "I just don't understand why God had to take him."

"He was a good man," nodded Mr. Cohen. "Who can understand?"

Mrs. Fenns' husband had died about four months earlier. He was a slow dier. He had been home ill for over ten years when he finally got around to it. During all those years, no one in the neighborhood had ever seen him. Nobody even knew what eventually killed him. Mrs. Fenns never talked about her husband's illness. But she loved to rattle on about how she had to wait on him constantly and how he refused to do anything for himself.

Mrs. Fenns lifted up the grocery bag, wrapped both arms around it and waddled towards the door. "See you tomorrow, Mr. Cohen."

"Have a nice day," he replied automatically.

I stepped up to the counter with the loaf of bread that I had just snatched from a shelf. "How are things going today, Mr. Cohen?"

"Good, Timmy, and yourself?"

"Okay." I went over to the cooler, took out a bottle of pop, opened it, and then grabbed a package of cupcakes from one of the shelves. I returned to the counter, opening the package of cupcakes and taking a sip of pop.

"You know, Lenny's home from school?" asked Mr. Cohen.

"Is he?"

Leonard went to the University of Illinois, which was located downstate in a small town. He was majoring in pre-med and was the same age as me.

"Yes, he's been home a couple of days now. He's doing very well in school, you know, a straight A student. We're all so proud of him. He's going to be a great doctor some day real soon."

"Gee, that's terrific, Mr. Cohen." I couldn't have cared less. Parents sound like such jerks when they brag about their kids.

Still, it was nice to see Mr. Cohen get excited. Although Leonard was the same age as I was, Mr. Cohen was considerably older than my father. Mr. Cohen must have been in his middle sixties. As he talked about Leonard, you could hear the wrinkles unravel from his voice.

A kid with an empty carton of bottles came into the store. I popped the last piece of cupcake into my mouth and leaned over the counter to toss the empty package into the garbage can.

"I'll have to give Leonard a call sometime, Mr. Cohen."

He was taking the carton of bottles from the kid along with a crunched up note. "You can see him now. He's over at the park playing basketball."

"Yeah, well, maybe I'll do that if I have time. I'll see you later, Mr. Cohen."

"We'll be seeing you, Timmy."

Mr. Cohen always said, "we," as if he were twins or something.

As I pushed open the screen door, I could hear Mr. Cohen's voice behind me, eyeing the kid with suspicion.

"Cigarettes, huh? Are you sure your mother wrote this note?"

I hadn't seen Leonard in about a year. When I was growing up, I didn't hang around with him much. Nobody did. One reason was that he didn't go to either the public or Catholic neighborhood schools. His father sent him to a private school, somewhere downtown. Even though Leonard wasn't richer than any of us—actually, his father made less money than most other fathers—the fact that he went to a private school made him seem richer. A lot of the kids probably resented him for that. I did.

Before Leonard even started grammar school, Mr. Cohen had told the entire neighborhood that his kid, Lenny, was going to be a doctor.

One day, when I was in eighth grade, I was in Mr. Cohen's store and I overheard Leonard tell his father that he had gotten sick in school that morning. Leonard said that he had spent the whole day lying in a regular hospital bed in the nurse's office. The nurse had told Leonard that his symptoms indicated that he had a touch of stomach flu. Leonard added that, medically speaking, the nurse seemed to basically know what she was doing. "Adequate," said Leonard, "she was quite adequate."

Unbelievable. Having a real nurse and a hospital bed right in your own school. I went straight over to Caepan's gas station. He was sitting with his feet propped up on his desk. I told him what I had just overheard.

"So what happens when you get sick at your school?" asked Caepan.

"I go up and tell the nun."

"And what expert medical advice does she give you?"

"She tells me to go back to my seat and put my head on my desk."

"Sounds like a good system to me," said Caepan. "If you don't pick up your head by three o'clock, she knows you're dead."

Another annoying thing about Leonard, when he was a kid, was that he never lied. All kids lie occasionally. I was an exception. I lied all the time. I lied even when the truth would have fit better, out of force of habit. My parents, who for years told me there was a Santa Claus, an Easter Bunny and that if I ate a good breakfast I'd grow up to be big and strong, became enraged whenever I lied to them.

When I was five years old, my father watched me pull off all my shirt buttons and then asked me if I had done it. When I said no, he got enraged, spanked me and then said it was very dumb of me to lie. I didn't think it was any dumber than him asking me if I had done something he had just seen me do.

Most kids are like that, at least sometimes.

Even if the evidence is overwhelming, they'll try and lie their way out of it. But not Leonard Cohen. He wouldn't lie even when he had a good chance of getting away with it. I don't think it was because he was all that honest or anything like that. He just couldn't be bothered. Leonard didn't seem to have the enthusiasm to lie.

But that afternoon, as I walked to the park, I envied Leonard. He knew where he was going, what he wanted to be and that was that.

When I got to the park, I saw Leonard standing alone on the basketball court, just dribbling the ball, and occasionally gazing up at the backboard.

Leonard had been a short, stocky kid. But, sometime around his fifteenth birthday, his pituitary gland went bananas and he grew eight inches in two years.

He hadn't seen me yet. He picked up the basketball, held it at waist level, and stared up at the basket. I could see him rocking on the backs of his heels. A strand of flesh and bone, wavering, but not quite willing to capitulate to the whims of a summer breeze.

When Leonard saw me approaching, he reacted by lobbing the ball up to the basket. The ball hit the hoop at a strange angle and bounced down towards me. I grabbed the ball and tossed it to Leonard.

"How're you doing, Leonard?"

"Hi, Conroy," Leonard said reluctantly. With Leonard, I always got the feeling that I had worn out my welcome before I even arrived.

"I was in your father's store today."

"Yeah?"

"He said you've been pulling straight A's."

"Yeah."

"That's really something."

"Yeah."

I had forgotten what an enthralling conversationalist Leonard was.

He casually dribbled the ball away from the basket as he went out to take a long shot. Leonard was obviously annoyed that I was even there. Screw him. I decided I'd stay and bother him a few more minutes and then leave when I felt like it.

"How's Barbara doing?" I asked. Barbara Gordon was a neighborhood girl that Leonard had been dating since sophomore year of high school. I don't think either of them had ever gone out with anyone else. She was now a student at a nursing school on Chicago's West Side. Barbara seemed to be a quiet girl who took all her orders from Leonard.

"She's doing okay."

I didn't bother asking Leonard how his older sister was. I knew he couldn't stand her.

"Looking forward to summer vacation?" I asked.

"Yeah."

Who needed this bullshit? "I'll be seeing you, Leonard. By the way, Mrs. Fenns sends her regards."

"Where did you see her?"

"In your father's store. She was telling him about how her marriage had been made in Heaven."

"If it was," said Leonard, "then God must have a strange sense of humor."

Leonard had worked for Mrs. Fenns when he was in high school, doing odd jobs around her house, cutting the lawn, stuff like that.

Twenty feet away from the basket, Leonard turned around, bent his knees slightly and shoved the ball through the air. He missed everything. I retrieved the ball a few feet away from the basket and shot it towards the hoop, missing everything. Leonard walked after the ball.

"Some marriages," he said, "are good only after they're gone."

He picked up the basketball, went over to a park bench and sat up on top of it. I walked over and stood next to the bench.

"Leonard, did you ever see Mr. Fenns when you worked for her?"

"No," said Leonard as he talked directly to the basketball wedged between his hands. "She kept the door to his room pulled over. I never even heard him. One day, I asked Mrs. Fenns what was wrong with her husband. It was a very ignorant question, I realize. But you have to remember, I was talking to Mrs. Fenns.

"She said the doctors didn't know but that they thought it might be some rare African disease that Mr. Fenns contracted during the war when he was fighting in the trenches.

"I told her that I was studying to be a doctor and that I'd be very interested in the symptoms. She was impressed by that. She got very serious and said that it was quite admirable that a young man would be so curious about his future profession. Curious, shit. I was nosy. Curious, nosy, what's the difference? So she told me the symptoms. I went home and looked them up in my medical textbook. If Mr. Fenns contracted that disease in an African trench, he was laying on somebody when he did it. He had VD."

"VD?" I started laughing. Leonard admitted a smile and then started laughing, too. My laughter was still withering into a few chuckles when Leonard started talking again. But he continued to direct his words to the basketball he held in front of him.

"The thing that bothered me," said Leonard, "was if I could tell from a medical textbook what he had, why couldn't the doctors? Another thing, Mr. Fenns had been in bed for ten years. At least, he had been home from work for that long. Mrs. Fenns said that he gradually ended up spending all of his time in bed. But the only way VD is going to kill you is if it goes untreated."

"Maybe Mrs. Fenns nagged him to death."

"Now that's a definite possibility," agreed Leonard. "Seriously, I think that man died of boredom. He probably just lost the will to live."

"You've discovered a new disease, Leonard. 'Fenns Syndrome.'"

"You can hardly call it a new disease when half the country's got it," said Leonard.

"Is it contagious?"

"Highly." Leonard bounced the basketball off the seat of the bench a few times. "When he died," continued Leonard, "the doctors told Mrs. Fenns, 'His heart stopped.' What a brilliant medical observation. They also chanted the national slogan of the AMA. 'We did everything we could.'"

"Was she upset when he died?"

"The next day she called me over to the house and led me past the door that had always been pulled over. I really wondered what I was going to see in there. But it was nothing unusual; a bed, a chest of drawers. Mrs. Fenns had her back to me. I thought that, maybe, she was trying to hide her tears. She pointed to a corner of the room. 'Leonard,' she said to me, 'the TV will go over there, the love seat along the wall . . .'"

EIGHTEEN

Dear God:

What would it be like if Christ came back today?

Signed: Conroy

Conroy:

Joseph would write a book, Mary would do shampoo commercials and Christ would appear on the Johnny Carson Show with a film clip of his latest miracle.

Signed: God

NINETEEN

During a sociology class, in junior year, everyone was requested to draw a man. A few days later, when the class met again, we were informed that our drawings were part of the research that a graduate student was doing for her thesis. She was studying the method whereby one can measure the mental age of an individual by the manner in which the person draws a figure of a man. My drawing indicated a mental age of three. Now if I had been asked to draw a freight car, it would have been a different story.

For little known to my friends, and the world at large, I once studied under one of the greatest pop artists of all time. A man whose works have crisscrossed the country for millions to view, whose achievements are so magnificent that blocks of traffic have stopped in awe to gaze upon them; a genius who has never done a painting worth less than twenty thousand dollars; an individual whose art can be found in almost every freight yard in the country. His name was Charley Day and he was a freight car painter.

Physically, he was not a large man, about five and a half feet tall. He was black, of better than average build, with a rectangular face slightly pushed in, which accentuated his unusually square jaw. When he worked he was always engulfed in gray coveralls, which began in the upturned collar around his neck and ended two inches below his shoe tops. His hands, when idle, rode along gently, buried deep in the kangaroo pockets that hung on the sides of his coveralls.

Capitol Freight Car Company, located in an industrial complex on Chicago's Far South Side, consisted of a number of oblong sheds wallowing in sand and gravel. Like most freight car companies, Capitol Freight Car Company did not build new freight cars, it simply rebuilt the old ones. Most of the cars on tracks today were originally built thirty or forty years ago and since then rejuvenated two or three times at a place like Capitol Freight Car Company.

Everyone at Capitol Freight Car Company, sandblasters, welders, riveters, carpenters, worked on the assembly line. At the end of the line were seven painters, none of them Charley Day.

Charley could be found in a small, wooden shed in an obscure corner of the complex. About half of the freight cars were diverted away from the other painters and sent rolling to him. Like most great artists, Charley demanded privacy when he worked.

The lord of this freight car manor was a guy named Bensen. He was a tall, well-built man in his late fifties with a sun-sliced face that gave him the appearance of being very tough. He was.

Superintendent Bensen wore a silver hard hat. His assistants wore blue hard hats. The five foremen wore red hard hats. The rest of the men all wore gray hard hats. Except for Charley Day who didn't wear a hard hat. And on those rare occasions when he bothered to talk to Superintendent Bensen, he didn't say "Mister" like everyone else did.

Charley Day's power over Bensen wasn't hard to figure out. Charley painted more freight cars than all the other seven painters combined, and he did a better job. In addition, he stenciled all the lettering and numbering on all the cars, and he built his own stencils. Yet, he still found ways to loaf—experiment, he called it—at least four hours a day.

In the June following my sophomore year of college, Capitol

Freight Car Company hired a number of college students for the summer vacation. It wasn't that the company really wanted help from the leaders of tomorrow, but Capitol Freight Car Company thought if they hired students they'd have a better chance of getting government contracts.

In order to make it tougher for the students to destroy the place, most of us were assigned to work with a regular employee. I was assigned to help Charley Day. He needed about as much assistance as the Rockefeller Foundation.

When my mind searches back through its files for snatches of that historical first day with Charley, I must admit it comes up with nothing. But even if that day could be relived, I doubt if it could unfold that intrinsic, invisible mesh that envelops two personalities and produces a winning combination. Who can explain the dual successes of Ferrante and Teicher, Hansel and Gretel, Laurel and Hardy, Day and Conroy?

Most likely, that first day was spent the same way most of them were. Me doing most of the talking and Charley Day doing most of the work, though he probably just worked on stencils. He didn't do any painting. That, I would have remembered.

On the second day, I was reassigned, with half a dozen other college students, to spread cement for the foundation of a new storage building. As we wallowed hopelessly in the stuff, a foreman in a red hard hat kept yelling at us. "Alright, you guys, shovel some over there. No, for Christ's sake, over there behind you." Superintendent Bensen would occasionally come out of his office, stand there with his feet braced apart, his hands on his hips and look down at us as if we were ants. His silver hat would catch the sun and would reflect through our cement-caked eyelids with its indelible message: "I am the Lord thy God."

Being a typical middle-class pseudo-intellectual, I absolutely detest physical labor. When I was younger, I used to rationalize having to do it by saying, in a heftier voice than usual, that "It keeps me in shape." In shape for what? Dying? One of the main reasons I had gone to college was to avoid work and I wasn't about to throw away the two years of schooling I had thus far accumulated by having a triple hernia as I tried to move around in that cement.

At lunchtime, I dragged myself over to Charley's shed. He was leaning over his drawing board, gently taping the torn sections of a wind infected stencil. The place was full of half-filled paint cans, used rags, bits of cardboard and turpentine cans. Paint smears speckled the wall.

"Charley, you've gotta get me out of there," I said. "They're killing me." He didn't even look up.

"What's the matter, kid, old Bensen working you too hard?"

I held up the backs of my hands to him. "Charley, do these look like the hands of a ditch digger? I'm an artist, a painter. These are the . . ."

Charley turned around and leaned back on the drawing board. "Okay, Conroy, I got the message. Don't worry, you'll be back over here as soon as lunch is over. Now, man, I gotta get back to this here stencil or Bensen's gonna have me shoveling that shit right next to you."

When the afternoon shift began, it must have been a thousand degrees outside. I kept looking towards that shed and for that man in the gray coveralls to come over and salvage what was left of me. I was even beginning to wonder if he was going to come. Really, why the hell should he?

Finally, about a half hour after we started, I saw Charley step out of the shed and come shuffling towards us. That slow, casual and confident way of walking that comes from knowing you're the absolute best at what you do. I used to walk that way through my back yard after playing ball off the Methodist church wall.

Superintendent Bensen was hovering over us in his usual God-like posture when Charley Day walked up to him. Charley stood next to Bensen, imitated his stance and began staring right along with him. There stood those two giants of Capitol Freight Car Company, side by side, watching us crazy college kids drown each other in cement. But, for a few moments, not a word passed between them.

Charley spoke first and he spoke as an equal, his head never turning towards Superintendent Bensen.

"I need Conroy, Bensen, he was a big help yesterday." That was enough to cause Bensen to do a double spin, which was exactly what he did. He turned and bellowed into Charley's face.

"Who are you trying to kid, Charley? You don't work half of the day as it is."

But the hot blast of air didn't phase Charley. He continued to look straight ahead as if the conversation wasn't worth his full attention. "Look, Bensen," he said, "I ain't one of the three little pigs. Huffin' and puffin' ain't gonna do no good. I need Conroy."

Charley turned and shuffled back towards his shed. The conversation was over. Bensen hesitated a moment, trying to put off the inevitable. Then he waved towards me. "Hey, you, Conroy, go with Charley."

At about 2:30 P.M., on that sun-burned June afternoon, while Charley and I were working on a cracked stencil, I heard it. CLICK, click click, CLICK, click click, CLICK, swisssh-badumpt.

"Well, kid," said Charley in a voice of resignation, "we'd better get it out of the way. Break time's almost here."

He walked to the door and surveyed the newly arrived freight car with all the perception of the sculptor viewing the uncut marble. He grabbed a huge barrel of paint, shoved it onto a coaster wagon, and pulled it out of the shed to the freight car.

Protruding out of the paint barrel was a six-foot-long spray gun consisting of two thin hoses running parallel to one another, ending in two long pipes, which in turn terminated in a flat coin-shaped face with two tiny holes. At the base of the pipe stems were two triggers, one controlling the paint pressure and the other regulating the flow of the air.

The idea was to keep the flow of air precisely balanced with the flow of paint. Too much air and the paint would be too thin. An insufficient air supply would cause the paint to thicken and run down the sides of the freight car.

All of this Charley explained to me as he locked a hose onto a pressurized air control outlet. Turning it on, he pointed the face of the gun downward, a few inches from the ground. Charley pulled one trigger, then another, then both. He repeated this a few times until he was satisfied with the combination of air and paint. He then lifted up the long spray gun and held it much as a flag bearer would carry the flag.

In college, the most "in" word for a student to use is "Why?" When I heard an instructor state that the essence of the universe was essentially such and such or that when it rains you get wet, if someone else didn't beat me to it, I would immediately yell "Why?" But somehow this man in the gray coveralls did not seem like an ideal counterpart for a prolonged discussion. So when Charley said "Step back" I did though I didn't know why.

He leaned the long spray gun to his left side. Then with one smooth motion, he swung it pendulum-style across the wall of the freight car, the head of the gun coming within a foot of the wall. Wissssssssssh. There suddenly appeared a five-foot strip of paint on the side of the freight car.

In my first moment's awe of Charley, I also discovered the freight car painter's worst enemy: wind. Although there was hardly any that day, there was red paint flying everywhere. It was covering every square section of the air that I had occupied but a few seconds earlier. There were mad red flurries in front of Charley; behind and on both sides of Charley. But none on Charley.

Although he seemed to be moving not at all, his feet were gingerly cutting in and out of the tiny wind currents created by the spray gun. Charley had all the moves of a great scrambler. Later, I found out that the other painters wore masks to avoid getting paint on their faces. And they painted indoors so they wouldn't have to contend with the wind.

Charley painted that entire freight car in about twenty-two minutes. The average freight car painter takes a little under two hours. We took our coffee break in Charley's shed.

"We'd better get back to work," said Charley as he crunched his empty coffee cup in his hands. "That car should be dry enough to stencil by now."

As we walked out of the shed, Charley pointed to a pile of stencils and told me to grab them. None of the stencils had the usual hooks in order to hang from the top of the freight car. I found out why when I lifted them up. They were covered with small magnets. I needed only to throw them up against the side of the freight car and watch Charley spray in the letter or number. Charley crowed, "Another Day invention, Conroy. Oh, that Glorious Day."

The weeks passed quickly with this DaVinci of the freight yard.

Slowly, my hands were being transformed into precision instruments capable of producing intense and monstrous works of art. I learned to manipulate the dual triggers of the great spray gun, to take into account a northeasterly wind that would come slithering down the wall that I was painting or for a westerly wind that would suddenly flare up behind my back. I learned to mix paints, or in Charley's more scientific terminology, to "mingle" paints. I was taught how to hold a spray gun properly, how to swing it, clean it. And I learned how to draw, cut, and measure stencils.

But more importantly, I began to absorb and reflect the personality of the master. I began to pick up that self-assurance, that cockiness that comes with greatness. I no longer wore my gray hard hat and, on more than one occasion, I was tempted to drop the "Mister" when I talked to Superintendent Bensen.

Charley Day wasn't all business. Normally, we'd paint and stencil ten freight cars a day. If Charley and I knew that a particular series had eighty freight cars in it and the beginning numbers were 223, we'd number the first car 22301, the second car 22302, and so on. One day, Charley decided that we were going to skip a number.

"Why are we going to do that?" I asked.

"They don't teach you much in college these days, do they, kid," said Charley. "It just so happens that when these freight cars come in off the road to be rebuilt, the first thing that happens to them is they go through the sandblasting shed. They're totally sandblasted. There isn't one mark of identification left on them. Do you get it?"

"Nope," I said.

"You just wait and see then," said Charley.

It didn't take long. Two days later, Charley and I were working on a freight car when Superintendent Bensen came stomping up to us.

"Say, Charley," demanded Bensen, "where's 38106?"

"I just paint them, Bensen, I don't babysit them."

"Look, Charley," said Bensen, "38105 came rolling up to the checkout point right on time yesterday and so did 38107. So where the hell is 06?"

Charley, who had been kneeling next to the freight car to get the low lettering on it, stood up and turned around in a complete circle. "Search me, Bensen, I haven't got it. You got it, Conroy?"

"Not me, Charley."

Bensen picked up the No. 6 stencil to see if it had been used recently. Then I knew why Charley had sprayed paint on the stencil the previous afternoon.

"Did you check the lunch boxes lately, Bensen?" Charley was referring to the act of confidence that Capitol Freight Car Company sometimes gave its men at the front gate at quitting time.

Bensen didn't bother to reply but simply went off and did the only thing a man in his position could have done; he called the police department to report a missing freight car. The next day, Capitol Freight Car Company's board of directors, in their gold hard hats, went searching around the grounds for a missing twenty-ton freight car.

Late one afternoon, Superintendent Bensen came bubbling into the shed. Bensen actually stepping into Charley's shed was totally against the law of gravity so Charley and I knew something was up.

"Hi, Bensen. What brings ..."

Bensen walked right by my familiarity and over to Charley. "There's a new group of freight cars coming over here, Charley, a hundred of them. The first one will be in front of your shed by tonight. But just paint them, don't stencil them."

Charley was stunned. "Why not?"

"Because," said Bensen with an accent of disdain I hadn't noticed in his voice before, "these are a totally different type of freight car than you're used to handling. We've split an ordinary car in half and inserted ten-foot beams. And we've raised the roof. If we made her any bigger, she wouldn't be able to turn corners. The stenciling's going to be huge and it's got to be perfect. So we're having stencils shipped in from New York and we're gonna hire a specialist, a sign painter, to handle the job."

Bensen took out a photograph of the freight car. On the left side of the car were two large letters, "I.W." Each letter threw off dense black-painted shadows. On the right side of the freight car were the words, "Illinois Western." Charley just stared at the photograph.

"Hell, Charley," continued Bensen, "I know you could do the job. But the boys in New York, they can't take chances."

It was the first time I had ever heard Bensen use the term "boys" to refer to the hierarchy. Normally, he would have just called them "bastards," but that day Bensen was wearing a white collar.

"I'll leave the photograph here," said Bensen. "Be careful with it, Charley, it's the only one the sign painter will have to work from." Then Bensen gloated out the door.

"What's so hard about stenciling that freight car, Charley?" I asked.

"It's the shadows, Conroy. It's real tricky to get that black paint to fall through that stencil in just the right way."

Charley looked around the shed at his arsenal of equipment. Old paint-scarred stencils, one piled on another, peered out of the rafters, hoping for one more moment in the sunlight. Buckets of magnets, sheets of cardboard and strips of plywood stood ready on the floor. Charley reached for his six-foot spray gun, which was mounted on the wall in the befitting manner of a knight's sword.

The four o'clock whistle was beginning to wail.

"You go home, Conroy, I got things to do."

The next morning I got to work at six-thirty, an hour early. There stood Charley, waiting for me.

"I finished a half hour ago, Conroy. Had the stencils done at about three this morning. Started painting as soon as the sun come out."

There it stood, the most colossal and beautiful freight car I had ever seen, colored a brashy, damning red, with the huge "I.W." and its foreboding black shadows on the left side and "ILLINOIS WESTERN" on the right.

"That's your 'Mona Lisa' Charley, no doubt about it," I said.

"I guess so, kid." Charley stood there a while, stroking his huge mahogany jaw, letting his mind and body soak in their achievement. Then Charley turned to me.

"I think it's about time for me to find another job," he said.

"I'm tired of painting these things. You know, Conroy," Charley continued, "once I'm gone, Bensen's gonna try and make life around here real tough for you." He handed me a slip of paper. "The stencils are in the shed and these are the dimensions. I've already gotten rid of the photograph."

Charley glided his fingers across the side of the freight car. "No sign painter, nobody's gonna replace you, Conroy, until you're good and ready to be replaced."

Charley stuck his hands deep into the kangaroo pockets of the gray coveralls, turned his back on the shed and shuffled toward the main gate.

And nobody did. The remaining ninety-nine "I.W." freight cars were painted solely by me, mainly because I was the only one who knew how. By September, when I left Capitol Freight Car Company to return to college, Bensen had hired five more painters to do the work of Charley Day.

Years later, parked at a railroad crossing, waiting for the train to go by. A familiar freight car, with its "I.W." emblem, rumbled past me. My mind raced back to Charley Day, that world we shared, and my last day in it.

I was in the office picking up my check. I asked Bensen if he knew where Charley was working now.

"Working? Are you kidding?" said Bensen. "He's probably still living off the money from the freight car he heisted."

TWENTY

There were only twenty minutes left before registration closed and I had to declare my major. During the past few weeks, I had given the decision plenty of thought. But all I had succeeded in doing was eliminating various subjects as possible majors.

Business and any kind of math were out. In first grade, the nun asked us to count our feet. I came up with a three digit answer.

Baseball wasn't offered.

In freshman year, I had virtually made up my mind to major in Sociology until I had taken a course from Dr. Lounders, who kept referring to the class as "You Whites," as if he was another color. He even did that to classes that had a lot of blacks in them. Dr. Lounders wore his three strands of hair in a "Natural."

Many things that made sense in sociology classes seemed to lose their logic once I got out of class. Riding home on the el one night, I wondered why the various sociology textbooks I had read and the lectures I had listened to didn't include studies or research on daily sociological problems that constantly preoccupied my mind. "The Social Implications of Surrendering Your Wallet."

"A Statistical Analysis of the Probability of Survival for Subjects Traveling on Public Transportation in the City of Chicago between the Hours of Two and Four A.M." "You Motherfucker: A Case Study of Stereotyping."

Majoring in English was a possibility until I took a poetry course. For five straight classes, we discussed the symbolism of three swans flying over a lake as described in a sixteenth century poem.

"Of course," said the professor as the discussion dwindled down into a collective coma, "if there had been two swans or four swans, the symbolism would have been so blatantly obvious. But three swans, ah, there's the challenge."

There were only ten minutes left before the closing of registration. I decided to major in speech and performing arts. No good. I couldn't fit all of that on the line provided. Psychology? But wasn't there math involved in there somewhere and, besides, I wasn't sure of how to spell it.

Then I thought of it, history. I quickly wrote it down and then sat back, proud of myself. History was the perfect major; easy to spell and I still had a half inch of space left on the line.

TWENTY-ONE

On a Saturday afternoon in early autumn, I was getting the props ready for the big performance, a Saturday night date with Sarah. Since Riverview, I had managed to get only a few dates with her. She was dating at least two other guys.

I had spent the past two hours washing and vacuuming the family car. Only the waxing was left. Slipping behind the wheel and starting the motor, I slowly drove the car along the curb towards the shade of a neighbor's tree. Plying the squeaky clean steering wheel with my fingers. A clean car always seems to run better. Shadows of an elm tree gently rolled over the hood of the car and slid up and over the windshield.

Mike Larkin, a guy from down the street, drove by. Years ago, he had been the first kid my age that I had seen driving around the neighborhood. It looked so strange seeing someone I knew, someone just like me actually driving a car. The sight had shocked me into realizing that hairy arms and corner taverns couldn't be far behind.

I was waxing the front fender a few minutes later when Leonard walked up to me. Apparently, he was in town for the weekend.

"Big date tonight, Conroy?"

"No, I went to confession this afternoon and this is my penance. The priest said, 'Say three Our Fathers, three Hail Marys and wash and wax the family car. And don't forget to clean the glove compartment.'"

"You Catholics sure are funny people. You probably laughed all the way to the lions. By the way, what's an 'Our Father?'"

"Jesus Christ, Leonard, don't you know anything?"

"Who's Jesus Christ?"

I threw the rag at him. "Don't give me that stuff, Leonard. I happen to know, for a fact, that they found your fingerprints on the cross."

"So what did you want us to do? Fine him a thousand loaves and fishes and give him six months probation? But enough of this religious banality. What are you doing tomorrow morning?"

"If I'm lucky, I'll still be on my way home."

"I'm taking my grandmother out to breakfast. Want to come along?"

I walked over, picked up the rag I had thrown at him, and shook the small stones that had latched onto the scabs of wax. "How is Grandma Cohen? I haven't seen her in a long time."

"Her arthritis is getting pretty bad," replied Leonard. "Anyway, you want to go?"

"How's she doing?"

"Okay. She's funny. Last Sunday night, they preempted the Lawrence Welk Show for a baseball game and she got so pissed that she kicked her slippers clear across the living room, one at a time."

Grunting as I rubbed the wax into the aging metal. "We're lucky," I said, "there wasn't mass rioting in the nursing homes of the nation."

"Look, do you want to go or not?" Leonard's mood had suddenly down-shifted. He was like that. One second, you could be kidding around with him and, in the next, he'd unexplainably unleash a flurry of words that would douse all of your enthusiasm for the conversation.

"What's the occasion?" I asked.

"She had her eighty-fifth birthday last week. The family threw a big party for her, but I was in the middle of registering for classes so I couldn't come back from school. I told her I'd take her out to breakfast tomorrow morning. It's a big deal for her. My parents can't come because they have to run the store. Grandma's always liked you so I thought it'd be nice if you came along."

"She likes me, huh?" My ego's always hungry. If an eighty-five-year-old woman, who I haven't seen more than a few times in the past five years, says she likes me, it makes my whole day. A fair indication of the kind of days I usually have.

"What time?" I asked.

"Ten o'clock."

"I'll meet you at your place."

"Fine," Leonard replied. Already, his antagonism was beginning to sink beneath the flow of our conversation. He began walking away.

"What are you doing tonight?" I asked. "Going out with Barbara?"

"Yeah," he said as he stopped walking for a moment. "Going to a show."

"Have fun."

Leonard resumed his walking. "Yeah, fun."

I would never have taken Sarah to a show. It would seem like such a waste; the two of us sitting in a darkened room and focusing all that attention on something other than each other.

TWENTY-TWO

"Sarah, your school friend's here." Mr. Faber pushed open the door for me.

"I'll be right down," I heard her reply from upstairs.

"Sarah got home late tonight from her job at the hospital," said Mr. Faber as he nodded towards the stairs.

"How are you tonight, sir?" I asked as I eased onto the couch.

The cushion on his easy chair was still rising in recovery when Mr. Faber sat back down in it and began staring at a television show. "Fine, and you?"

"Doing very well, thank you."

"That's good."

Brilliant conversation. As if either of us gave a damn. I could hardly say what he wanted to hear. "Believe me, sir, I have no intentions of violating your daughter, chopping her up with an axe and throwing her body in a river." If I was king, I'd make it a felony for a girl to keep her date waiting in the same room with her father.

I didn't blame him for hating me. How could a man like a kid who he believed was out to molest his baby pictures?

Mr. Faber was watching a documentary on porpoises.

"Looks like an interesting show," I said.

"It is."

I thought about how much I had to look forward to; getting married, having kids and watching porpoises on Saturday night.

About ten years later, Sarah came down the stairs. It was worth the wait. Thinking a lot about a person can do that.

We didn't have any previous plans so we drove around a while and went through the "I don't know, what do you want to do?" routine. Finally, I suggested the Prudential Building observation deck. Sarah liked the idea.

At that time, the Prudential Building was Chicago's tallest. The top floor contained a restaurant, whose prices, like the building, were high. Ringing around the restaurant, and about five feet lower, was an observation area. The entire floor was enclosed.

Sunlight was still lingering on the horizon when we arrived at the Prudential Building. Only a few people were walking around the observation area. Too late in the day for most families, too early in the evening for most dates.

The father of a family of tourists, however, was trying to convince his charges that this was a better deal than the cartoon movie they all wanted to see. "You do not," said the father emphatically, "travel all the way from Melville, Indiana, to Chicago to watch talking ducks." He waved his arms around him. "This is the high point of our trip. Get it, get it?"

"Now I know why all men are equal in the eyes of God," I said as I stared down at the streets below.

"Why?" asked Sarah.

"Because when He looks down at earth, they all look like ants."

"Some people look like ants when you're standing next to them," said Sarah.

"We're really ready to go tonight, aren't we, Sarah. Just raring to go. Fire one, fire two."

Her only reply was a smile.

Looking out at the city. "If I ever built a church," I said, "I'd build it right up here."

"Why?"

"Look at all the life you can see. Isn't that what religion's about?"

"Yes, I suppose so," said Sarah. "But most of the people I've met lately don't get religious until they feel a bottle dripping into their arm and a bedpan under them."

I could feel her words sliding me into a melancholy mood. That, I didn't want. "How can you be so high off the ground and still think about such depressing things?"

"You started it," she retaliated.

"See that building over there?" I pointed to a spot on the window.

"Which one?"

"Right there. The one that's crouched between that gray office building and that white hotel."

"Yes, now I see it," said Sarah.

"That's Engrim University."

"That's Engrim?" She sounded disappointed.

"What did you expect?" I asked, "a Notre Dame campus?"

"I didn't mean to offend you." She was serious.

"I'm not offended," I said. "I'm just kidding." I was, too, sort of.

"See that building just north of Engrim?" I asked.

"Which way's north?"

"Straight out," I pointed, "the one with the big antenna on it. See the small red flashing light? That's the antenna."

"Oh, yes, I do," said Sarah.

"That's the Kolton Building. They just finished building it about three months ago. I watched it go up. When I studied in Engrim's library, I could see it. I could hear it being built."

"You must have gotten quite a bit of studying done."

"Enough," I said. "I often wonder if I'll go by that building when I'm an old man and remember."

"Remember what?" asked Sarah.

"I'm sure I'll remember that, when I was a young man, I watched it being built. Nobody forgets something like that. But I wonder if I'll remember how my life was as it really is now. All the little details, you know. What I thought about. How I looked at life, who I ate lunch with.

"I doubt it," I said. "You never can. When you look back on your life, you always see it through the years you've lived since then. I think I'm going crazy."

I didn't, of course. I was just offering an excuse for my rambling.

"I don't think it, I know it," said Sarah.

"And you know what I kept thinking as I watched that building going up?" I didn't wait for Sarah to reply. "I wondered who was going to be watching it when it was being torn down.

"They made a big commotion, a big production out of building it. I read an article in the paper about how they used all these new engineering techniques in the Kolton Building and how the foundation and structure were super strong. As if it would never come down.

"That fascinates me. No matter what you build or how you build it, someday it's going to fall. I always do that. I look at a building, a person, I wonder when the end's going to come."

"Have you ever looked at me and wondered when I was going to end?" asked Sarah.

"No. I've thought about what kind of grandmother you'd make, but I've never thought about you not being here, I mean, not 'here' right next to me, but 'here' on earth. I mean, 'alive' . . ." Sometimes, even though my mind turns it off, my tongue keeps wagging.

"What kind of grandmother would I make?"

"A very good one."

We walked over to the west side of the observation deck. The fire of the setting sun filtered through bands of clouds that hung high on the horizon. As we silently watched, in the city below us, small scattered squares of yellow light grew boldly bright within the abyss of hulking skyscrapers. Lines of lamppost moons slowly awakened as the indifference of the night extinguished the orange glow of the setting sun.

Behind us, I could still hear the family from Melville, Indiana, hacking away at each other as they herded towards the exit. I wanted to turn around and tell them to shut up. But what could I say? "Would you please be quiet. We're trying to listen to this sunset."

Minutes passed. My hand was resting on the ledge when Sarah placed hers on mine. Immediately, I felt truly sorry for every one of the millions of people below who weren't me.

When she spoke, her voice was barely audible. "How can anyone whose day opens and ends with a miracle not believe in God?"

I wished she hadn't said that. I can't stand it when somebody takes something so beautiful, so universal, something that really belongs to everyone, and uses it for propaganda. I squeezed her hand and placed it on the ledge and turned towards her.

"You know," I said, "there are sections of this city where, at this time of the night, you can't even walk to the corner grocery store. Somebody might stab you to death for the milk and bread money. There are blind people, cripples, old people who no one cares about, lots of people no one cares about. Every day, a few people in this city throw away their lives; jump out of a window or step in front of a car. And for every one that does it, there are probably thousands who wish they had the courage to do likewise. Is all this brought to us by the same fellow who produced this evening's sunset?"

"You can hardly blame God for all the bad in the world," said Sarah.

"Why not? People like you try to give Him credit for all the good."

"What I believe in," said Sarah firmly, "is my business. I don't try to force my opinions on you. I made what I thought was an innocent comment and now, all of a sudden, you're acting so righteous. You're certainly very touchy tonight."

Tonight. She said it as if she had known me for years instead of a few months. Very nice.

I stuck my hands into my pockets but found no change. Got a dime for the telescope?" I asked her.

"You're something else." Sarah's voice was lighter now. "First you argue with me, then you try to take my money."

"This is only the beginning," I grinned.

Sarah mocked my grin as she handed me the dime from her purse. "Don't be too sure."

We walked over to the telescope a few feet away and I dropped in the dime. As I squinted through the telescope, I aimed it at a large building. Even though I couldn't see much, I made it sound good. "This is fantastic. A guy spends all that money for a luxury apartment and I can look through his window for a dime."

"Voyeurism's a beautiful thing," Sarah replied.

"This is neat. It really is. Want to take a look?"

"No thanks."

"Come on," I encouraged her, "you'll like it."

"Oh, all right."

Just as Sarah was about to look through it, the telescope clicked off. "You planned that."

"Don't you have another dime?"

"That was my last one."

"Don't worry about it," I said. "It was nothing to see anyway."

"A minute ago, you said it was."

"I lied."

"You do much of that?"

"No."

"Are you lying to me?"

"Yes."

By now, the observation area was knotted with people, mostly young couples like ourselves.

"Let's walk over to the other side," I suggested, "we can see the whole downtown area from there."

"Okay."

As I weaved and jostled through the crowd, I reached behind me and grabbed Sarah's hand. For just a second, it seemed as if she was pulling away from me.

When we got to the other side, we even had to wait for a front line opening at the window. Gradually, the reef of people eroded before us while the slow current of the crowd pushed from behind until Sarah found herself at the window ledge. I stood behind her, right behind her, and looked over her head at the city.

Below, the boulevards glittered with marquees, strings of street lights and the blurs of low beam traffic. Cubes of light sprinkled gawking skyscrapers as they sprouted out of the yellow electric mist. Black sky dripped into the crevices of the skyline.

"There was this woman who lived on my block," I said, "Mrs. Kaminsky. She worked downtown here, as a cleaning woman, on the night shift. Sometimes, I'd meet her on my way home from school. She'd be standing at the bus stop. If I didn't have anything better to do, I'd wait with her. She got a big charge out of that. Used to call me her 'little chum.' I was in second or third grade at the time. Didn't have too many friends so I made them where I could, even cleaning women waiting at a bus stop.

"She used to go on about how you could tell a lot about people from their wastepaper baskets. I was too young to know what she was talking about. She also used to tell me how she hated to work at night but that it was the only job she could get.

"The thing she hated most about it was that the rest of the world was always going in the opposite direction. The buses and trains she took to work were always empty. And there were plenty of them since they were on their way downtown to pick up the evening rush hour crowd. When she got downtown, she'd have to push through the homeward bound just to get out of the train station.

"At two in the morning, when she got off work, she'd walk down Michigan Avenue to the train station. Window shopping, alone. When she went to bed, she used to think about how everyone else would be getting up in a few hours to start their day."

"She told you all this and you were only in second or third grade?" asked Sarah.

"Yeah. That's strange, isn't it. She had a couple of kids herself, I think they were married and living in New York, so she must have realized that I didn't understand most of what she was saying. She probably didn't care. She probably just wanted to talk to someone, anyone, even me. Sometimes, you want to say something even though you know no one's listening."

"What's she doing now?"

"She was pretty old, close to retiring. Mrs. Kaminsky told me that the thing she wanted to do most when she retired was to go downtown in the middle of rush hour traffic, stand on a crowded bus, go shopping and wait in line for everything. Mrs. Kaminsky used to laugh when she'd tell me that. 'When I retire,' Mrs. Kaminsky would say to me, 'I'm finally going to go the right way.'

"As I got older, I started taking a different way home from school. I'd occasionally see Mrs. Kaminsky around the neighborhood, walking to the bus stop, at church or Cohen's Food Store, but that was about it.

"One night, at supper, my father mentioned that he had seen

Mrs. Kaminsky's obituary in the morning newspaper. He said
that it was really a shame because he had heard later in the day
that she had died of bone cancer and that she had been only six
months away from retiring."

"Bone cancer," repeated Sarah solemnly. "That's hardly 'going
the right way.'"

We stared for a few moments at the pockets of yellow floating
within the shadows of steel grids. "It must be strange," said
Sarah, "to spend years of your life cleaning offices dirtied by
people you never meet."

I didn't want to spend the night mired in melancholy. Silently, I
berated myself for even talking about Mrs. Kaminsky. A lesson
learned from "American Bandstand." Always follow a slow song
with a fast one.

"Did you know," I said, "that all of these tall buildings are
designed to sway a few inches so they can withstand strong
winds?"

"Yes, I did know that," replied Sarah smugly.

"Did you also know," I said not quite so enthusiastically, "that
during a thunderstorm, all of these buildings are repeatedly hit by
lightning?"

"I knew that, too."

"You certainly are smart," I said. "What don't you know?"

"I don't know why you're asking me all these silly questions."

I punched her gently on the shoulder. "Another knockdown for
the champ."

She punched me back, but not so gently. "That's because I
have lightweight competition."

Sarah stared out at the city again. "Speaking of thunder, I do
love storms; big, noisy ones. Snow storms, too. The kind that clog
up everything and make you stop and contemplate life in the
middle of what would have been a typical day. Sometimes, when
you have absolutely nowhere to go, you're forced to think about
where you've been and where you're going. I don't think I'm
making any sense."

"You are to me."

Sarah blushed and hesitated a moment before she continued
talking. "When I was a little girl, during a thunderstorm, my

sister and I would tell Donald, my younger brother, that the thunder was God yelling at people because they had been bad. We'd tell Donald that the only people who could hear the thunder were the ones that God was mad at. The next time it thundered, Donald would ask, 'Did you hear that?' We'd both look at him and say, 'Hear what?' Then he'd go running off to Mom and snitch on us. We'd hear her yelling as she came to get us. 'Are you two teasing Donald again?' "

"Just another example of women taking advantage of a man," I said.

"Another example?" Sarah asked suspiciously.

"That's right," I said, "another example. A male is born into this world and the moment he clears the womb, the first thing his mother says to him is, 'Why don't I see you more often?' He spends the next few years of his life being totally dominated by her. Then he goes to grammar school and, for eight more years, he's dominated by women."

"Most school administrators are men," said Sarah.

"Yeah," I countered, "but most of the day to day bossing is done by women. There are some male grammar school teachers, but not many. Women even make it a point to teach the girls better than the boys."

"I think the altitude up here is beginning to affect you," said Sarah.

"When I was in grammar school," I said undeterred, "we had spelling bees. Let's see," I said as I drew imaginary numbers on the windowsill. "We had about one every three weeks, which is about twelve a year for a total of ninety-three for all of my grammar school years. Out of all those spelling bees, the boys didn't win any. Not one."

Sarah looked at my finger smudges on the windowsill. "Apparently, they didn't do a very good job on you in math, either. You're off by three."

I rechecked my figures. "You're right," I said meekly.

"You know," she continued, "you're ignoring the possibility that women may just be smarter."

"You're right," I said, "I am ignoring the possibility. Now where was I? Oh yeah. Every time we'd have a spelling bee, we'd start out with forty girls on one side of the room and forty boys on the other ... "

"Eighty kids in a room?" Sarah interrupted.

"I came from a very large grammar school. Anyway, we'd start out with forty of each and within a few minutes, there'd be about thirty girls facing one boy, Danny Gutswater."

"Danny Gutswater, that was his real name?"

"How many grammar school kids did you know who used aliases?"

"There's one that should have," said Sarah.

"Danny Gutswater had that quality that all great spellers have. He was a fantastic guesser. He'd usually manage to pick off ten or fifteen girls before the nun finally nailed him. It was always on a technicality. He'd forget to capitalize a proper noun or he wouldn't repeat the word after he had spelled it."

"That's a very sad story," said Sarah mockingly.

"I wonder whatever happened to Danny Gutswater," I said.

"He probably grew up to be a dictionary."

"That's all right," I said. "Pulverize me with your witty remarks. It still doesn't change the fact that we men survive only under the most difficult of circumstances. Women control most of the world's wealth. They even have more freedom than men."

"More freedom?" asked Sarah incredulously.

"Sure, if a woman wears men's clothes, that's chic. If a man wears women's clothes, they lock him up. Even God likes women better. Far more males than females die in infancy. Women even live longer."

"More freedom? Are you kidding?" said Sarah. "Look at all the discrimination that goes on in the job market."

"That's about the only space in the scheme of things where a man actually dominates. And he knows, during his very brief time on earth, it's going to be the only chance he ever gets to even the score."

"I bet you were a real jerk in grammar school," said Sarah.

"No, I was an artificial jerk. Yes, of course I was. I never did anything. During eight years of grammar school, I only did my homework twice. And both times, I wondered why. The nuns and my parents used to constantly hassle me. It never occurred to me that if I did my homework, just a few minutes of work a night, life would have been considerably more pleasant. I know that sounds crazy, but it never did.

"There was a whole group of us. About nine of us. All boys. Every day, when the nun asked who didn't do their homework, we'd have to stand and mumble out the usual excuses. 'I left it at home.' 'The dog ate it.' 'I forgot.' Sometimes, you'd try and wait her out with a non-stop 'uuuh,' hoping she'd finally wave her hand at you and say, 'Oh, sit down.'

"When the nun really wanted to be particularly vicious, she wouldn't bother asking who hadn't done their homework. Instead, she'd start reviewing the homework assignment as if she just knew that everyone had done it when, of course, she knew damn well they hadn't. She'd keep calling on the normal kids to make us nine sweat it out. Eventually, she'd call on one of us nine and she'd act really enraged when she 'discovered' that he hadn't done his homework. Then she'd say, coldly, 'Anyone else who didn't do their homework, stand.' And the remaining eight of us would have to push ourselves up out of our desks for our usual dose of well deserved public humiliation. It was a delightful way to spend eight years."

"Why didn't you do such a simple thing as homework?" Sarah asked.

"Simple for you, maybe. I don't know. Perhaps, I was afraid I'd do irreparable damage to my brain, like learning something. Two plus two equals four, who needs it?"

Sarah looked down at my numerical smudges on the windowsill and then held up my hand and counted on my fingers. "One, two, three . . . you do."

I rolled my fingers into a fist and shook it slightly in her face. "Keep it up," I said, "and this is what you'll get."

Sarah pretended to bite my hand. "Did you know that human bites are more dangerous than animal bites?" she asked.

Pulling my fist away from her. "You mean, I'm going to get bitten again?"

"Very cute," said Sarah. "The remark, that is."

Elbows, shoulders and knees continued to goad us from behind. Gradually, Sarah and I shuffled our way back around to the northern side of the observation area where there were fewer people.

"See that darkened area over there, beyond all those neon signs?" I pointed.

"Yes."

"That's North State Parkway."

"You mean 'State Street' don't you?" Sarah corrected me.

"Nope. When State Street runs beyond the neon signs, it becomes 'North State Parkway.' Very classy area. You know who lives there, only two blocks apart? Hugh Hefner, founder of *Playboy* Magazine, and Cardinal Cody. Both of them in the religion business and doing quite well, thank you.

"One of them is selling life and the other one is selling death. Cardinal Cody's a lot more successful. After all, his company's over two thousand years old. Besides, unfortunately for Hefner, not many of us are capable of living. But most of us are quite capable of dying. At least Hefner only picks on people who can afford it."

"You had the *Baltimore Catechism* in grammar school, didn't you?" asked Sarah.

"Yeah, sure, who didn't?" The *Baltimore Catechism* was the book used in most Catholic school religion classes. It consisted of hundreds of questions and answers that we had to memorize. Stuff like, "Why are there three persons in the Blessed Trinity?" I don't remember what the answer was, but you'd have to memorize it and parrot it back, word for word, to the nun. The complete title of the book was, *The Baltimore Catechism, a Defense of the Faith.* I could never figure out who was attacking us.

"I spent all those years," said Sarah, "studying that material and now I can't remember any of it."

"Don't worry," I said, "it wouldn't do you any good even if you did."

"What do you mean?"

"I live behind a Methodist church. When I was in grammar school, one night after supper, I was walking the dog in the alley when I ran into this Protestant kid. He had gotten to the church early for some social function, but the building wasn't open yet.

"We got into this big discussion of religion. I hit him with all the stuff the nuns and priests had been telling me for years. How, if you're not Catholic, you can still get to Heaven but it's going to be a lot tougher. How Christ founded only one church, ours. All of that.

"But what I really had ready were all the answers from my *Baltimore Catechism.* The only problem was that the Protestant kid wouldn't ask any of the right questions. Instead, he pulled what I later discovered is a typical Protestant trick. He kept quoting the Bible. I couldn't argue with him. I'm Catholic. What do I know about the Bible? So I kept blabbing the stuff from the *Baltimore Catechism* and he kept giving me chapter and verse.

"This Protestant kid also kept attacking the Pope. He said that if the Pope was truly Christ's representative on earth, then it didn't make any sense that he was living like a king when Christ lived the life of a peasant. You know, the Pope's a very difficult guy to defend.

"About a half hour later, a buddy of his came along and told the Protestant kid that the front doors of the church were now open. Then the buddy asked the Protestant kid what we had been talking about. For a moment, the Protestant kid couldn't remember. I mean, he wasn't just saying that. I could tell. He really couldn't remember. Can you imagine that? Here I was, trying to save the bastard's soul and he was just shooting the bull."

"When I was in school," said Sarah, "I was told that if I wanted to save souls, I should go to either Africa or South America. No one ever mentioned your alley."

"They knew I had it covered."

"Did you ever make any converts back there?"

"Yeah, my dog. After that night, he wouldn't bite anyone but Catholics.

"Religion is organized lunacy," I said. "A few years ago, during a sermon at mass, this priest told us how we should love everybody. How stupid. Liking somebody, tolerating him, those are things you can control. But you can't make yourself love somebody, just as you can't stop yourself from loving somebody. Besides, love's a dangerous thing. A history professor I had once said that more wars have been fought over religion than any other topic. Love your neighbor even if you have to kill him to get his attention."

"Do you believe in God?" asked Sarah. Her directness momentarily stunned me.

"Do I believe in God?" An old trick. Repeating the question to give yourself an extra instant to think about it.

"I hope there's a God," I said. "If there was an election tomorrow on whether there should be a God, I'd vote yes. Living forever sounds like a good deal. But just because I want there to be a God doesn't mean there is one. Very few people, if they're honest with themselves, really believe there's a God the way, for instance, they believe there's another side of the world. Very few people."

"I believe there's a God," said Sarah, "as firmly as I believe there's another side of the world."

"I tricked you. There is no other side of the world. Chicago is all there is. The stuff you hear about other places is made up by some guy in my neighborhood."

"Did he also make you up?"

"You know what I believe?" I asked.

"No, what?"

"I believe we should go have some ice cream."

"Leave it to you to have a religion that melts."

Driving back towards Sarah's neighborhood, I felt strangely restless, as if I wanted to get out of my own body.

"You know who I envy?" I asked.

"No, who?"

"People who know what they want to do, what they want to be."

"What do you want to be?" asked Sarah.

A center fielder, that's what I thought, but I didn't say it. If you make a statement like that publicly, you'd better be sitting on Santa's knee.

"I don't know," I said. "I'm halfway through college and I don't know. There's this guy I know, Leonard Cohen, who wants to be a doctor. He's spent all of his life preparing for his career. He knows exactly what he's going to do with his life. I haven't the faintest idea of what I'm going to do with mine. Maybe I'll utilize my twenty years of preparation and go into the career of nothing."

"Do you have any idea what you want to do?"

"No, but I want to do something, something, for God's sake." I was really getting worked up. "I've been around twenty years and I haven't done a damn thing yet. . . ."

"I'm sure," said Sarah, "that you've made a fool of yourself a few times."

I glared at her for the few seconds that the torrent of city traffic would allow.

"Sorry," she retreated. "Seriously, though, you should relax. You're young. You have plenty of time."

"You're right," I said. "I forgot about that letter I got last week from God. 'Dear Conroy, relax, you've got plenty of time. I promise you.' "

"You're getting silly," Sarah said, annoyed.

"The trouble is," I said, "I don't think I'd want to do anything for a lifetime. That's quite a while. It's even a long time to live."

"You'd better get an extra big dish of ice cream. It'll help relax your nerves."

"I didn't know ice cream could relax you," I said.

"Sure. It'll make your nerves all mushy, just . . . like your. . . ." Her hesitation bloomed into a stop. I said it for her.

"Just like my brains?"

"Just like your brains."

Lashing into but, an hour later, lolling out of the restaurant.

"Now don't you feel better?" Sarah asked.

"You're right, I do. The ice cream really did the job. You'd make a great doctor."

"I know," Sarah beamed. "Take two scoops of butter pecan and call me in the morning."

I squeezed her hand tightly. She squeezed back, but not as hard.

We parked about two blocks down from her house. Although she was already sitting close to me, I put my arm around her and tried to pull her closer. Sarah moved, but only slightly. She began talking about how she had to get up early in the morning for mass.

Running her tongue across the front of her teeth, she asked, "Do your teeth feel funny?" An obvious attempt to convert the atmosphere into a more platonic mood.

"No, why should they?"

"From the ice cream. Mine do. Your teeth don't feel just a little bit strange?"

"Well," I said, "my *teeth* don't . . . "

Sarah's eyes widened in mild disapproval. "You're gross, you know that?"

"I didn't say anything."

"I know what you were thinking."

"You can read my mind, I suppose," I said.

"Yes, although the print's quite small."

It was nearly one o'clock. In a few minutes, I would have the assistance of someone who nightly nursed many a girl's friendly flickerings into ferocious flames of passion; a man whose voice was capable of creating a continuous chain of caresses. And all kinds of them, too, from the egg shell to the crusher.

Caepan had introduced me to Franklyn MacCormack a few years earlier. On Christmas Eve, I had stopped at Caepan's apartment to wish him a Merry Christmas.

I hadn't been to Caepan's apartment in a few weeks and I was hoping that he didn't have, as I suspected, one of those miniature Christmas trees that are about a foot high. Table top Christmas trees depress me. As if life wasn't big enough to handle a full-sized one. But I had figured that was what Caepan would have or he'd have none at all. When I walked into his apartment, however, I saw a monstrous twinkling Christmas tree that filled up half of his living room.

"Where are you going all dressed up?" Caepan had asked.

"Midnight mass. I wonder if God's up this late."

"He certainly is," said Caepan. "He's on the radio every night."

After midnight mass, I had listened to Franklyn MacCormack. His entrée had included casual conversation, reading his own poetry and playing original music from the big band era, all sweetened and served up by his deep, mellow honey voice. Caepan was right. I knew that if I ever heard God talk, He'd sound like Franklyn MacCormack.

But I could never understand how Caepan listened to Franklyn MacCormack alone. When I did that, I felt like I was at the show holding my own hand.

Sitting with Sarah that night, listening to Franklyn MacCormack weave his usual web of romance. "Why do I love you? I love you, not for what you are, but for what I am when I am with you." The Boswell Sisters, Al Jolson, Benny Goodman and Thou.

It was a good night, not a great night, but a good one. A very good one.

Thank you, Franklyn MacCormack.

TWENTY-THREE

Dear God:

Thank you for the gift of life.

Signed: Conroy

Conroy:

What gift? You know there's no such thing as a free lunch. You're paying for life every day. Pain, depression, bad weather, disappointments, sorrow, the blahs and every day you're getting older. What do you call all of that, fringe benefits?

I figured that if I just gave you life, you wouldn't appreciate it. Not that my charging you did much good. Most of you don't appreciate life anyway. You're too busy complaining about the price.

Signed: God

TWENTY-FOUR

S he'll be ready in a minute," said Leonard as he sat down sideways, looping his legs over the arm of an aging, overstuffed chair in the Cohen living room.

As I sat down on the couch, I could hear the sounds of the early Sunday morning crowd drifting through the door and up the few stairs that separated the Cohen Food Store from the living room. The few times I had been in Leonard's house, I always felt as if I were sitting backstage of a neighborhood play.

Mrs. Cohen came out of the bathroom, readjusting the apron that came up to her armpits. "Good morning, Timmy," she said, smiling as she walked across the living room.

"Good morning, Mrs. Cohen."

She stopped and stared furiously at Leonard. "Sit in that chair the right way."

Leonard obediently swung his feet around and dropped them to the floor.

Mrs. Cohen stared at him for a few more seconds and then continued towards the small stairwell that led to the store. When she went down the stairs and opened the door, a sliver of store noise exploded into the living room but was quickly doused by the closing of the door.

My words sprinted to fill the embarrassing silence. "What did you get your grandmother for her eighty-fifth birthday?"

"A savings bond."

"A savings bond."

I laughed and then said, with a mild dash of sarcasm, "Very funny, Leonard." It wasn't very funny, but it was funny.

"I hope you remembered," I said, "to get the birthday balloons and streamers."

"Of course, I did. And in her favorite colors, Mourning Black and Hearse Gray."

I stood up and stretched. "What a way to spend Sunday morning. Going out to breakfast with a guy who looks like Jack's beanstalk and sounds like Henny Youngman. And with an old lady who, when her favorite TV show is canceled, resorts to violence. I know she only kicked her slippers across the room. But that was probably all she was capable of doing. If she had had the strength, she probably would have torn the television set apart."

"Actually," said Leonard, "she did make a gesture in that direction. She tore up the TV section in the newspaper. She tore it up very slowly, but she did it nevertheless. And if you have something better to do this morning, why don't you do it?"

"Is that a threat?"

"No, it's a plea. And take me with you."

"No such luck, I'm here to stay," I said.

"Why don't we pick on your grandmother for a while?" asked Leonard.

"We can't, she's dead."

"How convenient. You probably arranged it just so I wouldn't be able to get even."

"So where are we going for breakfast?" I asked.

"A place called Samuel's near Halsted and Roosevelt Road."

"Nice neighborhood," I replied. "The waitress will probably add twenty percent to our check for protection. Why are we going way over there?"

"Years ago, that used to be Chicago's Jewish ghetto. My

grandmother raised her family there. Samuel's is one of the few places around now that was around then. She really wanted to go there today."

Just then, Leonard's grandmother, a small, plump woman in a print dress, toddled into the living room.

"Hi, Grandma Cohen," I said, "how are you today?"

She smiled. "I'm eighty-five, you know, Timmy."

"No. Grandma Cohen, I said, 'How are you, today?' not, 'How old are you?' "

Her smile deepened. "I heard you the first time."

When we got to the restaurant, Grandma Cohen insisted on sitting at a window booth. A forty-two-D-cup waitress handed us our menus. Leonard scanned it and then slammed it shut.

"I'm going to have liver and eggs," he announced.

Leonard was like that. He'd do something just to annoy the hell out of everyone around him. I hate liver. I'm sure Leonard knew that.

When I was a kid, I used to love watching those James Cagney movies where he'd be trapped in the warehouse by G-men, but nobody would be able to get him out but his mother. If that had been me, I would have never come out, especially for my mother. She probably would have been the one I was hiding from. But I knew they'd flush me out if they ever threw a piece of liver through the window.

"There's no liver on the menu, Leonard," I said.

"It may not be on the menu but all restaurants have liver," he replied. "What are you having, grandma?"

"The fruit's quite good here, you know," she said. The forty-two-D-cup waitress came over to the table to take our orders. Grandma Cohen looked up through the cleavage. "How are your melons this morning, honey?"

During the meal, Grandma Cohen did most of the talking. Her words revolved around the only worlds she had ever known; the neighborhood we were eating in and the one we had just left.

It was pretty dull stuff when Grandma Cohen talked about the neighborhood we all now shared. Because of her arthritis, Grandma Cohen had stopped walking around the neighborhood years ago. Her gossip might have been interesting if it hadn't been distilled by so much time. Neither Leonard nor I bothered to tell Grandma Cohen that half of the people she was talking about were either dead or had moved away.

"Television wouldn't have been so popular if it had been around when I was young," said Grandma Cohen. "Most people worked twelve, fourteen hours a day. They wouldn't have had any time to watch it.

"Your grandfather, Ben, worked as an ice man for forty years until he bought a small corner grocery store, only two blocks from here. It was the same size as your father's store, Leonard. The building was torn down years ago.

"Can you imagine that?" said Grandma Cohen quietly as she pushed the tea cup away from her, "my husband spent most of his life carrying fifty pound blocks of ice on his back, sometimes up four flights of stairs. Doing something all those years that doesn't even have to be done anymore."

Her words slowly dissolved into such soft sounds that both Leonard and I found ourselves leaning forward to hear them.

"A woman always has her children, but a man is what he does. Where's the meaning in a life like that?"

A few hours later, after we replaced Grandma Cohen back in the living room, Leonard and I took a walk over to Randall Park. On the way, at the corner of 111th and Drake, we met Steve Planter talking to a group of guys. He had just gotten back from Vietnam. Planter was telling them about how the war had to be won and how every man should be proud to give a year in defense of his country.

I had talked to Planter a few days before he left for 'Nam. He was terrified. After he got over there, his mother had told mine that Planter had managed to get a desk job and was nowhere near any fighting.

"Every day that I've been back in the States," said Planter, "I think about what I was doing exactly a year ago. This time last year, I was on guard duty. We had camped outside a small village about twenty miles north of Saigon. Not much happened that night, a few snipers, that's all."

As I stood there listening to Planter, Leonard gave me a hard nudge. "Let's get the fuck out of here," he said.

"Did Planter enlist?" asked Leonard as we walked towards the park.

"No, he got drafted," I said. "It doesn't surprise me to hear Planter talking like that. He always was a little empty-headed."

"A little empty-headed? The sonofabitch should have been drafted as a foxhole."

Neither Leonard nor I had to worry about the draft, at least for the time being. We both had student deferments.

Randall Park was one of Chicago's nicer ones; a dozen baseball diamonds, a few basketball courts, open fields for football or soccer, swings, monkey bars, teeterboards, plenty of full-breasted trees and park benches, all served on a platter of rich green grass, trimmed by a wide band of sidewalk.

Randall Park was only a block away from the Kool-Aid plant, which made a different flavor every day. As Leonard and I walked into the park, we could smell grape so we knew it was Sunday.

As usual for a Sunday afternoon in early autumn, the park was crowded with people. Every baseball diamond was occupied, three football games were running into one another and there was hardly a vacant rung on the monkey bars.

"With winter not far off," I said, "everyone knows these kinds of days are numbered."

"They're all numbered," said Leonard.

A symphony of sounds—children shouting, a ball crackling off a bat, laughter from a picnic blanket, shouts of excitement as a football was kicked, the gentle rustle of trees and the murmurs of old men on park benches—serenaded the sun as it gently warmed them.

Walking past the swings. "It must be lousy to be old," said Leonard.

"I suppose so," I said, "but your grandmother seems pretty happy. In fact, she seems happier than you."

I had never thought about it before, but Leonard did exist in an air of sad resignation, as if he could not relax and enjoy living because of the obligations of being alive.

"You're right," admitted Leonard, "but being old is still a lousy deal. It's especially rough on old ladies. Our society just won't let them grow old graciously. I get very depressed when I see an old lady wearing tons of makeup. It's so grotesque. They look like they're dead already.

"I read somewhere that the real function of makeup is that it acts as a sexual invitation. In some breeds of animals, for instance, parts of the female change colors during the mating season. It's depressing to see someone advertising so much when there's so little to sell.

"You know," continued Leonard, "my grandmother was old when we were born. I think that's one of the worst things about being old. Nothing really changes. In the past twenty years, I've gone all the way from nonexistence to what I am today."

Leonard held out his hands as if he was appealing for applause. "Ta da. It might not be much, but at least I've changed. But in those twenty years, my grandmother has just gone from old to older. The wrinkles got a little deeper, that's all. A holding pattern of decrepitation."

"You shouldn't call your grandmother 'old,' " I said. "The term is 'senior citizen.' "

"Bullshit." But Leonard knew I was just baiting him. "See what I mean?" he said. "No one likes to use the word, 'old,' because it stinks. 'Senior citizen,' " Leonard said disgustedly. "I can see some old guy saying, 'No, I'm not a senior citizen yet. I'm a junior citizen and my friend here is a sophomore citizen.'

"You know what the problem is?" asked Leonard. "The whole thing is designed wrong. It would make more sense if we were born old, got the rotten part out of the way and then grew young. At least that way, you'd have something to look forward to."

"That makes a lot of sense," I said. "With your system, we'd have eighty-five-year-old babies lying around."

"Don't get me wrong," said Leonard. "I'm not saying that old people are useless. I'm just saying it's sad that when they're old, they have to be old. You see what I mean, don't you?"

"Oh sure I do. How much plainer could you make it?"

"You know what I mean," Leonard assured himself. "Old people can be very interesting, like this morning. I enjoyed taking my grandmother out to breakfast. And I liked listening to her talk about all the years she's lived. . . ."

"Living history and all of that," I interjected.

"Exactly," said Leonard. "It's much better to hear about something than to read about it. History books waste most of their time on who was in power, what war was beginning or ending and the latest tariff act. But when you listen to an old person's words, you feel the fibers of their daily lives. Kids should spend more time learning from old people than from books. Maybe some old people could be taken out of nursing homes and put in libraries."

"That would make sense," I said. "I can see myself now getting a letter from the Chicago Public Library notifying me that I owe twenty cents on an overdue old lady."

"You know, Conroy," said Leonard, aggravated, but he held his words when he noticed that we were walking past some park benches. As usual, the benches were littered with old men. Unlike everyone else at the park that day, the old men were always there except when the weather got bad. But if the weather stayed warm and dry, they'd work a seven-day shift. Some of the old men were talking, but in a foreign language, so we couldn't understand them.

After we passed the park benches, Leonard began again. "Here we are, young men, living in the wealthiest nation in the world. We can do anything we want to do with our lives. But if we live long enough, we could end up like them, forced out of our own country by war, repression or economics, sitting on a park bench in some foreign country, waiting around to die."

I decided to give Leonard a hard time. I had nothing better to do. "What do you know about old men sitting on benches? For all you know, this may be the old men's major leagues of sitting. After all, this isn't sitting at the kitchen table, slouching in some chair in the living room or rocking on a lousy front porch." I yelled, "These are park benches, for God's sake. The real stars probably get to sit on the ends." Pointing towards the benches we had just passed, I said, "Very few people get the privilege to sit here, Leonard." I was almost screaming now. "These are the cream of the crop."

Leonard started to speak but then paused to review his reply, making sure the chosen words accurately summarized his feelings towards my comments. Then he spoke. "Fuck you."

"You know, Leonard, your problem is that you're too giddy.

No one likes a giddy person, especially a giddy doctor. I don't know much about medicine, but I suspect that giddiness is definitely frowned upon in the operating room. Don't you agree?"

Leonard said nothing.

We walked in silence for a few minutes. Then, "You know, Leonard, I do envy you. There are so many things I can do with my life, none of which excite me. I think that's the problem, too many choices. But you, you know exactly what you want to do."

"Yeah," replied Leonard disinterestedly. "Let's head home. My mother's having dinner around three o'clock."

"Okay. Say, why was she so ticked off with you this morning?"

"I told her that I probably wouldn't be coming home any more weekends until the holidays."

"Why not?"

"Once you've lived away from home, it's very tough to get used to your parents again," said Leonard. "They're constantly asking me where I'm going, who I'm going with, and what time I'll be home. Yesterday afternoon, my mother asked me why I didn't make my bed in the morning. I'm twenty years old and my mother is still asking me why I didn't make my bed."

"If you were fifty-two years old, but still living at home," I said, "your mother would be asking you why you didn't make your bed. Mothers are that way. I'm lucky. My parents don't bother me much. With seven kids, I get lost in the crowd. When I go out, the only thing my parents ask me is if I'm coming back and they always look disappointed when I say yes."

"Every time I come home from school, my parents drive me crazy," said Leonard. "Then you know what my mother said this morning? 'Your nerves are shot, Leonard. I think you're almost ready for a nervous breakdown.'

"What a stupid thing to say," continued Leonard. "Whatever happened to 'going nuts?' Don't people go nuts anymore? She thinks I'm 'almost ready for a nervous breakdown.' 'No, ma, I'm not quite ready yet. I have one more suitcase to pack.' "

That night, I left a question for Caepan in his mailbox.

Dear God:

Why do you let people grow old?

Signed: Conroy

Early the next morning, I retrieved his answer.

Conroy:

Although I've created all of you, I often find the way you think quite puzzling. For me, the most beautiful moment on earth is old people. They are my human sunsets.

Signed: God

TWENTY-FIVE

Riding home on the subway from Engrim, relishing the best high in the world, that Friday afternoon feeling. I thought about how I'd be seeing Sarah within the next few hours. There was an old woman sitting next to me. I started a conversation with her. I don't remember what was said except that she told me she got a ten percent discount where she worked and that she lived with her older sister somewhere on the South Side. I just felt like talking with somebody. I was absolutely delighted to be alive.

Mr. Faber still referred to me as Sarah's "school friend," but I now felt considerably more comfortable with him. We weren't exactly great buddies, but at least I allowed myself to sit all the way back in the chair when I was in a room with him. Lately, Mrs. Faber made it a practice to come out of the kitchen to say hello. I even kidded with Sarah's younger brother when he was around. He constantly told me the newest jokes that were making the eighth grade circuit. I didn't even bother laughing at the ones that weren't funny.

But I wasn't that friendly with them. I always kept a certain distance. Some guys, they date a girl and they just about become a member of the family. I hate that. If it happened to me, I'd feel like I was going out with my sister. When you're dating somebody, you never want things to become too casual.

That Friday night, we went to her girl friend's party. We didn't stay late, though. I was never big on sharing Sarah. Then we went over to a neighborhood hamburger stand.

I was getting back in the car with our hamburgers when both of us noticed that the back seat of a car parked on the other side of the lot was on fire. I started to get out of the car when I saw the owner already yelling at the guy behind the counter to call the fire department. Within seconds, a crowd had gathered around the burning car. Two or three minutes later, a fire engine came muscling into the parking lot.

But it was too late. The car was already flooded with flames. As a fireman jumped off the side of the truck, a young kid ran up to him and yelled, "Hurry, hurry, there's somebody trapped on the roof."

"Stick it, kid," the fireman blandly replied as he calmly reached for a hose.

Sarah and I were finishing our milk shakes when they put the fire out. "The food could be better," I said, "but considering the cover charge, tonight's floor show was superb."

"You think this was good," said Sarah, "you should have been here the night my father drove me and my girl friends home from a dance."

"What happened?"

"We were all in freshman year of high school. Everybody used to come here after the dance. But my girl friends and I weren't allowed to go home with boys so we had to be picked up by someone's father.

"That night, my father had been painting the living room and when he came to pick us up he was still wearing his paint clothes. He even had this weird little paint hat sitting on top of his head.

"At the time, my father was driving this car that was constantly falling apart. On the way home from the dance, one of the girls asked him if we could stop here for a hamburger. I could have killed her. I didn't want everyone who had just been at the dance to see me with my father dressed that way, driving that old junk.

My father bought hamburgers for everyone but, thank God, he stayed in the car. When we were ready to leave, I couldn't get one of the back doors shut. So my father got out of the car and proceeded to slam the car door thirty or forty times until it closed. When my father is frustrated, he has a habit of sticking his tongue out between his teeth," Sarah imitated, "like this.

"There he was, dressed in these ridiculous paint clothes, banging the door and sticking out his tongue. He was certainly beginning to draw a crowd. Finally, he got the door closed. But after he started up the car, it wouldn't shift into reverse. So we girls had to get out of the car, dressed in our best, and push him out of the parking space."

"No one offered to help you?"

"No way," said Sarah. "Everyone was laughing too hard. I was never so embarrassed in my life. I don't think I talked to my father for at least a week. He didn't even know what I was mad about. It's kind of funny now," she said, "but I can assure you that it wasn't then."

"Strange," I commented, "I never found your father that amusing."

"He says the same thing about you."

We pulled out of the parking lot and drove down Belmont Avenue. Waiting at a red light, I unconsciously lowered the volume of the radio so that I could concentrate on a girl in a short dress who was walking by the front of the car.

"Do you always turn the radio down," asked Sarah, "when you want to take a closer look at a pretty girl?"

I clicked off the radio and stared at her. "Yes."

She liked that.

A block later, one of my tires went flat. As we got out of the car, I handed my wristwatch to Sarah and told her that we were in the Indianapolis Five Hundred race, that our car had just pulled into the pits, and that we were now going to have to change the tire in record time in order to keep our hold on first place and end up in the winner's circle.

I had a rather messy trunk. It took me five minutes to find the jack. "Don't worry, kid," I said as I yanked the jack and the spare tire out of the trunk, "we're still going to grab that checkered flag. I've practiced changing tires ten hours a day for the past six months just in case this sort of thing happened. We'll be back out on that track in no time. Keep your eye on that second hand," I said as I struggled to pry loose the hubcap. "Every second counts."

Twenty minutes later, I was still trying to pull off the flattened tire. "Are you watching that second hand?"

"I don't need a watch for this," said Sarah, "I need a calendar."

Two hours later, we were back in the race.

"You better take me home, it's getting late," said Sarah. "I have to study all day tomorrow for a big test on Monday."

"Home? I thought we could go somewhere and talk for a while."

She smiled slyly. "I know how you like to talk."

"As long as you understand what I'm saying, that's all I care about."

"Did you remember the picture?" Sarah asked. The week before, she had gone shopping and had bought a small picture frame because it was on sale. Not until she had returned home had she realized that she had nothing to put in it. That night, when I had talked to her on the phone, she told me about the picture frame.

"Is that the type of picture frame that'll stand up on a desk?" I had asked.

"Yes."

"I'll give you something to put in it," I said. "You'll love it."

"Just what I need," Sarah had replied, "a picture of Timothy Conroy staring at me while I try to study."

As we drove along, I reached behind me and grabbed the manila envelope from the back seat and handed it to her.

"It's a picture of me, when I was five years old, sitting on a pony."

"How will I be able to tell which one is you?" asked Sarah.

"I'm the one wearing the hat . . ."

"Oh."

". . . And nothing else."

I stopped the car in front of her house. As usual, Sarah was sitting right next to me. As I put my arm around her, Sarah said, "So, you want to talk, nuh?"

Delicately, I kissed her. Sarah was not the kind of girl you could enjoy in gulps. For a lingering moment, she snuggled close to me, her lips occasionally brushing against the skin of my neck. The she sat up straight and pushed against me.

"Can't we just talk for a little while longer?" I asked.

"We can't start this, Tim, I have to get up early to study."

"Okay." I got out of the car and walked Sarah to her door where we continued the conversation.

Driving home, wondering if she'd like it. Imagining her sliding the plastic number twenty-six card out of the envelope and hoping she'd notice, as I did, that it was still wrapped in the fragrance of Betterman's Bakery.

Every night that following week, I talked to Sarah on the phone and waited for her to mention the picture frame or what I now hoped was in it. She never did. But on Saturday night, when I picked her up for our date, she met me at the door with a checkered flag.

TWENTY-SIX

The muggers were slowly melting away. Bread trucks were loading up. Over at County Hospital, the last victim of the night before was being sewn up. The whines of the expressways, which only a few minutes before had been at low tide, were now beginning to echo the trickles that would shortly swell into the morning rush hour. Even at the late closing bars, all the leaning elbows had gone home. Dawn was crawling over Chicago.

Although the sun was still bleary-eyed, I was already getting dressed for school. That morning, I had a philosophy exam and I wanted to get to Engrim University early in order to have some extra minutes to study. By the time I took the bus to the elevated train station, however, the first wave of the rush hour was already breaking.

Dr. Mandy, the philosophy professor, was about three feet tall and getting shorter every day. He lectured in a monotone voice at a level of about two decibels. Unless you sat in a front row seat, you'd neither be able to see nor hear him. It was the kind of class where you spent most of your time "Hanging the Butcher."

Walter Fenway, who sat in the second row, told me that one

morning he did lean forward and, listening intently, managed to hear Dr. Mandy for most of the class. Said Walter, "It was like picking up the telephone for an hour and listening to the dial tone. And as informative."

Dr. Mandy was a new teacher. The course had been listed in the class schedule as being taught by "staff." A new teacher is the worst. He behaves as if the entire world revolves around his course and assigns work as if his students live only to hear his words. A new teacher would find it difficult to believe that you actually went to bed without his notes under your pillow.

That morning, as I waited for the train, I kept one eye on the pigeons, hoping they wouldn't dirty my clothes. And the other on my fellow patrons, hoping they wouldn't steal them.

A few minutes later, I was standing on the train. One hand was clutching an overhead bar while the other held a paperback on Plato, which I was attempting to study. As usual, the train was shaking convulsively, causing everyone inside of it to vertically vibrate. My lower lip kept flapping over my upper lip and my bouncing eyes had just read the same line for the thirteenth time. A drunk was squashed in next to me. He was vibrating horizontally as well as vertically.

"Hey, kid," he mumbled to me, "you a college kid or something?"

I pretended that I didn't hear him.

He gave it another try, only this time much louder. "Hey, you a college kid, huh?"

"Yeah, that's right. I'm a college kid."

"What college you go to, kid?" He was on the verge of throwing up.

Knowing that the name of my school sometimes had that effect on me, I lied. "Harvard."

"Harvard? That's a pretty good school, isn't it, kid?"

"Yeah, I suppose it is."

Two stops later, he nudged me again. "Hey, kid, isn't it hard to get to Harvard on the Chicago Subway?"

"I have to transfer twice."

"Oh." He mumbled something about how he hoped I'd stay in school and really make a success out of myself and all of that.

Then he did something for which I was to be forever indebted to him. He turned around and got sick on someone else.

Coming out of the subway station with my nose still wedged between the pages of the paperback. I had just gotten up to street level, my mind ricocheting off one of Plato's philosophical droppings, when an acid voice with a little artificial sweetener scratched my ear.

"Hey, buddy, looking for a little action?"

She was a prostitute. She didn't look like one, but she was a prostitute just the same. In Chicago, any woman who talks to you first is either a prostitute or a Salvation Army worker. And this one didn't have any tambourine.

"Are you crazy or something?" I yelled. "For Christ's sake, I got an exam on this book in twenty minutes and you're asking me if I'm looking for a little action. It's only eight o'clock in the morning. What's the matter with you, huh?"

She started edging away. "You're a madman, you know that." The artificial sweetener was gone. Her voice was all acid now. She started walking down the street, looking suspiciously over her shoulder as if expecting to find me following her. I don't know why. The only thing I had to attack her with was my Plato paperback.

But the damage was done. One can go from the world of Plato to the world of a Chicago prostitute in a second. Going back the other way is quite another thing. I blew the exam.

TWENTY-SEVEN

You don't have to be a big shot to get police protection in Chicago. All you have to do is try and park with your date. If you go out and rape a girl or kill her, you'll probably get away with it. But if you're on a date, the moment you stop your car and turn off the headlights, you're under constant police surveillance.

Sarah and I would park somewhere for a while at the end of nearly every date. We never got much done, though. One reason was that we had a problem in communications. Sarah pronounced "Yes" differently than I did. She pronounced it "No."

Another problem was that we could never have any real privacy. We couldn't park on a side street because some neighbor would call the police to complain about a "suspicious" car. We usually ended up going to a parking lot that was located in a city park a few blocks away from Sarah's house. The parking lot was basically the local lover's lane.

Every fifteen minutes, a squad car would sneak around, usually with its lights off, while the cops stared through the back windows of the cars to see if everyone's head was above the seat. The Chicago Police Department didn't want anyone to have too good of a time, which proves how much cops know about such things.

Depending on the climate, both in and outside of my car, the windows would sometimes completely fog up. Then the cop would get out of his car and bang on my window with his flashlight. When I rolled my window down, he would flash the light in my face and ask, "What were you two doing?" A rather silly question for a man old enough to be a policeman.

The cop would then often ask to see my drivers' license. I don't know why. It wasn't the kind of moving violation that involved traffic court. "You have been found guilty of necking. Two more convictions and this court will be forced to revoke your lips."

I had a friend whose older brother was a cop. I once asked the older brother why a policeman would sneak around a park with his lights off, silently crawl out of his squad and tiptoe up to a car, leap up to the window and throw a flashlight beam on a young couple wrestling in the front seat of their car. He told me, "Why, to protect them from weirdos."

That parking lot certainly wasn't the honeymoon suite, but it was the only place that Sarah and I could have some semblance of privacy for any amount of time. Besides, like most four-wheel romantics, we were often too poor to pay for a drive-in, too young to go to an apartment and too scared to go to a motel.

The parking lot could be a very frustrating place. Occasionally, the police would enforce the weekend curfew and the park would close at midnight. Unfortunately, our passions would not.

Some nights, we didn't even have the sanctuary of the parking lot. If my father worked late or needed his car for something, I had to take the bus to Sarah's. Her father loved that. He once told Sarah's mother that he thought the Chicago Transit Authority was one of the most effective means of birth control.

One night, when Sarah and I drove into the parking lot, I had to swerve around several garbage cans that had been dragged out to the center of the lot. During the day, student drivers used the parking lot to practice.

It was a good night. Within a few minutes, all the windows were sweating with fog. About twenty minutes later, Sarah wanted to get going because she had to get up early the next morning for work. As I backed the car up, I heard the sickening sound of metal crunching against metal.

"What was that?" asked Sarah.

"Just a garbage can," I said as I put the car into "drive," pulled up a few feet at a different angle, then returned the car to "reverse" and backed up again. But again, I hit it.

I shoved open the door. "Why can't those goddamn student drivers put those garbage cans back where they got them?"

It was a squad car. A tough story indeed to deliver to dear old dad.

TWENTY-EIGHT

Dear God:

Is sex as immoral as everyone says it is?

Signed: Conroy

Conroy:

"Immoral," an interesting word. You're going to have to accept the fact, Conroy, that there are many things in life that are "immoral." Gambling, for instance, is "immoral" unless the state gets its cut. Making liquor is "immoral," unless the state taxes it. In fact, almost anything is "immoral," from walking your dog to buying cigarettes, unless the state taxes it.

Stealing is "immoral" unless it's legalized. (Talk to the Indians about that one.)

Killing is "immoral" unless, of course, you do it in a war or you're wearing a badge. If you refuse to kill in a war, then that's "immoral."

Sex is "immoral" unless the state licenses it and the Church blesses it.

My apologies. I do have a habit of rambling. I've just realized that I've given you a pretty good answer. Unfortunately, it has nothing to do with your question.

Conroy, I wanted you to see so I gave you eyes.

Signed: God

TWENTY-NINE

"Where were you on the night of March seventh?" Typical detective stuff you hear on television all the time. It's so phony. I hate it. Most people can't remember where they were three nights ago much less on a particular date. I know I can't.

The times you remember are the ones you're supposed to: Christmas day, the Fourth of July, your birthday. As you get older and occasionally look back, even those days drift together into one small blob of memories.

But you always remember the first time and the last. You remember your first day of school and the last. You remember the first time you went to the show by yourself and the last time you saw your grandfather. The first time you made love.

Most of the nights of my life have passed by barely noticed, like the black squares of rosary beads slipping through the wrinkled fingers in the last pew. But later, when I've looked back, I've realized that a few ink-colored seeds have taken root in my mind and have grown into oaken strength.

My dreams drift back and nestle in their branches. If those nights were suddenly not to be, I, who had come to lean on them, to relish those few surviving leaves of a young autumn that has passed and will not come again, would not know where I'd been. And I'd wonder, even more so, if there was anywhere to go.

Every Chicago winter delivers four gray weeks, with rare spots of sunshine, that are apparently the flipside of Hell. Teeth bared, the wind comes snarling off the lake with every intention of shredding the skin off your face. Numb since November, hands can no longer tell or care if they are wearing gloves. Snowmen, offsprings of childhood enthusiasm, are rarely born during these weeks.

Along with the human spirit, the temperature continues to plummet. The ground is smothered by aging layers of ice and snow. Looking at a magazine ad, you see a vaguely familiar blanket of green. Squinting back through months of brown snow, salt marked shoes, running noses, icy railings, slippery sidewalks and smoking sewers, you try to recall the feeling of grass.

February is four weeks of hanging onto the ropes, waiting to be saved from a knockout by the bell of spring.

One year, I was invited to Engrim University's "President's Ball," which was to be held on the first Saturday in February. I don't know why I was invited. Most of the students who received invitations were involved in a number of extracurricular activities; they participated in student government, belonged to various clubs, were presidents of fraternities or sororities, were doing extremely well academically or were, in some other way, pleasing the gods. I was never late with my tuition payments. Maybe that was it. Regardless, the President's Ball was to be held in the main ballroom of one of Chicago's swankiest hotels. I thought it was an excellent opportunity to impress Sarah with my importance.

A light snowfall was dotting the night air when I pulled up in front of Sarah's house. Heavy snow was in the forecast. The temperature was eight below and there was a twenty mile an hour wind. Pushing open the car door, kicking it shut, holding my ears and running for Sarah's house as the frigid air seared my throat and the wind razored across my face.

Sarah's father opened the door for me. "Cold enough for you?" He was a brilliant conversationalist.

"Yes, sir, it certainly is." I, too, have a way with words.

As Sarah came into the living room, I saw that she was wearing a black evening gown. Some girls, when they get dressed up, look kind of silly. Sometimes, they don't look much different than when they were five years old and tried the same thing. But Sarah looked very, very good.

Sarah's father said something to me and when I turned to reply, Sarah stepped behind me and went to the guest closet to get her coat. She left my sight an elegant woman and reappeared a moment later looking as if she was being swallowed by the Loch Ness Monster. She was wearing her favorite winter coat, an oversized blob of brown fluffy fur that rose up to her ears.

Both of Sarah's parents insisted on telling us to have a good time for at least ten minutes. By the time we got in the car, it had lost all the heat it had worked up driving over to her house.

I turned on the defroster and watched as the frost grudgingly backed off across the windshield. Feeling the cold steering wheel warm beneath my hands.

"That steering wheel must feel frigid," said Sarah.

"My hands are tough," I said as I clenched one into a fist. "They can take extreme cold. Remember, I held hands with you on our first date."

"You think you're funny, don't you?"

"No, I don't think I'm funny, but Donald Davis did. Actually, he thought I was crazy."

Old snow crackled as the wheels rolled away from Sarah's house. New snowflakes riddled the sky. Even the two ruts on the side street, carved out of earlier snows by previous traffic, were beginning to slicken. At the end of her block, I turned onto the main street and felt my back tires momentarily spin as they fought to grab the traction of the relatively dry surface.

"Who is Donald Davis?" asked Sarah.

"When I was nine years old, I was in the hospital for a week. Some kind of stomach trouble. He was my roommate."

"What made you think of him?"

"Didn't you notice? We just drove by a hospital," I said as I pointed to it down the street. "Donald Davis thought I was pretty funny. He did. When I was put in the room, he told me he had just had an appendix operation and he couldn't laugh because of the stitches. That's all I had to hear. I did everything I could to make him laugh. I told him every joke I ever heard. I stood on my head in bed. Took two bedpans, unused of course, and wore them as slippers. He was laughing constantly because of me. I think he had to spend two extra days in the hospital."

"You'd be a great comedian," said Sarah, "if someone could put your audience in stitches first."

"I would have hung out the window and exposed myself to get a laugh out of that kid."

"Small joke," replied Sarah.

"You know what I like about you, Sarah?"

"What?"

"You can't remember either?"

Sarah slid over close to me and ran her finger along the edge of my ear. "So you're finally taking me to a hotel, and the ballroom at that."

"Don't do that," I said. "It makes me nervous."

"Relax, I won't get you pregnant." Sarah remained sitting next to me, but she sat back defiantly and crossed her arms. "And to think my parents worry about you being too aggressive."

I put my arm around her and squeezed but I could barely feel her shoulders. The bulky fur coat had almost totally subdued her form. "Who would feel like making love to Smokey the Bear?" I said.

"I could use a laugh," replied Sarah. "Why don't you try hanging out the window . . ."

There was a long reception line of at least two dozen people standing in front of the ballroom's entrance. Most of the people in the line were older, probably administrators and professors. But a few of them were my age.

Sarah and I stood tangled in a crowd of people who were waiting to go down the receiving line.

"Now I know why they call this 'The President's Ball,' " said Sarah. "Everyone but the President of the United States is invited."

Just as we were about to shake the first hand in the reception line, I scanned down it quickly and saw only one face I recognized, that of Jack Avers. I knew him fairly well. He had been in a number of my classes.

Jack Avers was afflicted with what was a rare disease at Engrim University. He had school spirit. He belonged to dozens of extracurricular activities. Jack literally knew the words to the school song. The vast majority of students at Engrim didn't even know there was one.

Jack Avers was a nice enough guy but he had a very boring voice. I don't know why it was boring, but it was. No matter what Jack was saying, you didn't want to hear it. If he was on fire and screaming for help, your first impulse would be to yell back, "Oh, shut up."

Both the couple in front of Sarah and me and the one behind knew everyone in the reception line and were greeted accordingly. In front of us, we'd hear something like, "Hello, Bob, good to see you again. And who is this lovely lady?"

When our turn came, Sarah and I would get a flashed smile, two quick nods and a half-missed handshake.

Then as we were shoved along, behind us we'd hear, "Jim and Dolores, so nice of you to come this evening. You make a beautiful couple."

It was very embarrassing. For the first time in my life, I was actually looking forward to talking to Jack Avers. Finally, we stood in front of him. He reached out, grabbed my hand, shook it vigorously and said, "Danny, how have you been?"

The food was typical for a banquet, old lady portions and only coffee and one glass of water to drink. I can't drink coffee. The first thing it does when it slides down my throat is look for daylight. And there's no way I can properly eat a meal with only one glass of water.

In order for me to enjoy my food, I've got to correlate my eating with my drinking; so many mouthfuls, so many gulps. The old lady portions and just one glass of water threw my timing off. I was still slurping through my soup when I realized that I had already nearly exhausted my water supply.

They were serving green sherbert for dessert. Normally, I never skip dessert. A lot of times, for me, the meal is a boring preliminary for the sweetness that follows. But I've never been big on green sherbert. I always have the feeling that it started out another color. So instead of eating dessert, I went looking for a water fountain.

Sarah came with me. She often skipped dessert. I don't know why, she wasn't fat. Anyway, it was a good excuse for us to get away from the people at our table. They were real phonies. They spent the whole meal talking about all the people *they* knew in the reception line.

Music was provided by the "Harmonies," a group of Engrim alumnae who, according to the announcement, had performed at the last twenty-seven President's balls. They sounded as if they had played continuously.

Dancing with Sarah. "Having a good time?" I asked her.

"Yes, aren't you?"

"Sure I am. The crowd's hostile, the dinner was dumpy and the band's terrible."

"Well, pardon me," said Sarah.

"Do you realize," I said, "that I have spent nearly all evening with my arms around you. I've wasted the whole night doing nothing but this."

"No one's forcing you," Sarah said as she put both hands on my shoulders and pushed back subtly so that no one would notice. But I locked my hands behind her waist as I continued to talk.

"The entire evening wasted," I repeated. "It's not as good as wasting my whole life, but it's a start."

Sarah stopped pushing.

A few minutes later, we were dancing another slow song. Sarah's cheek was against mine. "Why don't we leave early?" I whispered.

"Why?"

"Why do you think?"

Sarah looked up at me as her face flushed into a smile. "You don't wear a long evening dress to go parking."

"I don't. But I was hoping you do."

Sarah grabbed my hand and began leading me through the crowd towards the coat room. "Let's leave," she said, "before that band desecrates a song I like."

When we drove out of the hotel's garage, we were welcomed by a savage snowstorm. Waves of cold wind rolled down the street as scratches of night peaked through the wall of falling snow. Prodding the car out onto the street, I saw that all traces of asphalt had been snuffed out by the snow.

"I hate this time of the year," stuttered Sarah as she tried to snuggle deeper into her coat. "The only day I want to see snow is Christmas. That's it."

"Christmas is okay," I said as I squeezed the brake down for a red light, "but it has its rotten moments, too."

"I suppose," said Sarah. "One thing that bothers me about Christmas is how they change the store windows the day after. They take down all the pretty Christmas displays and put up the spring fashions and New Year's is still a week away."

"I agree. It's sort of like they're saying, 'Thanks, suckers, now here's our next pitch.' "

Braking hard as I belatedly noticed that the car in front of me had stopped.

Sarah popped forward from the sudden stop, but had time to brace herself against the dashboard. "Perhaps it would be safer, Tim," she said as she settled back into her seat, "if you saved your philosophizing for warmer weather."

Stopping the car so quickly had killed the engine. I re-started the car and crept across an intersection.

"Maybe we ought to skip parking tonight, Tim."

"Why? It's still early."

"I know. But with this weather, it's going to take us forever to get home. Besides, there'll be too much snow to get into the parking lot at the park. And I don't want you hurrying."

"You think I'd take the chance of having an accident just to go park with you?"

"No, of course not."

She was wrong, I would.

"Don't worry," I said, "if we get home with a little extra time, fine. If we don't, we don't."

"Thanks, Tim."

When your whole body is pulsating with passion, that's when you have to sound reasonable to a woman.

I did drive a little faster than I should have, but I would have never really taken the chance of having an accident. Not that I'm afraid of dying. I am. However, I don't necessarily equate an auto accident with death. But having an accident does mean going through tons of garbage with your insurance company. I learned that when I had had a minor accident a few years earlier.

Die and it's over with. Bend a fender and you live in bureaucratic agony for years.

As we drove onto the expressway, I spotted a salt truck with a wide snow plow braced across its face. Immediately, I began following it. Pellets of salt clanged off the front of the car.

"Do you have to drive right behind it?" asked Sarah.

"We'll make better time." We did.

Both of us listened to the radio as I drove down Addison Avenue and approached her street. The park lay six blocks beyond. Waiting for Sarah's protest as I passed her corner, but she continued to sit in silence.

When we arrived at the park, the snow was falling with gracious serenity, no longer being flailed by a frantic wind. White ridges were calmly growing on tree branches. Billows of snow floated across the open fields of the park. The parking lot, normally visible from the street, was hidden behind a high crescent of white.

In the distance, I could see the backstop of a baseball diamond. Standing at the plate, glaring at the pitcher. Swinging the bat in short, menacing chops. Daring him to throw one by me.

"I wonder if there's anyone in there?" I asked.

"How could there be?" replied Sarah. "There's too much snow. Who would want to be in there?"

"Me."

"If you want to park that badly, let's stop on one of the streets near my house."

"And have some screwball in a uniform and a flashlight pounding on the window in five minutes? No thanks."

"I don't see where we have any choice," said Sarah.

"I can drive through that snow," I replied. "That would be no big problem. But do you realize if I did, we would be alone? Totally alone? We couldn't be seen from the street. And in a few minutes our tracks would be covered by the falling snow."

"You're crazy," said Sarah.

"Now you're sounding like Danny Davis."

"You are crazy." Solemnly, she asked, "Do you think you could do it? You wouldn't get stuck?"

"It's cold," I said, "so the snow is powdery. As long as I inch the car along, we won't have any problems."

"I don't know," she said, "it's awfully risky."

I knew I had her. "If you don't think it's a good idea, then we won't do it," I commented objectively.

"You don't think we'll get stuck?"

"No."

"What if we do?"

"I'll get us out, one way or the other." Obviously, a safe statement for me to make. If we did get stuck, sooner or later, we'd have to come out. Besides, even in Chicago, the snow melts in spring.

"You're not worrying about getting your father's car caught in there?"

"Not me." I was very worried.

"Okay."

A few minutes later, being with Sarah behind a wall of white. In front of the parkhouse, a few hundred feet away, a rope rang against the flagpole. Bells should always ring on such occasions.

Driving home with Sarah in silence. A screaming, ecstatic, hilariously delicious silence. Sarah sat curled up next to me, sighing her approval as my arm repeatedly squeezed her to me. Every time I stopped the car for a traffic light, she softly said, "I love you, are we home yet?"

Leaving Sarah's house and driving home. Snow continued to trickle from the sky as I pulled up to the front of my house. Instead of going in, I decided to take a walk. Actually, I did more running than walking. And a lot of jumping up and down, too. I would have done cartwheels except that I don't know how to do them.

When I got in the house, I still wasn't tired enough to sleep. It was a dumb idea, but I did it anyway. I called Sarah.

Listening to the first ring, hoping to God that someone else in the family didn't answer. One of their phones was in the kitchen and the other one was in her room.

I heard the phone being picked up just as the second ring began to twirl. There was a fumbling pause before I heard Sarah's sleep soaked voice.

"Hello?"

"I love you."

"Who is this?"

"Who is this? How many guys have said that to you lately?"

"Tim? What are you doing calling so late?"

"I just wanted to tell you that. That's all. So how have you been? I do love you. I really do."

Sarah laughed. "Danny Davis was right. You are crazy." Her voice turned serious. "Don't you ever change."

THIRTY

Dear God:

I am the world's greatest lover.

Signed: Conroy

Conroy:

No, you're not. I am. I've made everybody.

Signed: God

THIRTY-ONE

Standing just inside the main doors of Engrim, watching Weatherly as he tried to cross the street, which was immersed in morning rush hour traffic. Rain was battering the street. At last, there was a break in the traffic and Weatherly, his one arm wrapped around his books, and his head hanging low to avoid the rain, began jogging across the street. A cab that had just gone by Weatherly made a sharp U-turn. Weatherly almost ran into it. He yelled something at the cabdriver while simultaneously throwing up his hand and giving the driver the finger. The cabdriver who, by now, had driven a few dozen feet past the school, braked the cab, rolled down the window, and bellowed an obscenity at Weatherly. He responded by dropping his books on the rain-soaked street and thrusting out both arms, the middle finger standing high on each hand. The cabdriver, realizing that he was getting drenched by the blowing rain, rolled up the window as he yelled one final epithet at Weatherly and sped off.

The brief encounter had managed to tie up traffic in both directions. Dozens of horns were honking at Weatherly to get out of the middle of the street. Drenched, with rain even running off his ears, Weatherly calmly picked his books up off the street's center line and walked towards the front doors of the school. Engrim University has never bothered to offer a course in urban studies.

A few minutes later, we were sitting in the cafeteria and Weatherly was drinking coffee.

Even though it was still early in the morning, the cafeteria was mobbed. Since Engrim University was located in a heavy business district, it felt obligated to its students to set up barriers to discourage outsiders from using the cafeteria. Therefore, the prices were jacked up, the food was slop and there was one chair for every five students. Engrim didn't have an orientation week for its new students. It simply ushered them into the cafeteria and told them to sit down. There was bound to be someone of interest on the same chair.

Weatherly was still wet and shivering from the rain. His hands huddled around his coffee cup for warmth. "You know what I'd do if I was in charge of things?" said Weatherly.

"No, what?"

"I'd have a pedestrian in each city who had life and death powers over every driver. Nobody would know who he was. So every time a driver got the temptation to give a pedestrian a hard time, he'd never know whether that was the pedestrian who could have him executed."

"Yeah," I countered, "but some people walking around really ask for it."

"Fine. So give one driver in the city the same life and death power. If a pedestrian steps right in front of him, that driver can run him over, no questions asked."

"Sounds like there'd be a lot of dead people lying around," I said.

"You know how many people in this city got run over by cars last year?"

"No."

"Neither do I. But with my system, you'd cut the number in half. There's only one flaw in my system."

"What's that?" I asked.

"If the all-powerful pedestrian walks in front of the all-powerful driver."

"Like this morning?"

About half of the people in the cafeteria, like Weatherly and myself, were simply trying to stay awake. The other half were playing cards; pinochle, poker, the usual. Card playing was very big at Engrim.

Weatherly pulled the morning newspaper out from his folder and flopped it onto the table. "Late last night," Weatherly read aloud from the front page, "three people were seriously injured in a head-on collision at thirty-nine hundred south Lake Shore Drive. Oh, yes," he added, "four people were injured humorously."

"It was a dull weekend," said Weatherly as he continued to skim the front page, "only five people were murdered in the city."

"This is a slow time of the year for homicides," I said. "I learned in a sociology class that most murders happen between family members and friends and that they occur during those times of the year when people mix a lot. Therefore, the murder rate goes up at Christmas time and in the summer along with the temperature."

"Then the solution is obvious," said Weatherly. "We should ban families and friends, cancel Christmas, stop wasting money on sociologists and start spending more on air conditioners."

"Where did the murders occur?" I asked.

"One happened in the Robert Taylor Projects. Some karate expert resisted an armed robbery. Witnesses said the karate expert tried to chop the mugger in the throat. Police estimated that such a karate expert probably swung his arm at the speed of nearly one hundred miles an hour, about five hundred miles slower than the bullet that went through his head."

"Did you know that the Robert Taylor Projects are one of the largest in the world?" I asked Weatherly.

"What a dumb name," he said, "Robert Taylor. Who the hell is he? Probably some political crony. I worked with a guy once who lived there. He never heard of Robert Taylor either. The place is such a goddamn hellhole, at least give it a name that means something to somebody."

"What would you suggest?"

"How about 'Louie the Pimp Housing Project'?"

Weatherly opened the newspaper to the society page with its

usual assortment of wedding pictures. "This past Saturday morning," Weatherly read, "Jane Blessel, daughter of Mr. and Mrs. Thomas Blessel of North Arlington Heights, became the wife of Mr. William Leland II, son of Mr. and Mrs. William Leland of Chicago, at a simple ceremony at the Third Presbyterian Chapel in Highhills, Illinois. The bride wore a gown of white satin trimmed with Chantilly lace, seed pearls and sequins on the bodice and floor length train. Bridesmaids, wearing...." Weatherly interrupted himself.

"What bullshit. Why don't they write about the really important moments." He looked down at the newspaper and pretended to read. "Last Saturday night, Jane Blessel, daughter of Mr. and Mrs. Thomas Blessel of North Arlington Heights, lost her virginity to Mr. William Leland II, son of Mr. and Mrs. William Leland of Chicago, during a simple ceremony in the back seat of his Pontiac. The bride wore a smile ... "

Carol Foltz sat down at our table, but not willingly. She didn't like Weatherly. But it was the only empty chair she could find and her coffee was getting cold and her sweet roll was beginning to stick to her fingers.

Carol Foltz had on ten-year-old shoes, a twenty-year-old dress, and a thirty-year-old hairstyle that sat atop a one-hundred-year-old mind.

It was rumored that her family had a 1947 calendar still hanging on the wall. According to Mr. Foltz, if it was good enough for 1947, it was good enough for now.

A couple sitting at the table next to us were putting on their own passion play. But if she was from a large family and he didn't own a car, where else?

"That's disgusting," said Carol Foltz.

"Why?" inquired Weatherly.

"It just cheapens a girl, that's all. How can a boy respect a girl if she allows him to treat her like that?"

"Did it ever dawn on you," asked Weatherly, "that she might want to be treated like that?"

"Well, uh ... even if she does, she shouldn't allow it. A girl like that is going to have a difficult time getting married."

"Why?" asked Weatherly.

"As my mother has often told me," said Carol Foltz assuredly, "why buy the cow when the milk's free?"

"Isn't that a line from the balcony scene of Romeo and Juliet?" asked Weatherly.

After quickly consuming her coffee and sweet roll, Carol Foltz grabbed her books, mumbled a few nondirectional good-byes, and hurried off to class. As soon as she left, Weatherly tapped me on the hand and pointed to a girl that was standing at another table halfway across the room.

"See that broad? That's the one I'm going out with now."

"Nice looking girl," I lied.

Weatherly noticed my lack of enthusiasm but was unperturbed.

"The closer you get, the uglier she gets," he said. "But she only lives ten blocks from me."

For many, that was the love story at Engrim University. It didn't matter what a girl looked like, or was like, as long as she lived fairly close to you. Chicago is a big place and it seemed to get a lot bigger on Saturday night. No one wanted to spend any of those few free weekend hours in the lanes of some expressway. For Weatherly, love ended at 59th Street.

Somewhere between my first bite of sweet roll and my last sip of hot chocolate, Weatherly redirected the conversation into one of his grand theories. He began expounding on why he had chosen to attend Engrim University, more generally a commuter school, rather than having gone away to college. It was a frequent topic of conversation at Engrim. Commuter students constantly itch with the suspicion that they are missing something by not having gone away to school. The boys are afraid that living at home so long will turn them into weirdos and the girls have nightmares of marrying the boy who lives four doors away who's an apprentice butcher.

"Go to a school like Engrim," said Weatherly, "and when you get out, it's much tougher for somebody to make a sucker out of you. You learn to kick somebody's ass around the block instead of the other way around. That's an education."

"What do you mean?" I asked.

"Almost everyone ends up working a job in the city," said Weatherly. "So if you go to school in the city, work part-time jobs in the city, you're that much more ready. For instance, this morning, when I picked up a newspaper at the newsstand on State Street, there was this little old lady standing next to me. She had a purse in one hand and a five-inch hat pin in the other that she was hiding under her shawl. She's probably been carrying that hat pin around for years just hoping for the chance to run it through a purse snatcher or some other annoyance. And that news vendor makes more book in a week than any literary press in the country. The cop I passed on the way to school was ticketing certain illegally parked cars and ignoring others, because some people have paid off and others haven't. You believe all of this, don't you?"

"Sure," I replied.

"I'd bet that a lot of kids who've gone to out of town schools wouldn't believe it," continued Weatherly. "They might say they did, but they wouldn't really. They're naive. They live in a world of theories. Almost no reality. The typical college town has very few old people, little kids, or other people who are working regular jobs and aren't into the college scene. Those kinds of towns are incubators for four-year liberals. That's not an education, that's a fantasy trip. If I had wanted that kind of an education," said Weatherly, "I would have sat in front of a mirror for a few years and asked me what I thought."

THIRTY-TWO

It was almost a nightly ritual. Running in low gear, short strides, the knees barely bending, listening to my gym shoes lick the sidewalk as I ran through the neighborhood streets. Feeling my muscles yawn, glad to be away from the hours of studying.

I imagined myself trotting in from the outfield after I had just leaped high above the wall to snare a home run ball. The fans were going wild. I could care less. What the hell, that's what I was paid to do.

As I ran by the houses, I could almost hear the thoughts living inside. Living room lights and the flicker of a television. Already guessed the ending. Wondering if there's anything better on. Who took the sports section?

Kitchen light. Quietly opening the refrigerator to get a glass of milk. Carefully sliding a piece of chocolate cake from under the cover and hoping that the slight clatter doesn't draw a crowd.

Basement lights. Doing the wash. Searching for that nearly empty gallon of lacquer left over from one of the bedrooms a few years ago.

I could have called Sarah from home and often did. But with

nine people in a house, only a trip to a pay phone could guarantee more than a few minutes of uninterrupted conversation.

Since it was after nine-thirty, the drugstore was closed. The next nearest phone hung out in a booth, in front of a bus depot, a few blocks away from my house. When I got there, as usual, the folding door fought back as I shoved it aside. Picking up the receiver, it felt cold in my hands.

I rubbed my hand over the ear piece to warm it up and then dropped in the coins and waited for the dial tone. Nothing. I slammed the receiver down on the phone and then picked it up and listened again. Still no dial tone. A punch to the midsection, right in the middle of the directory assistance card, and dial tone popped on.

Sarah's mother answered.

"Hello, may I speak to Sarah, please?"

"Just a moment," her mother replied. We both knew who each other was but we sort of pretended we didn't. Not a very polite thing for me to do, I admit. But I didn't have anything to say to Mrs. Faber. Worse yet, if I thought of something to say, or Mrs. Faber did, I'd be spending time talking to her when I could have been talking to her daughter.

I don't remember what Sarah and I talked about that night. I don't even know why I remember that specific night. There were hundreds of others just like it. We shared our day with each other, I'm sure of that. Little things. I might have told her about what had happened at my part-time job or talked about friends of mine she knew. She'd tell me about her day and, sometimes, things about her family. Maybe, about how her brother was now playing first-string for the school basketball team.

That night, I'm sure we talked about the upcoming weekend. We would be celebrating eighteen months of knowing one another. Celebrating anniversaries was hardly new to Sarah and me. We did it on a monthly basis. But an eighteen-month anniversary was, of course, a very big deal.

In such weather, when I'd prop up my toes and they'd no longer be able to feel the tops of my shoes, I knew I'd soon have to end the conversation. That night, a wind that I had barely noticed when I had left the house was now shearing through the air vents of the phone booth.

"I've got to go," I said over the noise of the wind. "Remember, I love you."

"What did you say?" asked Sarah.

Louder, "I love you."

"What?" she asked again.

Shouting, "I love you."

"Once more?" asked Sarah meekly.

She had understood every time. "I've got to go."

"Don't be mad. I just like the way you say it."

"I've got to go?"

"No, of course not. I like the way you say, 'I love you.' "

"What did you say?"

"Good night, Timothy."

"I love you."

"I love you, too."

I liked that. Sarah never said "and" before it.

Running home. Strengthening my stride as the cold wind snapped against my ears. Watching as houselights were turned out as if the wind were hushing them into darkness.

That Saturday night, we went to Willowbrook, a restaurant that featured big band music and ballroom dancing. It wasn't a real expensive place, but it wasn't cheap either.

Sarah and I danced the first dance of the evening. She clung to me as I wrapped my arms around her.

"You know," I said, "we don't have a song."

"So?"

"Every couple should have a song."

"We have a number," said Sarah as she softly drew a "two" and then a "six" on my back. Sarah had superb fingers.

"That's different," I said as I hugged her tighter. "You can hardly say, 'Hey, listen, they're playing our number.' "

"You can if you're at a bingo game."

"But wouldn't it be nice if, every time we heard a particular song, we thought of each other?"

"Every time I hear a beautiful song, I think of you."

The music stopped. "What would you like to do now?" I whispered in her ear. I expected her to say something like having a drink or going into the restaurant for dinner.

"Let's go park."

I had just paid the price of admission, which included the cost of two dinners, and was wearing a freshly pressed suit and a new shirt bought specifically for the evening. I had spent over an hour driving to the place and had even gone to the trouble of buying Sarah a corsage.

"Okay."

Later that night, driving home. "You crushed my corsage," said Sarah as she tried to fluff up the flowers.

"There's always a price to pay for passion," I said.

"Would you stop at that gas station up ahead?"

"Why?"

"I need to use a washroom," said Sarah. "After that, we can stop for something to eat."

"All I've been doing tonight," I said in mock exasperation, "is taking care of your biological urges."

"I think I'd like a hamburger."

"Will you marry me?" I didn't mean to say it. I had thought it a thousand times, but I still hadn't meant to say it. I was almost tempted to look around the car to see who had.

In the past few weeks, I had actually thought about saying it. When I did, I decided, it would be at the pinnacle of a perfect evening. We would waltz across a cloud-covered dance floor and I'd dazzle her with my charm. I would take a ring out of my pocket and on it would be the number "26" glistening in diamonds. Looking straight at her, I would ask her to marry me and she would softly reply, "Yes." Then I would slip the ring on her finger, thus crowning the most romantic moment in the history of mankind. The rest of the evening would be personal so I'm not going to go into it.

Instead, we were driving to a gas station washroom and talking about biological urges. I congratulated myself for such great timing.

Sarah hadn't answered. I had no choice. I actually had to say it again. "Will you marry me?"

"If I do, will you buy me a hamburger?"

"I'm serious."

"I'm sorry."

"Will you?"

"When?"

"I don't know. I still have a lot of school left. And it would be nice to have a little money before we got married. But that's not important. But . . . I haven't even got a ring for you."

I pulled the car over to the shoulder of the road. "It was a silly question wasn't it?"

"Yes, it was."

Stepping on the accelerator harder than I should have. The car jerked back onto the road.

"Would you like a silly answer?" she asked.

"Sure." Hoping.

"Yes."

On the following Monday afternoon, right after my last class, I walked over to a bank near Engrim. Feeling fantastic as I strolled through the lobby. Now my life had a place to go. So this was what growing up felt like. Stroking the glow as I relived the conversation we had had on Sunday afternoon.

"I thought of the perfect place for a honeymoon," Sarah had said.

"Where?"

"Tenseed, Wyoming. A few years ago, a neighbor of ours went out there with his brother-in-law and built a big hotel because the town was expecting a mining boom. The boom never came. Our neighbor moved back. He said that town's the most boring place in the world. There's absolutely nothing to do."

"So why would you want to spend your honeymoon there?"

"Boy, are you dumb."

"Oh."

I stepped up to one of the teller's cages. "I'd like to open a joint account." Filling out the proper forms and taking it back to him. I opened the account with the minimum amount, three dollars.

"Now you understand," he said emphatically as his head hung low checking out the forms, "that with our system, you are responsible for recording each deposit and each withdrawal so that you are aware, at all times, of the balance of your account. You also understand that, concerning taxes, you are responsible . . . "

Walking through the lobby and out of the bank, feeling my high regurgitate into sobriety. I stared at the names on the savings account book: "Conroy, Timothy M., Faber, Sarah T." Remembering the can of paint that got knocked over in the garage years ago. My father came raging into the kitchen and looked straight at me. "Are you responsible?"

Talking in the washroom line. The nun came up from behind me and grabbed me by the back of the neck. "Are you responsible for all this talking?" She shook me. "Are you responsible?"

Recalling the first time I watched my little sisters for my mother when she went to the store. "Remember, if one of your sisters is kidnapped or run over by a car, you're responsible. Remember, you're responsible."

Crossing over a bridge that spanned the Chicago River on my way to the subway station. Recalling what my Aunt Carla had said a few months ago when my cousin, Raymond, got married. "After all," she had told my mother, "he's twenty-three. It's time he settled down."

Below me, along the shore line, a young boy tossed a paper cup into the river. Ripples of water splashed across the brim. Within seconds, the cup filled, bowed to the water and sank. I imagined that cup drifting down through layers of green to black until it slipped into that soil of slime at the bottom of the river. Waiting while time and indifference decomposed it into nothingness. Drifting through layers of green and black. Drifting. Settling down.

That night, I didn't call Sarah.

THIRTY-THREE

Dear God:

Today, in my philosophy class, a guest lecturer proved, through the use of logic, that You do not exist.

Signed: Conroy

Conroy:

Ask your professor to explain to you why sunshine feels good on your face and snow does not. Have him write on the board the logical explanation of laughter. Ask him to list the reasons why pizza and beer taste good together. What are the logical factors that allow a bumblebee to fly? According to all aeronautical theories, it cannot.

Everything in the universe makes sense to me. Why shouldn't it? I'm God. But very little makes sense to you humans because I deliberately made you considerably dumber than me. Why look for trouble?

By the way, a few years ago, there was a guy in New York who logically proved that the earth does not exist. Just to make sure, he wrote down all of his calculations and checked them over. But as he already knew, his reasoning was correct.

To prove his point, he jumped out a twelfth floor window. On his way down, to make absolutely sure his thinking was logical, he again reviewed his facts and again found no error in his thinking.

He now firmly believed he was right. But when he hit the ground, he made just as big a splat as anybody else.

Logic and reality don't have much to do with one another.

Signed: God

THIRTY-FOUR

Making the crumbs for major league baseball. During one summer, I worked at Mother Martha's Wholesale Bakery House. Mother Martha made buns and rolls for hotels, restaurants, hospitals, nursing homes and other institutions. She also made all the hot dog buns for her two biggest customers, the Chicago White Sox and the Cubs. Mother Martha's was a small factory, employing only about fifty people.

The air inside Mother Martha's was always hotter than the outside air that surrounded it. Batches of hot, freshly baked breath would drift from the ovens through the plant, seeping into the pores of the employees and reaming out tiny droplets of sweat. Lunch came at midnight. Dessert was three glasses of water and a salt tablet.

I was a bun packer and worked the night shift, which began at four P.M. and usually ended at five the next morning.

The night shift was thirteen hours of standing on the assembly line, grabbing hot dog buns as they went by, one squeezed between each finger, and slapping them into the empty box that laid, open mouthed, on a narrow metal shelf that ran alongside

185

the conveyor belt at waist level. Two more handfuls of hot dog buns filled the box, which was then placed on another conveyor belt that led to the wrapping machine.

Occasionally, instead of spinning a suit of cellophane around the box, the wrapping machine would spew out a mangled blob of cardboard and bun. Then the wrapping machine would pop a noise that sounded suspiciously like a burp.

As I worked, I would occasionally glance up at the narrow windows that were located along the top rim of one of the high walls. The luster of the late afternoon summer sun would gradually melt into the gray stare of sunset which, in turn, would deepen into the dimness of night. About nine hours later, the process would reverse itself. It was the only announcement we got that the old day had passed away and another had been born.

If the White Sox or Cubs were playing a team that was as bad as they were, only a few hundred hot dog buns would come bobbing over the assembly line belt. But if the New York Yankees were coming to town to play the White Sox in a Sunday doubleheader, the Wednesday night shift at Mother Martha's wouldn't end until early Thursday afternoon.

One Wednesday night, as we packers picked up and boxed one wave of hot dog buns after another, I yelled, out of desperation, "Doesn't anyone go to watch the damn game?"

José, a Puerto Rican who was working next to me said, "It's the kids. A couple of weeks ago, I took my two boys to a game. They spent all afternoon supporting the vendor."

Mother Martha's Wholesale Bakery House was owned by a guy named William Jesop, who came by twice a week to check the books. Supposedly, Jesop owned a number of wholesale bakery houses as well as a few dozen hotels.

There were five foremen and Haterfock, the plant superintendent, who was in his middle forties. He worked, literally, twenty hours a day, six days a week, even though, unlike the rest of us, he was paid a straight salary rather than an hourly wage.

Haterfock had never married, although it was rumored in the plant that he once had something going with a crescent roll. He lived with his younger sister's family.

Haterfock spent his twenty hours a day getting on everybody's nerves: peering over bakers' shoulders as they stirred the dough, getting in the way of the oven men as they yanked the hot pans out of the ovens.

One night, I was tying up boxes and piling them in a corner. Haterfock came up to me and said, "No, no, you don't tie them that way." He demonstrated, "You tie them this way." I didn't ask what the difference was. I knew. None. But I said nothing. You don't tamper with a man's religion.

Haterfock loved to stand next to the conveyor belt and poke a finger into an unsuspecting hot dog bun. "Goddamn," he'd bellow over the loud hum of the assembly line. He'd hold aloft the hot dog bun that was still impaled on his finger and he'd roar, "This bun's too goddamn soft," or "This bun's too goddamn hard." Whatever.

Often, he'd say, "Are these the kinds of buns that Mother Martha can be proud of?" The man didn't even realize what he was saying.

One night, as I grabbed hot dog buns off the conveyor belt, I saw Haterfock standing a few feet away from me. He was sneezing all over the place. One of the foremen suggested that Haterfock go home and take care of his cold.

"And who's going to do all of my work?" asked Haterfock as he blew into his handkerchief.

"I'm sure," said the foreman, "that if you show me what has to be done that I, and a few of the other men, can take care of it."

"You guys aren't capable of doing my job," Haterfock said disdainfully, and loudly, so that everyone could hear him over the noise of the plant. "Nobody can replace me."

Standing with Eddie Lieb, the night foreman, at the bus stop, our deflated muscles aching from the fourteen-hour shift we had just finished. Warming ourselves in the light of the infant sunrise that had yet to be trampled by the waking world. As the bus was pulling up to the curb, we saw Haterfock drive through the intersection on his way home.

"That guy's going to work himself to death," I said.

"That's what everybody keeps saying," replied Eddie Lieb. The words came slowly on the heels of a yawn. "Every couple of days, someone says that about Haterfock. It's kind of like predicting rain. Say it long enough and, sooner or later, you've got to be right."

It was sooner. Haterfock went home and dropped dead in the shower.

When I punched out the next morning, I noticed that Haterfock's time card was still in the rack. Slowly, I pulled the card up out of its slot and stared at the last set of numbers punched on it, "4:42 A.M." Strange, it seemed as if it would have been more upsetting to the scheme of things if someone had ripped up that card than the fact that Haterfock had dropped dead. The least important thing on that time card was the name. Cross it out, write another name in, and the card would function just as well.

Eddie Lieb walked up behind me. "You don't have to worry about that card, kid, Haterfock's punching that big one in the sky now."

Lieb laughed as he reached around me and dropped his card into the time clock. I mumbled something about how I had grabbed Haterfock's card by mistake and shoved it back into its slot.

Eight weeks later, when I quit my job at Mother Martha's Wholesale Bakery House to go back to college, William Jesop, the owner, still hadn't bothered hiring anyone to replace Haterfock.

Nearly a year later, on my way home from school, I met Eddie Lieb on the bus. We reminisced about the usual stuff. I asked him who replaced Haterfock. "Gee, kid," he said, "I forgot all about that. Until you mentioned it just now, I never realized that nobody was ever hired to take over his job. You know," he said quietly, "Jesop didn't even go to the guy's funeral."

As we rode along together on the bus, Eddie Lieb continued to talk about the world of Mother Martha's Wholesale Bakery House, but I couldn't hear him over the noise of the assembly line and the bellowing words of Haterfock. "Nobody can replace me." He was right. Nobody did.

So much for being a company man.

THIRTY-FIVE

Going to a wedding with Sarah. Some girl friend of hers. Sarah knew her from high school.

We didn't go to the church because both of us had to work. But on our way to the reception that evening, Sarah kept talking about these two guys that she and this girl friend had double-dated with a few times. The guys were best friends and all of that. One of them still wrote to the girl who had gotten married that afternoon. They were, of course, "just friends." Anyway, these two guys had joined the Marines on the "buddy" system. The system guaranteed that the two "buddies" would always be in the same platoon. Terrific.

In his latest letter, this one guy told Sarah's girl friend that his unit was involved in heavy jungle fighting, that about half of the unit had been killed and almost everyone else, including him and his buddy, had been wounded. Neither of them expected to survive another month.

I'm sure she wasn't aware of it, but Sarah was making me feel very guilty. Those guys were the same age as me, had lived pretty much the same lives as I had. Yet, they were twelve thousand miles away in a jungle fighting for their lives and my biggest problem was getting through a few boring hours at a wedding reception. No doubt about it. I'm a mental case. When times are bad, I wonder why they couldn't be better. And when they're good, I feel guilty because I'm not miserable.

"How many people do you think are here?" I asked Sarah as we moved through the crowd towards the coatroom.

"I don't know," Sarah said curtly. She already knew I wasn't too thrilled being there. A few minutes later, for lack of something better to say, I guess, I asked the same question.

"I told you, I don't know," Sarah said. "This isn't a ball park, they don't announce attendance figures."

"The White Sox should draw so well."

Sarah's older married sister, Nancy, had also been invited. She and her husband had earlier agreed to meet Sarah and me at the bar. After we met them, we found a table with four open places.

Nancy was a very nice person but she had habits that would drive you crazy. When we were standing and talking at the bar, and even when we sat down at the table, she would constantly reach over and brush off her husband's shoulder. I can't stand it when someone touches somebody else that way. As if the guy was five years old or something and had to be dressed in the morning. He should have broken her arm off. Granted, her husband did have a fantastic case of dandruff. But it wasn't falling that fast. Besides, it's bad enough having dandruff without someone tapping you on the shoulder every five minutes to remind you.

There were four other couples sitting at the table. Two of the couples apparently knew each other well, especially the men. They were jerks. The one guy kept telling the other one how they both would have ended up on skid row if it hadn't been for their two "little women."

"You know it's true, Jack," the one guy said to the other. "You and I are doing all right. But we wouldn't be where we're at if it wasn't for these two fine women of ours. If they didn't keep us on the straight and narrow, make sure we did what we were supposed to do, and keep us from drinking ourselves to death, Jesus, who knows what kind of lives we'd be living today."

He sounded like he was talking about his mother. The two

women just sat there, blushing at the proper moment, and soaking up all that shit.

The guy sitting next to me, who was about my age, and the girl on his other side, had both come to the wedding separately.

"I just broke up with my fiancée," he said to me.

"Oh, that's too bad," I replied as I shoveled in some beef.

"Had everything all set," he continued. "Even bought a house in the suburbs. Three bedrooms."

"Very nice," I said.

"No two ways about it. I'm going to have to get married soon."

"Why?"

"Like I've told you, I've already bought a house." He turned to his other side and introduced himself to the girl sitting next to him. Three months later, he married her.

We left early. On the way home, Sarah sat against the door. "If you sit any further away," I said, "you're going to have to run alongside the car."

"What was wrong with you, tonight?" demanded Sarah. "You hardly talked at all. You didn't feel like dancing ... "

"I don't like weddings." I knew I should have padded that statement, but I didn't feel like bothering.

"Does that include, and I mention this only as a remote possibility, ours?"

"No. And don't give me that stuff about ours being a 'remote possibility.' "

"I'm beginning to wonder. If you didn't want to go tonight, you should have told me. I would have gone alone."

"If you had, right now, some guy would be trying to sell you a three bedroom house in the suburbs with a lifelong mortgage."

"What are you talking about?"

"Nothing."

"I don't understand it. What is your problem?"

"Weddings are so phony," I said. "They're so sterile. At all weddings, they serve the same kind of food, play the same kinds of music, take the same kinds of pictures, even the poses are exactly the same, and say the same kinds of dumb things. You know what I heard one woman say to the bride tonight? 'Just as long as he takes good care of you, nothing else matters.' Does this girl think she got married or adopted? What about happiness? Isn't that what marriage is all about? Two people getting married because that way they'll be happier than if they didn't. You don't need a mob scene for that."

"It's a time when people want to share their happiness," said Sarah.

"I'll bet the only two people who had less fun tonight than us was the bride and groom."

"That's not necessarily so and you know it."

"True, but it's a damn good possibility."

"All weddings are not alike today," said Sarah. "People are writing their own vows, choosing their own music. Some couples are even getting married outside."

"Like in parking lots?" I asked.

Sarah ignored my attempt at humor. "I really don't know what your problem is."

"It's all so phony, the bride wearing white."

"What," said Sarah, exasperated, "is phony about that?"

"The bride wears white because she's supposed to be a virgin . . ." I began.

"Oh," interrupted Sarah, "so if she isn't a virgin . . ."

"It doesn't matter. The point is that wearing white implies that a woman who's a virgin is 'pure.' Therefore, a woman who has had sex is not pure. My mother's had seven children. I don't consider her impure."

"They are talking about having sex before marriage," said Sarah. "But it's only a symbol, tradition, that's all."

" 'They,' who's 'they?' The government, right? It's against the law to kill somebody, unless we do it in a war 'they' want to fight. It's illegal to make liquor unless 'they' tax it. You can't gamble either unless 'they' get their cut. And having sex with somebody is immoral unless 'they' give you a license to do it. That's what was wrong with the wedding, tonight. These two people were announcing to the world, and seeing that crowd, I think most of the world personally attended, that they were now going to be going to bed with each other on a regular basis. Making it official. Breaking the bottle across the bow. That's nobody's business. Marriage is making public what is basically private."

"What about children?" asked Sarah coldly. "Doesn't the government have the right to make sure that the children of these 'private affairs' are given some sort of stability in their lives?"

"If the government was so concerned with 'stability' in young children's lives," I said, "then one of the most fatal diseases among children wouldn't be something called 'parents.' The government has very little interest in improving our lives. They want to regulate them. In other words, keep our lives dull. What better way than marriage?"

I pulled the car up to the front of Sarah's house. "There's something very wrong with society."

"I don't know about society," said Sarah, as she shoved open the car door, "but there's certainly something very wrong with you."

I sat there for a moment, watching her walk hurriedly towards her front door, waiting to see if she'd look back. By the time I realized that she wasn't going to, she was already on the steps of her front porch. Quickly, I got out of the car and ran towards her house. But it was too late. Sarah had already gone in and closed the door. She didn't answer when I knocked.

THIRTY-SIX

Dear God:

Why were we put on this earth?

Signed: Conroy

Conroy:

Because I couldn't find any other place to put you.

Signed: God

THIRTY-SEVEN

Saturday night. Sarah was going out with someone else. There was no way I was going to stay home and mope around the house all night thinking about her. I had called up Leonard and we agreed we'd make it a night of mating at Mother's.

Driving up to the North Side of the city to meet Leonard. Thinking about her. The radio announced it was seven o'clock. I imagined her, giddy with anticipation, hurrying home from work so that she'd have more time to get ready for him. As she rushed around her bedroom, her mother would occasionally stick her head in and say, "It's about time you went out with someone else besides that boy, what's his name, Confloy?" Sarah would be so preoccupied about what dress to wear, what color lipstick and did she have too much makeup on or not enough, she wouldn't even hear the question.

Walking with Leonard down Rush Street, the main artery of Chicago's night life district. Although the temperature clung to the low fifties, a cold, stabbing wind refused to admit that April had indeed arrived in Chicago. The mating bars reveled in the springtime. They had no dancing girls or banjo music. But they had lots of young single people, most of whom were "trying to find themselves" but who were quite willing to forgo the probable disappointment in such an inquiry by finding someone else. Most who went felt vaguely uncomfortable but then no species has it easy. Salmon swim a thousand miles upstream for the same thing and then drop dead the moment they satisfy themselves. At the end of a night of swimming upstream through various Rush Street mating bars, you only felt like you had died.

"Why?" I asked Leonard, as I spread my arms out in front of me, "are we the lucky ones? Why, out of millions of people, are we walking down Rush Street loaded down with youth, good looks and class? Money in our pockets and plenty of time to look for gorgeous girls? Why are we the lucky ones who . . ."

"Because," said Leonard as he yanked the plug on my enthusiasm, "we haven't got anything better to do."

Shoving my hands into my pockets. "Precisely."

Spring had definitely arrived on Rush Street. The barkers weren't simply sticking their heads out from behind the doors anymore, shouting as you went by. They were back on the sidewalks again, making sure not to step on the cracks. "Hey, you guys," one of them said to Leonard and me, "Wanna see a great show? Right this way."

We stepped into the doorway of the Hi Belle, a joint that featured girls, dressed only in pasties and G strings, dancing on the bars. Engrim University was only two blocks away from the Rush Street area. A year before, after a late night class, I had taken a walk on Rush Street. And, like this night, I had stepped into the doorway of the Hi Belle. Nothing had changed. The grandmother wallpaper with the flower design still wrinkled along the wall. The place was still crawling with Medicare patients and office boys getting their giggles watching some young body with an aging face and a six-inch appendix gash under her right rib shuffle around the stage. Psychedelic lights gave her the appearance of a slow moving cartoon character.

Continuing down the street towards Mother's, we stopped in and sat down at the Red Garter to listen to the plectrum banjos maul some dogmatic melodies such as "Heart of My Heart" and "Bicycle Built for Two." The only concession the Red Garter had made to the arrival of spring was that it had added "In the Good Old Summertime" and "Take me Out to the Ball Game" to its repertoire. Big deal!

I was sitting there with my beer, singing "Let Me Call You Sweetheart" when Leonard nudged me. "Come on, let's get out of here."

"Let's just sing this one out," I said.

"I don't know the words."

"You don't know the words to 'Let Me Call You Sweetheart'? "

"No," replied Leonard.

"What do you Jews do at weddings?"

"We break glasses and eat Christian babies." Leonard started to get out of his chair.

"Hold it," I said. "I think that's the next number."

Waiting in line to get into Mother's. When one is too old for sock hops and fraternity parties and does not particularly care for computers and church dances, there is little territory left for hunting. Lunch room cafeterias and libraries aren't open that late and one inevitably sifts down to those dim arenas of the mating game, the mating bars of Rush Street. And on Rush Street, Mother's was the main arena. On the heavy wooden door was Mother's emblem, the exposed rear end of a fat woman.

Glancing at my watch. Eight o'clock. Imagining him walking up to Sarah's door. I didn't know his name or anything about him. But I was sure that he was the most handsome, charming, intelligent, and wealthiest man in the universe. In other words, Sarah was finally dating someone in her own league.

I could see her father vigorously shaking hands with him and thinking, "What an improvement!"

Sarah's younger brother listened mesmerized and she gazed up at him lovingly as he shyly admitted that, yes, the headline in the evening sports section of the newspaper was accurate. That very afternoon, in the closing seconds of the game, he had indeed scored the winning touchdown to clinch the Big Ten Title for his school. Gamely, he tried to hide his limp as he opened the door for Sarah and gently took her arm to escort her down the stairs. "Still seem to be a little stiff from the game," he smiled apologetically.

The instant the door closed, Sarah's mother ran to the phone, called at least a dozen banquet halls, and asked each one what they charged per plate for weddings.

It never occurred to me that very few colleges play football in the spring.

Leonard and I got past the two I.D. checkers at the door and headed down the long wooden flight of stairs that lead to Mother's. Almost every bar around Rush Street had two I.D. checkers to make sure you were of legal drinking age.

The guy who took your I.D.'s first was usually a congenial, smiling little fellow who had color in his cheeks and a crease in his slacks. Every fiber of his razor-cut hair was where it should have been and if he hadn't been totally convinced that he was making the world a better place to live by working as an I.D. checker at Mother's, he would have undoubtedly been a missionary helping the less fortunate build better bathrooms.

His partner usually wore a fourteen-by-fourteen-foot body dressed in grease-blotched skin, wrinkled teeth and body odor.

If the I.D.s looked legit to the friendly fellow, he would hand them right back with a smile. If he had any doubts, he would give them to his cohort, who would not be smiling.

"What's your mother's middle name?"

"My mother's middle name? Let's see, I think it's uh . . ."

"What year was your father born in?"

"What year was my father born in. Well, if he's forty-six now . . ."

"Here." That's all he would say as he shoved the I.D.s back at you.

You could have gotten smart with him. "Oh, please, sir. Please let me in so I can give all my money to Mother. How about if I just give you my money. Do I have to be of legal age to do that, huh? Oh, please take my money. Ooooh, pleeeeeze." You could have done something like that. But you would have never done it again. Or anything else.

Behind us, a thin girl in gold slacks didn't make it with her I.D.s. She "forgot" her middle name.

"Can't let you in if you don't know who you are," quipped the little friendly I.D. checker. If she had known who she was, would she have been coming to Mother's?

In decor, Mother's was a typical Rush Street mating bar. Not including the dance room in back, it was about twice the size of a bungalow living room, and was covered by a plaster ceiling that was a mess of chips and points. The wooden floor was seasoned with sawdust and there was a shoulder-high ledge running across the wood-paneled walls on which the patrons could rest their drinks or themselves.

While Leonard went searching for the bathroom, I looked at Mother's Polaroid Poster. A lot of the mating bars had "fun clubs" that anyone could join. The clubs would go on periodic journeys of joy and would then slap up a Polaroid Poster to let all the dull slobs who didn't pay their money know just what a really great time they had missed.

Each of Mother's snapshots had a Magic Marker caption scribbled in under it. "Here are Bob and Dolores riding up on the ski lift. Hope you two don't come down too fast. HA! HA! HA!" "Here's Big Ned with his best friend. Is that a Schlitz or a Budweiser, Ned? HA! HA! HA!" "Here are all the girls feeling sorry for poor Bill who broke his ankle on the slopes. We think Bill did that deliberately just to get a little attention. HA! HA! HA!"

Leonard came up behind me. "I went on one of those last winter."

"Really, I didn't know you skied."

"I don't."

"How was it?" I asked.

Leonard put his finger on a snapshot. "Here are Bob and Dolores coming out of the motel room. Bob is smiling. So is Dolores. She gave him a gift. But it's a surprise. He doesn't know it yet. Hope your Clap is the right size, Bob. HA! HA! HA!" Leonard pointed to another picture. "Here's Big Ned on the ride home, barfing all over the bus. Say, Ned, is that Budweiser or Schlitz? HA! HA! HA!" Jamming his finger against another Polaroid, Leonard commented, "Here's poor Bill after his accident on the slopes. Notice how the entire left side of the brain is exposed and how Bill's eye, which was somewhat loosened by the fall, is hovering over his navel. We think Bill did that deliberately just to get a little attention. HA! HA! HA!"

The dust-orange lighting drifted down from the sixty-watt bulbs and was trapped against Mother's ceiling by a rising carpet of cigarette smoke, causing the dust-orange lighting to spill down into the corners, giving the entire room a hellish lustful hue.

In the center of Mother's was a large triangle-shaped bar. The true heart of Mother. Even though it was only nine o'clock, all but two of the stools around the bar were already occupied.

Leonard and I sat down and tried to get the bartender's attention. A few seconds later, one of Mother's goons tapped us both on the shoulder. "Would you two gentlemen mind giving up your seats to these ladies?" Behind him were two girls who appeared to be in their mid-twenties. They looked down self-consciously at the floor.

"Sure," I said as I slid off the stool and tossed a smile in the girls' direction. Leonard didn't bother smiling. The girls sat down on the stools and mumbled "Thank you" to both of us as we stepped back a few feet behind them into the crowd. One of the girls called the other one Sarah. I wondered if she was related to my Sarah and if she was, would she tell Sarah what an exciting night I had. Then I realized it was going to be a long night. "It's the last name," I said to myself, "that makes people related, not the first one, Wizard."

Mother's, like all Rush Street mating bars, had a Victorian rule, which stated that a woman who was standing could take a bar stool from a man who was sitting if all the other stools were taken.

"Such an undemocratic practice," said Leonard, disgusted.

"Maybe," I said, "someday, a bastard child of Mother's will take his case to the Supreme Court."

"I can just hear the court handing down the decision," said Leonard. " 'It is unconstitutional for Mother's Bar to compel a patron to surrender his stool to some lousy broad simply because she has no other place to park it. This practice constitutes discrimination on the basis of sex. And Mother, most of all, should know better than that.' "

Ten-thirty, entering prime time at Mother's. Not a male posterior was at rest. Tears leaked through half-clenched eyes and ran down cheeks as cloud formations of solid nicotine bumped into everyone's eyeballs.

"Do you really think somebody could meet a girl in a place like this and end up marrying her?" asked Leonard.

"A couple of years ago, a friend of mine from Engrim did."

"I wouldn't buy a tie under these lighting conditions," said Leonard.

"Neither would my friend."

A few minutes later, Mother's opened her back room. Leonard and I drifted in to see what was going on. A "Live Music Every Night" sign hung from the ceiling. On stage, an electronic web of musical instruments and flesh was lashing out and lopping off earlobes. In front of them, a mob of amoebas moved, each in its own constricted pattern. Shoulders bumping, eyes staring, hands pushing. All of it sliced by an occasional "Excuse me, excuse me, could I get through here?"

Standing by the far wall was a bald-headed man who had probably been coming to Rush Street for the last twelve years trying to get something to click. He seemed to be waiting for a slow dance and wondering why he didn't see anyone around any more that he knew.

Through the haze of heads, I saw what faintly looked like an attractive girl. She was standing with a few of her girl friends, watching the crowd. Like the bald-headed guy, like almost all guys, I suppose, I prefer slow dancing. I waited for a few minutes but the band kept bashing out fast songs. Finally, I figured the hell with it and I walked over and asked her. Probably, she didn't actually hear me but presumed what I had said. She didn't say anything, but just nodded and moved out into the crowd.

One reason I hate fast dancing so much is because I'm so lousy at it. All I do is move my shoulders up and down, bounce a little and turn around every now and then. I can't think of anything that makes me feel dumber than fast dancing. She was a good dancer, though. She could really move it.

Seeing Sarah move. Gracious yet bold strides that set into motion ripples of sensuality.

The music was so loud I didn't even bother trying to talk to her. I wanted to, though. That's the way you really get to know someone.

But this girl wasn't looking for a great conversationalist or Fred Astaire. Whatever she was looking for was either very high or very low. As she danced, she stared either straight up at the ceiling or straight down at her feet. On one of my turn-arounds, I turned around and she wasn't there. I could see her eight or nine people away, staring down at her feet, still dancing.

Discovering the only thing that could make me feel dumber than dancing fast: dancing fast alone.

I walked back to Leonard who had watched the whole thing. "Isn't there a song," he asked, "that says, 'Breaking up is oh so hard to do?' You make it look rather easy."

"Too crowded," I said as Leonard and I, in single file, weaved around people as we walked back to Mother's front room. I waited a few moments while Leonard's chuckles wore away the humor of my dance floor desertion. Then, in a professional tone of voice, I asked him over my shoulder, "Did you get a good look at her, Leonard? She looked a little heavy to me."

Leonard moved close behind me to make sure I couldn't miss his evaluation. He delivered the words casually, "Twenty pounds away from greatness."

A beerman was quickly approaching us. He was wearing a pocket apron and he was smiling, naturally. He was so goshdarn happy to be a member of Mother's happy family that he could hardly stand it. Naturally.

Jingle . . . jingle . . . jingle. With every step he took, the change in his pocket apron beckoned all to come to him. He was the Good Humor Man of Mother's.

To me, pocket aprons always mean "Gyp." From the church bingo game, to that thief at the hardware store and the floating summer carnival that sets up in that prairie down the street. Pocket aprons are a good thing to stay away from.

"Can I help you, sir?" the beerman asked Leonard who looked over to me. I shook my head. "Yeah, one beer," said Leonard.

The beerman turned towards the bar in the center of Mother's, raised his arm and held up his index finger. "Draw one," he yelled and began twisting in and out of the now massive crowd to pick up his beer. He came back through that sweltering, jarring, elbow-in-the-face mob with the beer raised high in his hand, smiling all the way. Naturally.

By a little after eleven o'clock, human flesh was packed into almost every inch of Mother's. "Let's head over to Rush Up," I said, "the girls have got to be better than this."

Leonard and I started squeezing past shoulders toward the

four-letter word flickering through the lung-strained mist. EXIT EXIT EXIT.

I could see Sarah and him dining and dancing in a ballroom high above the city. I didn't know if there was a place like that anywhere in Chicago. But I was convinced that, even if there hadn't been one before tonight, there was one now. They were dancing, full body press, and when the music stopped, she whispered to him that she hated to go back to the table because she'd have to leave his arms. He pulled her even tighter, rested his chin on her head, and told her that she'd never leave his arms again. Arms clasped behind each other's backs, they strolled out onto the balcony. Below them were the lights of the city. They looked into each other's eyes and . . .

"Make way!" One of Mother's boys shrieked as Leonard and I tried to shuffle through the crowd toward the staircase that led up to the street. He was rolling in another barrel of beer for the bar. Raucous roars of cheer went up, not unlike those accompanying dropped trays in high school lunch rooms. Saliva drippings could be heard everywhere. "The serum has arrived," said Leonard, "you can always depend on Mother."

A guy in front of us began doing a soft shoe to some tune his friend was tapping out on his beer glass to celebrate the new arrival. Sawdust brings out the soft shoe in people.

Up those long wooden stairs, past the two I.D. checkers. Walking down the street, past Butch McGuire's, another popular mating bar. One of Butch's hired help was warning a would-be customer, "Only girls and guys with dates are allowed in. We already got too many guys. We gotta keep a balance in there."

"What's Butch running," yelled the would-be customer, "a bar or an ark?" His witticism was met by silence and he moved on.

Leonard and I continued walking past The Depot, Pat Haran's, and Bourbon Street. Everything in sight was moving. Even neon signs seemed to be swaying to the people prancing beat of Rush Street.

Another block of barkers, prostitutes, school teachers, secretaries, leering conventioneers, bored college students, cursing cab-drivers and whorey-eyed teen-agers and we were at Rush Up. But the girls weren't any better and the search went on.

"We haven't seen an attractive girl all night," I said as we came down the stairs of the sixth or seventh mating bar that we had visited that night.

"You're right," said Leonard. "Not one of them's been Sarah."

Leonard was staying for the weekend with a fraternity brother who lived on the North Side, so he didn't drive home with me. Noticing the time on a clock that stuck out from the corner of a bank. Nearly two o'clock. Making a left when I should have gone straight and driving a few miles out of the way. I eased the car around a corner and then slowly drove past Betterman's Bakery, reliving the moment we met. What were they doing now? Parked in a lovers lane? Our lovers lane? No, he had too much class for that. A motel room? No, she had too much class for that. I saw them lounging in a lavishly furnished room before a roaring fireplace, sipping wine and nibbling on one another's ears. His place! With his dough, he probably had so many "his places" that his biggest problem was deciding which one to take her to. The luxury apartment on the Lake Shore? The mansion tucked away among the rolling hills and forests? The lovers' loft high atop one of his skyscrapers? She had already called her mother to tell her she'd be a little late. Somewhere around Tuesday. Her mother understood. There was no hurry. Any time within the next three months would be fine.

Pushing open the door of my house, I stopped and listened a moment. Everyone was asleep. I gave it no thought whatsoever as I walked through the darkness, picked up the phone and dialed Sarah's number. The phone was picked up within half a ring. It was Sarah who asked hello. Her voice was very awake. I had not even considered the possibility of someone else answering.

"It's me, Tim. So how are you doing?"

There was a long, steaming pause. "What do you want?"

"My evening was very nice, thank you," I said, "and yours?"

I suddenly realized the insanity of what I was doing. "Hey, I'd love to chat with you a while but it is late. I'll be talking to you," and hung up.

What a dumb thing to do. I didn't want to think about it. Turning on the television set but there weren't any programs. I left it on anyway. I liked the way it looked. A splice of snowstorm in a darkened room. I looked for a book and found one on a lamp table but I didn't bother to turn on a light. Pacing back and forth across the living room with the book gripped in both hands. I debated about going into the kitchen and checking out the refrigerator. I wasn't hungry, but I thought it might be interesting to just take a look around.

The phone rang. I almost literally dove for it. There was an extension phone in my parents' room. My mother and father had totally opposite reactions to a phone ringing in the middle of the night. My mother would think someone had died and my father would want to make sure someone did.

It was Sarah. "Tim, I don't know if things are going to work out between us. Perhaps, it would be best for us if they did not. But I do want you to know that I love you, too."

THIRTY-EIGHT

The last day of college: Two final examinations, one in the afternoon in psychology and the other in the evening in a research course that all graduating seniors were required to take. That morning, before I left the house, I checked the want ads. There were no jobs for outfielders.

Sitting in my last college class, looking out at the glittering lights of Rush Street. The sassy yellow light of the classroom banged against my eyes. Driven by a shortage of patience rather than of time, my hand wrote furiously through the pages of the bluebook.

I finished the answer to the last question and checked over the examination and the bluebook again to make sure I had answered everything. Then I latched my hands onto the side of the desk and dragged myself out of my seat.

Jack Avers, from a seat behind me, whispered, "Don't forget, we're meeting in the cafeteria."

"That's where I'm headed," I replied wearily. A few sluggish steps later, I handed the examination to the professor and stepped into the darkened hallway.

Engrim University closed early on Friday nights. All the evening classes were scheduled to end at nine-thirty P.M. but, because of the final examination, our teacher had given us extra time.

Pushing the button and listening to the elevator rumble up through eighteen floors to get me. As I rode down, I tried to savor the feeling of the ride. This would not be the last time, I knew that. After graduation, I'd come back to the school, not so much to see how it had changed, but to see how I had. But there would never be a ride through this limbo again.

Already, that night, the old skin of my college years was beginning to peel away from me. Like one's dying, I suppose. While still breathing, you develop an objective point of view of your own demise; as if, by becoming a bystander, you can remove yourself from the actual proceedings.

In the cafeteria, only a few lights continued to ream through the high tide of the night's shadows, which had already submerged most of the room. I got a cup of hot chocolate from the vending machine and sat down at a table that was beneath one of the streams of light. Watching Weatherly move towards me through the mire of confused tables and displaced chairs.

"How did you do on the exam?" I asked.

"Who cares? That's it. Finished. I passed and that's all I care about."

Although he had done everything possible to avoid it, Weatherly was finally graduating. He didn't panic when he received the news. He simply enrolled in graduate school. His draft board, unlike mine, would extend student deferments to include graduate school. Weatherly was going to have to get a job, though. He was running out of money.

My draft board was composed entirely of retired members of the V.F.W. Only one of them had ever gone to college and he was quoted in a neighborhood newspaper as saying, "College students don't deserve deferments. I went to college and I know it's a total waste of time. During those three weeks, I didn't learn a thing."

Weatherly went and got a cup of coffee and then sat down across from me.

"You going to the graduation?" I asked him.

"I have to. My parents would kill me if I didn't go. They want to make damn sure I get out of this place. How about you?"

"Yeah, it's a big deal for my parents, too. I don't mind going. How many times do you graduate from college? It's just that graduation ceremonies are so impersonal. They don't seem to have anything to do with the four years it took you to get the degree."

"What do you want them to do?" asked Weatherly, "hold the ceremonies on an el platform?"

"Not a bad idea. I remember my first day here at Engrim. That first day of orientation week when we were all sitting in the auditorium. They told us we were 'The leaders of tomorrow.' "

Weatherly stared into his coffee. "Tomorrow's in trouble."

"Right after graduation, I've got to start looking for a job," I said.

"Me, too. Our degrees, especially with our majors in history, are certainly going to be a big help," said Weatherly sarcastically.

"A college graduate has the inside track on a lot of jobs," I replied.

"Yeah, but our degrees haven't trained us to do a damn thing."

"A college degree isn't designed to 'train' you, it's meant to educate you," I preached. A few months earlier, the same topic had been discussed in one of my classes. I proceeded to parrot my professor's opinion.

"A university isn't supposed to be a training camp for big business. We came here, not to be 'trained,' but to be educated, to think. We've had to memorize some facts but, more importantly than the 'how,' we were supposed to learn the 'why' of things. A proper college education teaches us to challenge life, to ask questions . . ."

"I see," interrupted Weatherly, "like, 'Why can't I get a job?' "

"If you think education's such a waste of time, why are you bothering to go on to graduate school?"

"You know why, the draft. But I'm going to get my master's degree in business. I'm tired of my life not showing a profit."

Weatherly took out a cigarette from the pack in his shirt pocket, lit it, and flicked the match onto the floor. "Hey, do you remember Betty with the big ones?"

"Yeah," I laughed, "that's some nickname to get stuck with. I haven't seen her around in quite a while."

"She quit school."

Every September, there were fewer faces to remember. Unless it was a close friend, you didn't even realize that person was no longer around.

"When did she drop out?" I asked.

Weatherly reworded my question. "When did 'they' drop out? I think it was during sophomore year. I'm surprised the school didn't charge her double tuition."

"Remember Servallion?"

Weatherly didn't answer me for a moment. Then he took a quick sip of his coffee. "Yeah. God, this coffee's terrible."

Six months after meeting her through a forgotten anthropology book, Bernie Servallion dropped out of school and married Brenda Sandling. A few months later, she was pregnant.

By being an expectant father, Bernie hoped to avoid the draft. It didn't work. He was sent over to Vietnam. He learned to enjoy being in the army and, while in Vietnam, decided to make the service his career.

He wrote a letter home to Brenda telling her of his decision. She threatened divorce. He wrote back saying that the army offered him a good career and an early retirement.

The argument was settled by a land mine.

Weatherly took another sip of his coffee and then gently bit his tongue between his teeth. "Why do I always burn my tongue on hot coffee?"

"Because it's very difficult to burn it on cold coffee?"

"Witty," said Weatherly, "Jesus Christ, are you . . . Hey, do you remember Mike Provost?"

"No, I don't think so."

"Sure you do. A short, blond-haired guy. Real muscular."

"Oh, yeah. He dropped out?"

"Yep, two summers ago," said Weatherly. "We were both working at Kale Book Store on Lake Street. We spent most of our time doing paper work or moving books from one shelf to the other. Real excitement.

"On our last day, Provost told me at lunch that he had decided he was going to stay on full-time for a year and then go back to school. He wanted to earn money for a car. He said he was going to continue taking classes at night. For a while, he did, too. But then he quit completely.

"I was in Kale Book Store a few weeks ago. Provost's assistant manager now. He thinks it's the end of the goddamn world."

"Do you know whatever happened to Carol Foltz?" I asked.

"You mean Carol 'Why buy the cow when the milk's free?' Foltz?"

"That's the one."

"She's working full-time during the day and going to school at night since she got engaged to Mark Gicepi. He's a graduate student now. He discovered that old Carol could type. With all those term papers to do, he fell in love with her seventy words per minute."

"That's very fast typing for a cow," I said.

"When they got engaged, she asked Gicepi not to buy her an engagement ring so that when they got a house, he could use the money to buy her a washing machine instead."

Weatherly put his left hand down on the table, spread his fingers, stared at them and said, "My what a gorgeous washing machine. Just look how it sparkles and catches the light."

In a rattling voice, the landing elevator announced the new arrivals: Jack Avers, Donna Condon and a couple of other seniors. Avers had a dental floss personality. He was the same guy who had stood in the reception line at the President's Ball and had humiliated me in front of Sarah.

Avers was a philosophy major. He had once told me that he had written a 348-page philosophy by which he planned to live his life. Later that same day, I told Weatherly about it. "Three hundred and forty-eight pages!" said Weatherly. "He could have done it in three words: 'Be a shithead.' "

"How about a round of coffee for everyone? I'm buying," beamed Avers.

"As you can plainly see," said Weatherly, "Conroy and I already have coffee."

"Then how about seconds?"

"Fine," said Weatherly resignedly. I nodded my agreement. I

just didn't have the energy to say no. Within seconds, Avers skipped back with his first delivery. After depositing the filled coffee cups on the table, he turned and headed back towards the coffee machine.

Weatherly picked up his notebook from the table and said, "You know what's going to happen to these notes that we've been taking for the past few years? They're going to follow us around in cardboard boxes until we die."

"Would you mind explaining that?" demanded Donna Condon as she picked up the coffee cup that Avers had placed in front of her.

"I have a cousin who graduated from college years ago," said Weatherly. "A few weeks back, I helped him move and I asked him what was in these two big cardboard boxes that we had just dragged out of his basement. He told me they contained his college notes and some of his college books. I asked him why he didn't throw them out and he said that he didn't know why, but that he'd probably never throw them out."

As Weatherly finished talking, Jack Avers arrived back at the table with his second load of coffee cups propped gently between the fingers of his hand.

"What are you going to do with your notes?" Weatherly asked Avers.

"The notes from tonight's class?"

"No," said Weatherly, "I mean the notes you've taken for the past four years. Have you still got them?"

"Sure," replied Avers. "I store them in a cardboard box in my room at home."

His words sparked a round of knowing nods and chuckles from everyone except Weatherly who hesitated only momentarily before asking Avers another question. "Why are you going to keep them?"

"For reference," said Avers. "No, that's not true. I put a lot of work into them. I don't know. I'm just going to keep them, that's all."

Avers sat down and as he continued to talk, the brightness of his voice, which had been temporarily overcome by Weatherly's questioning, returned to his words.

"Wouldn't it be nice if everything could stay exactly the same as it is tonight?" Avers immediately realized the lunacy of what he had just said and quickly added, "At least for a while?"

"What do you mean?" asked Donna Condon.

Avers stumbled for an answer, but I knew what he meant. Avers was basking in the warmth of the moment. A warmth that had taken four years of friction to produce. But now it was over, more so for Avers than the rest of us.

Avers had relished his college years. They had created a routine that he thoroughly enjoyed. When he was an old man, he would still be reheating anecdotes that had been spawned in his college years. He didn't want to think about it but he realized it was true. The others had accepted college as a temporary stage, not a way of life.

Avers knew that his college world would end on such a night as this. Like stepping off a cliff. One day, it would exist and the next day, it would not. I felt sorry for Avers. Engrim University was his outfield.

But in a way, except for Weatherly and Donna Condon, we were all in sort of a lousy mood as we felt the first pains of post-college withdrawal symptoms. For sixteen years, we had trod through the tunnel of formal education. But as time shoved us around the last curve, that strain of cockiness that thrives in the darkness of security was beginning to wilt. That night, already, we were squinting and flinching with self-doubt as we stared at the oncoming glare of reality.

College was the ideal place to talk about how you were going to conquer the world, and how you couldn't wait to marry the one you loved, because you still had a good excuse as to why you hadn't yet. After all, you were still only a student.

Donna Condon was one of the few that truly delighted in seeing the end. Hers was a black and white world that allowed for no shades of gray where spores of indecision could breed. Two weeks after she graduated from Engrim, she was getting married to her high school sweetheart. They were then moving to Washington, D.C., where they both had jobs waiting for them at the State Department.

Weatherly, too, seemed to have no fear of graduating. But I had always known he was a zebra.

I thought about the incoming freshman class that was still three months away from Engrim: people starting college with lifelong friends they had yet to meet, wives and husbands they had yet to marry. New generations would hinge on forgotten books, typing skills and bakery lines.

Donna Condon, becoming impatient with Avers' mutterings, looked up at the clock and announced, "I've got to get going. I have a lot to do tomorrow." She got up out of her chair and began picking up her books from the table.

"Wait a minute," said Avers. "I've got an idea. Why don't we all go down to the Pizza Pot on Rush Street and celebrate?"

"I'd love to," said Donna Condon as she continued to pick up her books, "but I have a very busy day ahead of me."

"How about the rest of you?" asked Avers.

"Not me," replied Don Lipkowski. "I have to get up early for work."

"Me, too," said some other guy whose name I didn't know.

That left only Weatherly and me. I wouldn't have minded going if there had been a group. But I had no desire to have my feelings minced between Avers' glibness and Weatherly's cynicism.

"I don't think I can make it, either," I said. "I'm tired. I'd like to get to bed early tonight."

Weatherly said nothing.

"Oh, that's okay." Avers spoke the words as if it didn't matter. "Maybe, we can all go some other time." He knew there'd be no other time.

A few sips of coffee later, we were all moving through the cafeteria, pushing chairs out of our way and tossing good-byes to one another. Weatherly and I were the last ones to reach the doors. I stopped and looked back at the table, dotted with coffee cups, that we had just deserted. The fat spike of light above the table, now polluted with cigarette smoke, continued to whirl in the darkness.

"I wonder who turns out the lights?" I asked.

"Conroy," said Weatherly emphatically, "you're out of college now. Quit asking stupid questions."

Weatherly and I didn't go straight home. He had taken his father's car to school that night. We spent a few hours driving around the city, occasionally stopping at a neighborhood tavern or a singles bar.

As we drove towards the Far South Side on the Dan Ryan Expressway, Weatherly said to me, "Is there a blue spiral notebook on the back seat?"

I looked back. "Yeah."

"Will you get it for me?"

"Yeah, sure." I went to reach for it.

"Don't bother, " said Weatherly. "I can do it." He reached behind the seat and, as he occasionally glanced at the road, flipped through the pages until he found a small piece of paper that he retrieved and stuck into his shirt pocket. "Some broad's phone number," explained Weatherly, "I didn't want to lose it."

Such casual driving on the Dan Ryan Expressway would have terrified me a few years earlier. But not any more. In the past four years, having spent hundreds of hours driving the Dan Ryan, I knew another pro when I saw one.

An experienced Dan Ryan driver, such as Weatherly, could easily simultaneously tune his radio, adjust the heater, eat pretzels out of the glove compartment, check the rear view mirror, jump lanes, blow his horn, hit his brakes, and still find the time to look through a spiral notebook in the back seat.

We ended up in an all night restaurant at about three in the morning. It was the only place we could find that was open but it was a real dump; an upset stomach with a door on it.

While Weatherly and I waited for our orders to be served, we amused ourselves by watching a drunk at the counter. There was a plate of scrambled eggs and a cup of coffee in front of him. The drunk's head would wobble around a few times and would then dive-bomb towards the plate of scrambled eggs. Each dive, however, was abruptly aborted as, just before contact, the drunk was able to stop his head from falling.

Finally, he lost all control and his head plopped into the plate of scrambled eggs. A waitress ran over to him and yanked his head up. The drunk spoke very deliberately, hoping that he'd sound more sober. "I wanted to see if these eggs had enough salt on them."

A cop, who was sitting at the other end of the counter, got up and escorted the drunk out. As the cop pushed him through the door, the drunk looked back at him and said, "You know, I'm thinking of taking the policeman's exam."

When our sandwiches were placed in front of us, Weatherly took off the top piece of bread and began eating it. He always ate a sandwich from the top down as if he had to make sure, for himself, what was in it.

"So what are you going to be doing in the fall?" asked Weatherly.

"I don't know yet."

"You told me you were thinking of going to graduate school."

"Yeah, I did. I applied to three different ones, too. I was accepted by all of them. No scholarships, though, and I don't feel like borrowing the money. Besides, I really don't know what I want to do with my life."

"How about living it?" offered Weatherly.

"You know what I mean, Weatherly. How old are you, now, anyway?"

"Twenty-five."

"And you're still in school, riding the bus for student fare."

"So what?"

"When my father was twenty-five, he had already spent three years as a combat soldier in Africa and Europe, was married and had two kids, owned an apartment building and worked two jobs. He was, you might say, an adult."

"He was, you might say, a nut," said Weatherly. "No offense intended."

"But that's the way it was for everyone, then," I said. "People had things to do and they did them."

"So who's stopping you?" asked Weatherly. "Go over to Africa and Europe and fight for a few years. Come back, get yourself a wife and two kids, make sure one of them's not too bright, like yourself, buy an apartment building and get two jobs."

"You can't fake it. Besides, I'm not saying that's what I want. I'd find all of that boring. But the point is that, even if my father's generation didn't have a voice in deciding what had to be done, at least they had things that had to be done.

"I was talking to a graduate student last week who's thirty years old," I said. He still doesn't know what he's going to do with his life and it's almost half over. You know what he told me? 'Life's a game and you've got to prepare yourself for it.' When you're thirty years old, you're in the game, like it or not. By the time he's ready, the goddamn game's going to be over."

"Don't worry about it," said Weatherly calmly.

"I feel this tremendous compulsion to get somewhere," I said, "and I don't even know where I'm going. Some day, I'm afraid I'm going to be fifty-five years old, sitting on a curb and saying to myself, 'I wonder what I'm going to be when I grow up.' "

Weatherly popped the last piece of crust into his mouth. "Sounds okay to me."

THIRTY-NINE

The day after graduation. Going downtown. Getting a job. Giving them the business. I had worked numerous part-time jobs downtown during my college years, of course. But this was my first attempt at getting a full-time job down there.

During one school year, I worked in a small advertising agency. Their major client was Filler Up, a tar-like liquid that was "guaranteed to have you gain as much weight as you want, where you want." The only way Filler Up worked was if you ate the bottle and then you only gained eight fluid ounces.

Originally, it came in two different flavors, chocolate and vanilla. Having been put in charge of testing the new banana-flavored Filler Up for taste quality, I gave a sample to all the secretaries. For the next three days, not a typewriter key clicked in that advertising agency. Every one of the secretaries was home sick. In explaining her illness to her boss, one of the secretaries told him that boats in Honduras weren't the only ones who made banana runs. I was fired. Good-bye fat paycheck.

I had also worked part-time for the post office, which presumed nothing when it came to the intelligence of its employees. The hallways of the building were divided by a fat yellow line. On the right side of the line was a long arrow pointing down to the words "Walk Slowly This Side."

My first interview that morning after graduation was with Kabby's International Food Company. I was interviewed by the personnel man, Arthur Turner III, whose parents were obviously doilies.

"You know," he squeaked primly, "Kabby's is the world's largest producer of food."

I imagined people walking through Kabby's offices waving their fingers yelling, "We're Number One." I was going to ask him who was Number Two, God? But I didn't.

"I know that, sir," I answered. "I see your advertising all the time."

Doily Junior was delighted with my reply. I obviously had spent plenty of time hanging around food shelves, preparing myself for my life's career.

"We're looking for young men with a lot of experience," said Doily.

Naturally, I thought to myself. "Wanted, recent college graduate with ten years of experience."

"Yes, sir," I replied.

"Now," he said smiling, "just what do you know about food?"

"Well, I've been eating it all of my life."

Going to Akex Steel Corporation for an interview. Not only was the personnel manager willing to hire me, he even had the first eight years of my life planned out. "We'll start you out in Pittsburgh as a foreman on the night shift. In three years, if things continue to work out, we'll switch you to Newark, put you in the office. Then, if you continue to be happy with us and we continue to be happy with you . . ."

He smiled knowingly as a light chuckle rippled through his words. The message was clear. He just wanted to let me know that he obviously realized it was absurd that a great guy like me might not "work out" but that he was obligated by company policy to state the possibility.

" . . . we"ll put you into the sales division of the company. After that," he leaned on the desk and said solemnly, "it's up to you."

I had a suspicion that he expected me to jump up, salute him, put on my hard hat, run out the door to my phantom jet somewhere on the runway, and fly to Pittsburgh just in time for the night shift.

"By the way," he said, "you're not at least six feet, one inch tall, are you?"

"No, I'm not."

"That's what I thought. We'll have to put you in our retail sales then rather than our wholesale division."

"Why is that, sir?" I didn't care, but I could tell that he expected me to ask the question.

"All our wholesale representatives have to be at least six feet, one inch tall. These men deal with our distributors and Akex Steel feels that big men will give the company an image of strength."

"I see." I didn't. Having been beaten up regularly throughout my life, I considered myself somewhat of an expert on strength. I had never noticed a correlation between power and size. Shorter people had often pulverized me. My mother for one.

He was such a fast talker that I couldn't interrupt him. Eventually, he paused to reload his lungs and I told him that I had to get going because I had an appointment for another job interview later that morning. He was miffed but I didn't care. Working the night shift in a steel mill. That's what I had gone to college to avoid.

Finally, I got a job at the Thomas Patterson Public Relations Company. I was hired because someone else had quit their job twenty minutes before I had walked through the door. Later, I discovered that Mr. Trenkel, the man in charge of hiring, got very nervous whenever there was an unfilled position, no matter how unimportant it was. Therefore, Mr. Trenkel tended to hire the first warm body that came through the door. His job interview could have consisted of taking your temperature.

No one, least of all me, knew exactly what my job was. My title was assistant executive production manager. Long title. Short paycheck. Caepan had warned me about such things. "Remember," Caepan had said, "you can't eat a title." I never did meet the executive production manager I was supposed to be assisting. Mr. Trenkel had told me that the job description stated that I would be writing articles, press releases and other copy for various clients. That sounded reasonably interesting to me. I've never minded writing. Actually, I spent most of my time doing research for various pamphlets that were being created, proofreading, and putting together audio-visual materials such as tapes, graphics, and films for presentations to clients. Not exactly the outfield.

During my first week on the job, Mr. George Rebe, Junior, the head of Thomas Patterson Public Relations Company, invited me out to lunch. He extended this courtesy to every new employee. On the anointed day, his secretary escorted me into his office, informed me that Mr. Rebe was at a meeting that was scheduled to end shortly, and that I was to make myself at home. I looked around his office. It was done in the usual blanket of brown decor. As I attempted to "make myself at home," I tried to remember what room in my house had a desk the size of a tennis court.

A few family photographs, an intercom, a desk set, a telephone, and a glass paperweight all sat unperturbed on their regal bed of walnut. I thought of my own small desk whose surface was already scaled with "in" and "out" papers. At a very early age, George Rebe, Junior, had demonstrated his ability to make sharp business decisions. He had chosen George Rebe, Senior, as his father.

On the front of his desk was a black sign with gold lettering: "George Rebe, Junior, President." A lie. That sign might have said a lot of other things and still have been true: "Owner," "Boss," "King," "Everything you see is mine," but not "President." "President" certainly sounded better, though. As if George Rebe, Junior, was such a great guy that everyone in the company had elected him to tell them what to do. It's always a good idea to give the illusion that you're the people's choice.

George Rebe, Junior, wasn't a bad guy. I had only met him briefly a couple of times before the day I was supposed to go out to lunch with him, but he seemed like a pleasant enough fellow. Besides, how many heads of companies have a policy of taking every new employee out to lunch? I was impressed.

About a half hour later, Mr. George Rebe, Junior, came into the office. He was a man in his early sixties whose well developed chest was sinking into his stomach. He had been married and divorced two or three times but had never had any children. Supposedly his alimony payments equaled his payroll. He usually tried to avoid playing around with the secretaries in the office. He usually failed. When I stood up to meet him, he grabbed my hand tightly and pumped it so vigorously that I thought he was going to shake my shoulder right out of the socket. Mr. Rebe was one of those who used handshakes to prove his hormone count.

"How about Berghoff's Restaurant?" he suggested.

"Fine, sir." What did he expect me to say? No, even though you're the boss and you're paying for it, I want to go to the Walgreens down the street. I've already reserved the two end stools at the counter. Formalities like that kill me.

Mr. Rebe patted me on the back as he ushered me through the door but quickly stepped around me so that he could lead us through the maze of office aisles to the hallway and the elevators. I couldn't figure out why he was taking such a round-about route until he stopped at Nancy Kimberly's desk. She was one of the secretaries in Accounts Receivable.

Nancy Kimberly was the kind of girl you'd move over for on your deathbed, even if you were dead. If Nancy Kimberly couldn't bring you back, then Heaven had to be two of her.

"How are you today, Miss Kimberly?" Mr. Rebe asked cheerfully.

"I'm fine, sir," she gushed. "And you?"

"Good, good. Now you have a nice afternoon."

"I will, sir. And you, too."

"Thank you, Miss Kimberly, thank you. I'm sure I will now."

Mr. Rebe just stood there for a moment and smiled at her. Self-consciously, she returned his grin. He patted the top of her desk a few times before continuing our walk. Did he know something I didn't? A secretary's desk is a highly erogenous zone? Pat her drawers and she'll follow you anywhere?

I felt like a jerk standing there. A few days earlier, at the water cooler, I had tried to start a conversation with Nancy Kimberly. It was like trying to set fire to a rock. Now, I had to watch while this sixty-year-old, pot-bellied man waltzed her around with his words. The flow of his voice was just a little too smooth to be fatherly. The difference between sounding as if you'd like to sign adoption papers or a hotel register.

Standing with a group of people waiting for the elevator. Two massive girls stood directly in front of the elevator doors. They must have thought there was food coming up. One of them was eating potato chips and talking so loudly that she was forcing everyone around her to listen. She was going on about how her mother-in-law was going to have to learn to get along without her and her husband over there every night.

"On Monday nights," she said, "Bill and I do the shopping. Tuesdays, there are certain television shows that I absolutely refuse to miss. Wednesday nights, I go out with the girls and Bill visits his aunt . . . " Her friend simply nodded, chewed her gum, and said, "Uh-huh."

My ears were getting out of breath. I didn't want to listen but her words were slamming so loudly through the crunches of potato chips that I didn't have any choice. She was getting me very depressed. She continued to talk as everyone shuffled onto the elevator and rode down nineteen floors.

" . . . How can that woman expect me to be over there every week?" the fat girl exclaimed between potato chips as she lumbered off the elevator with her "Uh-huh" friend. "My time is valuable. I have a million things to do."

A pathetic voice behind me said it. "And every one of them involves eating."

During the meal, Mr. Rebe talked mostly about the business. I was very uncomfortable. I don't like eating around people I can't relax with. When I eat, I get very involved with my food. In other words, I'm a slob. When I was a kid, my mother always told me to put twice as much on my plate as I planned on eating. She figured that half of it would never get to my mouth. Of course, I've improved since then, but not a lot. When it comes to eating, I'm just not very coordinated. It's not a case of my left hand not knowing what my right hand is doing. I don't think my left hand even knows there is a right hand.

When dessert arrived, Mr. Rebe finally started talking about something else other than the Thomas Patterson Public Relations Company. He was also beginning to act very tired. During the meal, he had had a couple of glasses of wine and had also done a lot of talking. He was probably tired from both.

"Last Sunday afternoon, I went to a party," said Mr. Rebe. "It was a rather dull affair until I met this Dr. Troberly, a biology professor, as I recall. A delightful fellow. Very funny man. He was making my whole afternoon worthwhile. But then, around four o'clock, he walked into our host's den, sat down on the couch, and died. They called an ambulance, but it was too late."

Mr. Rebe shoved his spoon into his chocolate mousse. "And I was having such fun. Of all the days in that man's life, he had to die last Sunday afternoon. You know, Timothy," Mr. Rebe said as he talked with his mouth full of chocolate mousse, "there are many things in life that are very difficult to understand."

We sat in silence as we continued to eat our dessert. Mr. Rebe rimmed the bottom of the decanter with his spoon as he said, "That man was the life of the party and he died."

Just as I thought, it was all a joke. I waited for the confirming smile. It never came.

Later that afternoon, I went down to the second floor with Mr. Valesky, one of the men I worked with, to pick up some pamphlets. After we stuffed them into envelopes, we were going down to the first floor to mail them. It was nearly quitting time and we were both in a rush to finish the job. At least I was. I had the door to the stairwell half opened when I noticed Mr. Valesky standing at the elevator. He was an old guy, but he was in good shape, certainly in good enough shape to walk down a flight of stairs. I went over and stood next to him.

"You've hooked up with a great company, you know that?" he said adamantly.

"Have I?"

"Sure you have. They have a great pension plan. I've been with them forty years. A year from this April, I retire. How many more months is that? Sixteen?"

"I guess. Let me see ... "

"Yeah, it's sixteen months. I'll be sixty-five. Boy, am I going to start living then."

God must have heard me. The elevator came.

Forty years, I thought to myself. A guy who had been born on

the same day that Mr. Valesky had started working for the
Thomas Patterson Public Relations Company was now nearly
twice as old as I was. Forty years of riding buses, coffee breaks,
watching the clock, staff meetings and eating lunch at noon even
though you weren't hungry. My entire college career, four years,
was probably little more than a blur to him.

Forty years. You could murder quite a few people and get less
than that.

FORTY

On a hot August afternoon, stopping in at Mr. Cohen's for a bottle of pop and a banana. I was in a rotten mood. I had nothing to do that day. Nothing that I had to do or wanted to do. No pleasure or pain. Just a day packed with blah to look forward to. I really didn't need the pop or banana. I just felt like taking a walk and, besides, Mr. Cohen was a pleasant enough guy and I thought I'd shoot the bull with him for a while.

"Is Leonard home?" I asked Mr. Cohen as I put the change on the counter.

"He's gone," Mr. Cohen replied abruptly as he scooped the coins into his palm and dropped them into the cash register.

I was surprised and rather offended. I didn't think Leonard was leaving for medical school until later in the month and I certainly expected him to say good-bye to me before he left.

"He's left for New York already?"

"What New York?" said Mr. Cohen. "He's moved out. Up to an apartment on the North Side." He turned his back to me and began refilling the cigarette rack.

I recalled the conversation that Leonard and I had had earlier in the summer about the friend up on the North Side who might sublet his apartment.

"Why did he do that?" I asked. "He's just going to have to move out in a few weeks. Leonard's still going to New York, isn't he? Or has he changed his mind and he's going to a medical school in Chicago?"

"What medical school?" said Mr. Cohen as he continued to refill the cigarette rack. "My son, Leonard, going to medical school? My son, Leonard, doing something worthwhile with his life? My son, Leonard, making his father proud of him? Why should he bother? What's it to him? He has his own life to live."

In all the years I had known Mr. Cohen, I had never before heard antagonism in his voice. It was making me feel very uneasy. I really wanted to get the hell out of there. But, first, I wanted to get Leonard's phone number.

"Do you have a number I could reach him at?"

"No. He hasn't got a phone yet."

"His address?"

"No . . . " Mr. Cohen reconsidered. "I think it's on a piece of paper next to the cash register. Thirty-eight something Leomont Street."

I leaned over the counter, memorized the address and then began walking out of the store. Mr. Cohen was still facing the cigarette rack with his back to me.

"Thanks for the banana and pop, Mr. Cohen."

"Thank me? Why thank me? You paid for them. You don't have to thank me. You don't owe me anything."

I went home, borrowed my father's car and drove up to the North Side.

Finding Leonard's building in an unshaven, worn coat-with-most-of-the-buttons-missing neighborhood. As I walked up the stairs, I passed an old man sitting on the top step. He didn't even look up at me as I walked past him. In the lobby, I found a small piece of paper with "Cohen" penciled on it taped below a buzzer. I pushed the button and put my hand on the door, waiting to be buzzed in. Nothing. I pushed the button again. Pulling on the door. It was unlocked. I walked down the hall, stopped in front of 1A and knocked. I could hear someone moving around inside.

"Who's there?" Leonard finally asked.

"It's me, Leonard, Conroy."

Leonard opened the door and I stepped into a small room. To my left was a door that lead to another room, which I presumed was a kitchen. A naked mattress sprawled in one corner of the room while a card table and two folding chairs were set up in another. Behind them stood a radiator. Partially opened cardboard boxes were lined up beneath the room's only window, which faced a brick wall. I could hear the toilet gurgling what sounded like its death throes. Faded speckles of dried paint lingered around the edges of the floor, which sagged like a tired trampoline. A large crack had ripped along one wall.

"I'm sorry," said Leonard, "but the butler position has already been filled."

"Not amusing, Leonard." I was really aggravated with him. And with me. At the same time, I felt sorry for both of us.

When I was a kid playing baseball, Leonard was studying the bones of a skeleton that his father had bought from a medical store. Already, especially on certain days, when I had dropped three fly balls in a row and a grounder had popped out a few teeth, I had suspected that my baseball ambitions just might be delusions. More than a few parents, mine included, were fond of asking their children why they couldn't use their time "more constructively" like Leonard Cohen.

I had both admired and despised Leonard for that cocoon of security he spun around his life. He had played sports only for recreation and played better than some of us who took them much more seriously. He laughed when we talked about making a career out of a game. He never bought a baseball card, saved a stamp or started a coin collection and was truly puzzled as to why anyone else would. Leonard once asked Peter Lollar, who was taking guitar lessons at the time, why he bothered to learn to play something when he could buy records of someone who already knew how to do it well.

Everything in Leonard's life, sometimes obviously, sometimes not, eventually funneled down to that one commandment that had made up the center of his universe. "Thou shalt be a doctor." Leonard was going somewhere while the rest of us kids were just going along. Now that I had seen where he had actually arrived, I didn't know whether to feel smug or sad.

"So what the hell are you doing living in this dump?"

"Dump! Are you kidding? This is a very elegant building." Leonard looked around the room. "The decor, you like it? Early Ghetto."

"Come on, Leonard, what's going on?"

Leonard flopped down on the mattress. "That's the problem. I haven't decided to 'go on.' I may decide to . . ." he dramatically emphasized the next two words, " 'go on' to medical school. Then again, I may decide not to 'go on.' Either way, *I'm* going to decide what I'm going to do. It's not just going to happen.

"A few days ago, when I was helping my father clean up the store, I tried having a heart-to-heart talk with him. Unfortunately, he was lacking the prerequisite. Maybe we both were. I don't know. I told him I wasn't so sure I wanted to go to medical school. He was so shocked he almost dropped a case of returnable bottles. I didn't think anything could surprise my father that much. He got really mad. I mean, mad. He started telling me how he and my mother had sacrificed all those years to put me through school. How they always gave me spending money so I wouldn't have to work a part-time job when I was at school and take time away from my studies."

A phone rang as I straddled one of the card table chairs. "I thought you didn't have a phone, Leonard."

"I don't. That's next door." He tapped his knuckles against the wall over his head. "Very thin walls. The first night I was here, that phone woke me up. I thought maybe the last tenant forgot to have his phone taken out. I was so sleepy that I walked right into a wall on my way to answering it. What was I talking about?"

"Your father."

"Oh, yes, my father. So he started telling me what being a doctor meant to him. I'll give him credit there. He didn't give me a lot of crap about helping the sick. He talked mostly about the money, the prestige. But one thing he talked about struck me as weird."

"What? The privilege of looking under women's dresses?"

"You're sick, you know that, Conroy." He laughed a little. "Amusing, but sick."

"I've heard the rumor." I said.

"You know how one little thing on a job can drive you crazy?" Leonard said.

"How would you know? You've never worked any jobs besides very rarely helping your father in the store."

"I had a part-time job down at school for a while, working in the cafeteria. I never bothered telling my father about it. The one thing I hated about that job was cleaning out ashtrays. I didn't mind any of the other stuff—doing dishes, cleaning off tables—but I hated having to wipe out ashtrays. Well, there's something about my father's job that he hates; waiting on people."

"Then why the hell doesn't he do something else for a living?" I said defensively. It's not pleasant discovering that the man who sold you penny candy when you were a child would have just as soon stuck it in your ear.

"Because the last three job offers he's gotten would have put him in too high a tax bracket," said Leonard. "What choice has he got?"

"You're right," I admitted.

"He doesn't really mind waiting on people," Leonard corrected himself, "he hates to wait while they're making up their minds what to buy. You know, bringing up something to the counter and then deciding to take it back for another brand. Or standing in front of the soup section for five minutes trying to choose between Chicken Noodle and Tomato . . . "

I thought to myself that I was indeed lucky that Mr. Cohen had allowed me to survive my childhood. I could see myself standing in front of the penny candy case poking my finger against the glass as Mr. Cohen hovered over me from behind the counter. "I'll have two jawbreakers and one stick of licorice. Two black jawbreakers. No, make one of them red. No, make them both red. No, I think I'll skip the licorice. No . . . "

"For my father," continued Leonard, "that's one of the big deals about being a doctor. Having people wait for you. All those people sitting in your reception room waiting until *you* get time to see them."

"That's absurd," I said. "Your father actually said that making people wait was one of the best things about being a doctor?"

"He didn't come right out and say it," said Leonard. "But as he talked about it, I could see the fiendish glee pouring out of him at just the thought of someone waiting for him for a change. And if not for him, at least for his kid."

I got out of the chair, walked over to the window and stared at the brick wall only a few feet away. "Nice view."

"You should see it at sunset."

I turned around and leaned back on the windowsill. "Maybe we could get everyone in the neighborhood to cooperate. Instead of just walking in and buying something from your father, we'd have everybody make an appointment with the understanding that they'd have to wait at least a half an hour when they got there. And they'd have to create at least one problem to talk over with him. 'Well, you see, Mr. Cohen, it's my asparagus. It just doesn't feel right.' "

"And he'd get to charge ten dollars for a pack of cigarettes," added Leonard.

"Why not?" I replied. "But there's a problem."

"What?"

"It'll probably catch on. People love to be degraded. Other stores will start doing the same thing. They'll take away business."

"No problem," said Leonard. "We'll form a union, but we'll call it an association. That sounds much better. We'll call it the American Merchants Association, AMA for short. We'll tell everybody that my father has spent over twenty years of his life learning how to sell food and that he only has a relatively few earning years to get back all that investment of time and money. And we'll tell them that without proper food and people like my father who know a lot about it, they'll die. Then we'll convince a few people in government to pass the right kind of laws and there goes our competition."

"Think it'll work?" I asked.

"You'd be surprised," said Leonard. "You'd be surprised."

"What about Barbara?" I asked.

Leonard slowly got up off the mattress and started into the kitchen. "Want some coffee?"

"No thanks," I replied as I followed him. "You didn't answer my question."

"Where did I put my coffee cup?" Leonard said to himself as he glanced into the sink and then began flipping open cabinet doors.

"You only have one cup?"

"I know you don't like coffee."

All the shelves were completely bare. He even looked in the refrigerator.

"Why don't you check the stove?"

"Don't be silly," he replied. "Now I remember." He went into the bathroom and came back a moment later with a large porcelain cup dangling from his finger. "Went to bed quite late," explained Leonard. "At that time of night, one sink looks pretty much the same as the next."

"Could you flush the one you put it in?" I asked.

"You know, when I went to the toilet, I did notice that my feet didn't touch the ground."

"What about Barbara?" I asked again.

He began filling a pot with water. "After my 'discussion' with my father, I went to her house and told her that I was seriously considering not 'going on' to medical school. I think she almost went into a catatonic state on me. I say, 'I think.' With Barbara, it was hard to tell."

"You know, Leonard, I don't know Barbara that well. I mean, I've known her for years, but I've never really gotten to know her . . ."

"Unfortunately," interrupted Leonard, "I can say the same thing."

"I'm serious, Leonard."

"So am I."

"She's always treated you like a god."

"I know. It must have been very rough on her. God handing in his resignation."

"You've dominated her for years."

"I know that, too. I always used to think that was to my advantage. No goddamn woman was going to tell me what to do. Unfortunately, she didn't tell me much of anything, about me or herself." Leonard poured the boiling water into his cup and stirred until the brown silt disappeared from the top. "Sure I can't offer you anything?"

"What? Water?"

"Hot or cold?" Leonard gestured towards the living room. "Let's go sit at the card table." He proceeded slowly so as not to spill his coffee. But his long legs sneaked in a gait and a few drops of the hot liquid splashed out. Leonard slid into the chair, put both elbows on the table and propped up his head with his hands. "I spill enough coffee in a day to keep most people awake for a month."

"You were talking about Barbara," I reminded him as I sat down in the other chair.

"It's amazing," he said. "I dated her all those years. We talked to each other. Not constantly, maybe not even a lot. But we talked. We must have. Apparently, neither of us was saying anything."

"Or neither of you were listening."

"Probably both. She cried that afternoon. She asked me how I could give up a profession that meant so much to me. That made me mad. 'Give up what?' I asked her. 'Give up something I never had? I'm not a doctor. I'm just a guy with a college degree who happened to major in biology and who planned on being a doctor.' Barbara was astonished. She lived so much in the future, as I did, I suppose, that she always looked upon me as a doctor already who just happened to still be in the process of completing his training. It's very depressing to see someone discover reality.

"She loved Leonard the doctor. If she had to make a choice between the two, I don't think it would be Leonard."

"You think she went into nurse's training because of you?"

"Sure," said Leonard. "White on white. A matching set. You know what she said to me? She said that I should seriously reconsider not going to medical school because doctors were the most important people in our society. I was flattered. It's no small thing having your ego inflated by a woman you've known as long as I've known Barbara. For the first time, in a long time, I really started feeling good about us. But then, like a real ass, I asked her what she meant. She told me that when Ann Landers has a problem that even she cannot solve, she always tells the person to see their family doctor." Leonard began tracing his finger through the puddle of spilled coffee. "I felt so dumb, so sad. I almost apologized to Barbara for taking up so many years of her life."

A low hissing streamed from the radiator behind us. I waited for Leonard to say something but he didn't even seem to notice. Finally, I said, "Leonard, why's the radiator making that noise?"

"The heat's on."

"In August?"

"There's something wrong with it."

"Obviously."

"I talked to the janitor about it." Leonard was still thinking about what he had said rather than what he was saying.

"What did he say?" I asked.

"I don't know. I don't speak Italian."

Leonard went over to the window and opened it up even higher. "There's one big advantage to living here," he said. "When you go outside, the whole world seems air conditioned."

"Who are your neighbors?"

Leonard pointed towards the kitchen. "I've only met one of them. He's a guy about my age." Leonard returned to his seat at the card table. He turned the chair sideways to the table so that he could stretch out his legs. "A delightful fellow," said Leonard cynically.

"A real jerk, huh?"

"No, he really is delightful. I've talked to him a few times. He had a delightful childhood and a delightful four years in high school. He had a delightful time in college and, right now, he's having a delightful time leading the 'single life.' He has no doubts that he'll meet a delightful girl and that they'll have a delightful marriage with two perfectly delightful children. He'll be a delightful grandfather with delightful grandchildren and he'll die with a delightful smile on his face. And I don't think he's faking it," lamented Leonard. "He seems to thoroughly enjoy life and doesn't even have to work at it to feel that way. All of his memories are good ones. He looks forward to the future yet enjoys every day. And the worst part is I like him. He's really a delightful guy. All in all, he's a delightful pain in the ass."

"Where does he work?" I asked.

"Downtown at the commodities exchange. He probably deals in delightfuls."

The room was beginning to get extremely warm. "How could the other tenants stand this all summer?" I asked.

"I don't know," replied Leonard. "Let's go next door to my friend's. Maybe there's some way of shutting it off that I don't know about."

We went down the hall and knocked on Mr. Delightful's door, but there was no answer. "Might as well try this door," said Leonard as he turned around and knocked on apartment door 1C.

"Who lives here?" I asked.

"I don't know."

"Yes?" A young woman's voice from behind the door answered the knock.

"Are you getting heat in there?" asked Leonard.

"I'm sorry, I can't hear you."

"I said," boomed Leonard, "are you hot in there?"

"I beg your pardon?"

"Interesting neighbor," I observed.

"I mean," stuttered Leonard, "is your radiator giving off heat? And if it is, is there any way to shut if off?"

"I already called the janitor," the voice replied, "and he's on his way over to fix it."

"Thanks," answered Leonard.

As we walked back to his apartment, I said, "Not only does she have a sexy voice, she speaks fluent Italian."

"No doubt about it," said Leonard, "I'm going to have to check out Apartment 1C." When we got back to his apartment, the radiator's hiss was already fizzling out.

We sat down again at his card table. "Want more coffee?" asked Leonard.

"What do you mean 'More?' I haven't had any yet."

"Oh, want some?"

"No thanks."

"I think I'll have another cup." He sprung up and returned a moment later with his cup refilled. Spilling a few drops of coffee as he put the cup down on the table.

"So what now, Leonard? Where do you go from here?"

"I start looking for a job Monday. Work for a while. Give myself some time to think. I'll probably decide to 'go on' to medical school next fall. Maybe, I don't know."

"What about the draft?" I asked. "You're going to lose your student deferment aren't you?"

"Yeah. I'll just have to take my chances." Leonard quickly changed the subject. "How's your job? You like it?"

"It's all right."

"What do you do?"

"I'm not too sure."

"Seriously, what do you do?"

"I told you, I'm not too sure." I wasn't. So far, I had been doing mostly busy work; photocopying, filing, reading some brochures published by my company. In the eight weeks I'd been there, I had written only a few small blurbs for clients.

"Did you need any letters of recommendation to get it?"

"No," I said. "I happened to apply for a job on the very day that someone else quit. I just got lucky."

"Do you think you would have needed letters of recommendation?"

"I suppose. But you have those, don't you?"

"Yeah, but they're all concerning medical school," said Leonard. "Do you think letters are that important?"

"No, I don't. But when I was looking for a job, a couple of personnel directors that I talked to thought they were. They said I should try and get as many letters of recommendation as possible in my file so . . ."

"So people who actually meet you won't have the awesome responsibility of deciding whether or not you're a shit."

"Precisely. They also said that the longer the person who writes the letter knows you, the more impressive the letter is."

"Great," yelled Leonard as he jumped out of his chair and began pacing the room. "I'll go back to Mrs. Kremper, my kindergarten teacher, and ask her for a letter of recommendation. 'Dear Prospective Employer: I can highly recommend Leonard Cohen for a job. He knows how to handle blocks and he doesn't wet himself. On most days.'"

"What kind of job do you want, Leonard? What do you want to do?"

He began pacing faster. "I don't know, I don't know." He turned on me. "What the hell do you want to do? Stay at that goddamn public relations firm for the rest of your life?"

"Easy, Leonard."

"Sorry." He sat down on the mattress but kept his feet on the floor. His bony knees framed his face as he stared at me. "Well, what do you want to do?"

"I've thought of being a writer, a novelist. You know, write books." Sure, I thought of it. When I was standing in right field and had just dropped the first fly ball that had been hit to me in the past four months, I thought about a lot of things.

"Really? I never knew that."

"Yeah," I said. "My seventh-grade nun thought I had a flair for it."

"Well, that's certainly a good reason to devote your life to a career."

"Who's talking about life?" I asked. "I just said I'd like to try it. But it's very tough to get published."

"Being dead helps."

"Maybe I'll write a book and then kill myself."

"What if they wanted minor revisions?" Leonard didn't wait for my answer. He got up off the mattress and began pacing again.

"What kind of job do I want?" he asked himself aloud. "What do I want to do?"

"Maybe," I said, "some day I'll win the Nobel Prize in literature."

That slowed Leonard down slightly. "You know, when I was a kid, I used to dream that I'd win that in medicine."

"Too bad they don't give one in the category of indecisiveness."

Leonard began increasing his pacing tempo again. "I'm not so sure I'd accept it."

His pacing now carried him into the kitchen and back to the living room again. "What am I going to do? I've got to get a job. How can you enjoy Saturday and Sunday if you don't have to go to work on Monday?"

"What are you talking about? You've loafed all summer."

"I wasn't loafing, I was resting because I was planning on going to medical school. If you have nothing to go to, then it's loafing."

As Leonard walked by the room's only closet, he toyed with the doorknob. It came off in his hand.

"My uncle's a city building inspector," I said. "If he ever saw this place, he'd condemn it."

With the doorknob still in his hand, Leonard stood with his back to the mattress and allowed himself to topple back onto it. His lanky frame bounced slightly a few times before settling down. Closely inspecting the glass doorknob as if it were a crystal ball, he said, "Too bad there aren't life inspectors. They could come around, look at your life and say, 'Sorry, your life is unsafe for occupancy. You're going to have to tear it down and start over.' Then they'd slap a 'condemned' sticker on your forehead and that would be that. All very neat. No decisions to make. Too bad there aren't any of those."

"You can say that?" I asked, "after a childhood dominated by adults, sixteen years of formal education, and now, as you're about to enter the job market?"

"You're right," said Leonard as he put the glass doorknob down on the floor, "too bad there's so many."

A few days later, Leonard called me on the phone.

"I won't have a phone until Friday," he said, "but I just wanted to tell you I got a job. Wait until I tell my father. He'll love it."

"What are you doing?"

"I'm driving a bus. 'Dad, I've got a job and I'm so important, people are waiting for me on every corner.' "

FORTY-ONE

Dear God:

   Is there an expiration date on childhood ownership?

Signed: Conroy

Conroy:

   I once had a son. When I felt that he was no longer an "old boy," but was now a young man, I gave him a letter: "Dear Son: Ever since the day you were born, I have made your life worth living. Make no mistake about it. I have done everything for you. And during all those years, just by being my son, you have made life worth living for me. I would have lived without you, but I would have never lived so well. Let's call it even. And if we see each other after today, let it be because we're friends, not family."

Signed: God

FORTY-TWO

Riding on the bus with the two top buttons of my shirt open and the tie hanging loose. I sat tall in my seat so that my face caught the full force of the window breeze. Although it was already late afternoon, the livid sun continued to blister my patch of earth as it staggered towards the cover of nightfall.

Not until the motion of the bus completely died at my stop did I bother to get up. As I stepped off the bus, droplets of perspiration began swarming over my now unprotected face. I readjusted my sport coat, which hung from the index finger, over my back. Before crossing the street to Caepan's, I quickly stopped in at the discount store on the corner and bought a rubber ball. If I got home in time, I thought I'd go out in the alley and throw the ball off the Methodist church wall for a while. I didn't do much of that anymore.

The sticky sweat of the blacktop grabbed at my shoes as I walked past the gasoline pumps and into Caepan's office. I glanced into the garage and saw Butcher asleep under the back end of a Ford panel truck. Caepan was sitting on a high stool near the pay telephone. In one hand, he gripped a small

245

rectangular blob of machinery while the other hand delicately probed it with a screwdriver. The top of Caepan's desk was buried under scrambled grease-stained papers, a few empty coffee cups, a parts catalog, two flattened potato chip bags and a half dozen flashlight batteries. The big bottom drawer was pulled out to accommodate empty pop bottles.

"So how's the new job?" Caepan asked without looking up.

"Terrific. Today, I reorganized the receiving department, got two new accounts and financed another merger."

Caepan looked up at the clock on the wall. "And all of that took you until nearly six o'clock?"

"Long lunch," I said, "business, you know."

"How's Nancy Kimberly?"

I had forgotten that I had told Caepan about her. "She's okay. The boss, Mr. Rebe, is putting the make on her, quite successfully, I think. I don't understand it. He's old, bald, fat and not very good looking to begin with. I'm young, virile and disgustingly charming. The guy's been married three times and plays around constantly. She must know that. Everybody in the office does. Yet, she acts like she goes for him."

"She probably does," said Caepan. "And if your description of him is as accurate as your description of you, he undoubtedly looks like Clark Gable."

"All right," I admitted, "I've exaggerated things a bit. But I still don't understand how a girl like Nancy Kimberly can be attracted to a guy that old, no matter what he looks like. Believe me, Mr. Rebe is just an average-looking sixty-year-old man."

"Mr. Rebe happens to have a fair amount of the strongest aphrodisiac known to mankind," replied Caepan. He waited a moment and when he didn't hear me ask him to explain himself, he said sarcastically, " 'Aphrodisiac' isn't a type of salad dressing. It means, 'sexual stimulant.' "

"I know that." I didn't.

"Mr. Rebe has a certain amount of power," said Caepan. "Anybody with money does. I had a cousin out in Colorado who used to manage a farm for some rich guy. When I went out there, he gave me a tour of the place. In the barn, I noticed that each of the horses had a huge stall all to himself. It seemed like such a waste of space to me. I mentioned it to my cousin. He said to me, 'These are stallions, you know, healthy male horses.' I asked, 'So what?' He explained to me that you can't allow stallions to get together because they'll beat each other's brains out. He said their sex drive makes them do that. Stallions have such a strong sex drive that they're not allowed to be in public places unless they're gelded. You know, unless all the important parts are cut off.

"In the wild, the strongest stallion takes all the females for himself. The weaker stallions, the old ones, the young ones, all the losers, roam around together, but without any mares. That's the way it is with many species of animals. The most powerful male gets all the action. Same thing with people except, as usual, we humans have messed up the natural course of things."

"Oh, I get it," I said, feigning enlightenment. "If you're a horse's ass, like Mr. Rebe, then you win all the women."

"If you were getting it," said Caepan slowly, "you wouldn't be complaining to me."

"Go on," I said emphatically.

"With human animals, young guys usually have the advantage with women because of their youth, looks and all of that." Caepan stopped tinkering with the piece of machinery for a moment, casually looked me up and down and then said, "Notice that I did say 'usually.' "

I smiled blandly as Caepan continued.

"But when a young guy runs into an older man with money, with power, he's had it. Today, more than ever, money counts more than muscle. Arm wrestle a wallet and you'll lose every time."

"In other words," I said, "what the sex manuals say is true. Most women do care about the size of your wallet."

"Precisely," said Caepan. "You learn fast."

"Yeah, too bad I forget faster."

"Look at it this way," said Caepan as he put down the screwdriver and shook the small piece of machinery to see if there was anything loose. "Imagine how much money old Rebe would pay to buy a few years of your youth."

"You're right. At least a dollar-eighty."

"At least," agreed Caepan. He got off the stool, gently placed the piece of machinery down on it, dropped his hand into a side pocket, and wiggled his fingers around, looking for the right change. "How about a bottle of pop?"

"Sounds good to me. By the way," I said as we walked out towards the pop machine, "I notice that your desk doesn't look quite the same as Mr. Rebe's."

"That's because I use mine for different reasons than he does," said Caepan. "That desk is where I put a cup of coffee or a bottle of pop that I've decided to finish later. It's a good place to rest my feet. I've even slept on it a few nights. Once, I used it to prop up the side of a truck when the jack broke. At closing time, I drag it behind the front door because one of the locks is broken. About a month ago, some guy ran over Butcher's food dish so now I feed him out of one of the drawers."

"You're right," I said. "Mr. Rebe doesn't get that kind of mileage out of his desk. I don't think he even owns a dog." With bottles of pop in hand and knees up to our chins, Caepan and I sat on the curb of the concrete apron that encircled the front of his office. I took the rubber ball out of my pocket and put it down next to me. A young breeze rambled through the neighborhood as the sun skidded from its pedestal towards the edge of the earth.

"I bet he has a big desk with barely anything on it," said Caepan.

"How did you know?"

"He uses that office for only one thing, intimidation."

"Intimidation?"

"That's what desks are all about," said Caepan. "The same's true of offices, especially the ones with bookshelves."

"I don't follow you."

"Years ago," said Caepan, "your boss would intimidate you by grabbing you by the collar or threatening to fire you or punching-in your face. But that kind of stuff is too obvious for today. 'Sly' is in. So when you walk into your boss' office, he's sitting behind a huge desk in a big, plushy chair. You get to sit in a little chair, if you're allowed to sit at all, and whisper your prayers to him."

"Why don't you have an office like that?"

"If I want to scare the hell out of somebody," said Caepan, "I call Butcher. When was the last time you were afraid of getting your foot chewed up by a desk?"

"It's been a while. You know, a few days ago, before quitting time," I said, "I was with this old guy named Valesky, who's been working for my company ... the company," I quickly corrected myself, "the Thomas Patterson Public Relations Company, for the past forty years. Can you believe that? Forty years! He's retiring in about a year and a half and you know what he told me? 'I can hardly wait. I'm really going to start living.' Start living? What's he been doing for the past sixty-three years? God, that's depressing."

"For the average guy," said Caepan, "the odds are almost even that he won't even be alive when he's sixty-five."

"You're kidding."

"Am I laughing?"

"How do you know?"

"What do you mean?" said Caepan as he clunked down his nearly empty pop bottle on the concrete next to his feet. "You think I spend my whole life with my head under the hood of a car? I read it somewhere." Sometimes, Caepan got very touchy when you implied that, just maybe, he didn't know everything.

"You know, when you're a kid," I said, "every year of your life is different. One year, you're a sixth grader. The next year, you're in seventh grade. There's always some sort of progress being made. Every year is new. But when you get older, the years start running together. They're all the same. Is that all I have to look forward to, the 'Valesky' years?"

"Maybe it seems," said Caepan, "no matter what age we are, that we've spent most of our lives in grammar school, because we have." He plunked his index finger against the side of his head. "Up here, this is where the clock is running. And the older we get, the faster it runs. Somewhere along that time track, it was the early twenties for me, your mind jumps from the local to the express."

"You're right," I said. "When I was a kid, Christmas didn't come once a year, it came once a lifetime. I must have spent ten years in first grade."

I took a sip before continuing. "I never believed I was going to grow up. When I'd complain about something, my father used to tell me, 'Wait until you grow up, then you'll see how tough life is.' Or the nun would say, 'You'd better study or you won't be able to get a job when you grow up.' Grow up. What kid really believes he's going to grow up? I was a kid today, I was a kid yesterday and I was going to be a kid tomorrow.

˙"All of us kids worried constantly about death, but not about growing up," I said. "The nuns and priests used to tell us that we'd go to either Heaven or Hell when we died and that death could be just around the corner."

"One Monday morning, we came to school and were told that one of our classmates, James Damond, had been killed by a car on Sunday afternoon. A few years later, Mack Cosca, who was so tall he always had to sit in the back of the room, died of pneumonia. But we never showed up one morning for school to discover that one of our classmates had become thirty-five the previous afternoon.

"No, when I was a kid, I never really believed I was ever going to grow up." I looked down at my bottle of pop and my rubber ball. "And I was right."

I waited for Caepan to say something in my defense, but he didn't. Instead, he did something that he never did before or again. He talked about himself.

"My old man was loaded with dough, did you know that?"

"No, you never told me."

"Yeah, well, he was. I mean, loaded. Tons of the stuff."

"What did he own?"

"Companies, I don't even know how many."

"What kinds?" I asked.

"Who knows?" replied Caepan. "They had names no one could remember and made things no one knew about. One of his companies had an entire division that made tiny plastic washers used in assembling children's toys. Sounds fascinating, doesn't it? The old man owned about a dozen cars ... "

"He was loaded, wasn't he?"

"I already said that," said Caepan, obviously annoyed. "As far back as I can remember, I was always tinkering around with his cars. When I was a kid, he thought it was cute. But when I was still doing it when I was supposed to be going to some university, the old man wasn't so amused. He kept asking me, 'When are you going to grow up?' I didn't know what he was talking about. Finally, I realized what he was saying: 'When are you going to give up?' "

I wanted to know more about Caepan and the family he had never before mentioned. Did he have any brothers or sisters? Where did they live? Did he ever see any of them? But Caepan didn't volunteer any more information, so I didn't ask.

Caepan locked up and we walked home. I talked about the White Sox pitching staff. Caepan explained the problems he encountered with the car he had worked on all afternoon. Neither of us listened much.

FORTY-THREE

Driving downstate to the University of Illinois on a yellow autumn day, past fields crowded with braids of cornstalks. Their parched colorless skins crackled lightly as they swayed in the breeze of this after-life called fall. Leonard had asked me if I wanted to go along with him to see the homecoming game. I told him I'd go if I could get out of a "previous commitment." "Hey, Ma, you mind if I clean the basement on Sunday instead of Saturday?" When we got down there, Leonard was supposed to meet a number of his fraternity brothers, whom he had graduated with, at some local tavern before the game. They had set up the meeting on their last night in the frat house the previous June.

I had been to the University of Illinois a number of times before and always found it mildly depressing. Walking around the campus, past the dorms, the open fields and the fraternity houses made me aware of what I had missed by not going away to school. Not that I had a choice. I hardly had enough money for bus fare to Engrim much less for tuition to a state school. Leonard had gone to the University of Illinois on a debate scholarship. When I had heard about that, I really felt stupid. I never knew they gave scholarships for such things. When I was in high school, I argued all the time. But today, you've got to be an organization man. Do something for the pure love of it and all you have to show is a disfigured body and a rearranged face. Get into organized arguing and you'll get a four-year ride through college.

An hour outside of Chicago, I was already regretting that I had agreed to go with Leonard. And the closer we got to his university, the more monotonous it appeared the day would be. Listening to the highway scars pummeling the tires, I could see Weatherly sitting in the Engrim cafeteria with the morning newspaper spread out on the table, reading my personal stock market report to me.

"Boredom up two thousand points while enthusiasm experienced another day of decline. Stupid decisions continues its steady climb, which began twenty-two years ago."

"Say, Leonard, did you get your bike back?" Two weeks earlier, Leonard's bike had been stolen from his storage locker in the basement.

"Oh, yeah, sure," he replied as he began to accelerate out of a small town speed zone. "It was only a test. When I went downstairs yesterday, I found a note attached to my bike from the thief. It read, 'Had this been a real theft, you would have been out of a bike, turkey.' "

"Just asking," I said defensively.

"Okay, so you asked. I answered," said Leonard.

He was in an extremely rotten mood. The previous day, he had gone for his army physical. His parents were quite upset over it. On the day they found out, I had gone into the store to buy a bottle of pop and Mrs. Cohen had even forgotten to put on her body length apron. I don't think I had ever seen her before without her apron. It was embarrassing. She might as well have been nude.

Mr. and Mrs. Cohen were constantly calling Leonard, trying to get him to change his mind about not going to medical school. If he was drafted, of course, he wouldn't have the choice of changing his mind.

Earlier in the morning, before we left on the trip, I had asked him what had happened at the physical. Leonard had said that he didn't feel like going into it but that he'd tell me about it later in the day. I was almost positive he had passed.

I had gotten lucky. Because of some clerical error, my draft board had given me a student deferment that went six months beyond the date of my graduation. There were still a few months left on it. Knowing that sooner or later I'd have to go for the physical, I was very interested in knowing what had happened to Leonard.

The Vietnam War was already going strong when I had graduated from high school. Being a typical high school kid, I could hardly wait to 'do my duty.' Since I wasn't too sure of what I wanted to do with my life, I had considered postponing college, enlisting in the army and giving myself some time to think. Until I talked to Caepan.

"If you are a corpse, you won't be able to think," he had said. "Go to college for four years. Then if you still want somebody to blow your head off, don't worry, there'll always be plenty of people around willing to do you the favor."

Caepan had been right. In four years, my enthusiasm had mellowed into cynicism. Now, like almost everyone else my age, while the members of Congress sat in Washington passing various laws designed to get me into the army, I sat at home and searched for legal and physical flaws that would keep me out. So far, I was winning. College had kept me out of the war for the past four years. If the war was still going on when my deferment ran out, I planned on taking one of a number of possible courses of action: flattening my feet, dislocating my knees, putting braces on my teeth or becoming a priest or a pervert, any one of which was deferrable. If the war was accelerating, I'd do all of them. Actually, I had a bad strip of vein behind one knee that I was hoping would keep me out. A friend of mine had the same thing and he had already been deferred. I guess the army figures there's nothing worse than having a defective leg blown off.

Leonard and I were already an hour late by the time we parked the car and began the two block walk to the tavern. Leonard took quick, impatient steps and I had to hustle to keep up with him. His earlier melancholy mood was now blossoming into merriment.

"What a great feeling to be walking in this town again," said

Leonard. "A lot of great memories here. A lot of them. You'll love my fraternity brothers, Tim. Great guys and a lot of laughs."

But when we got to the tavern, only one of Leonard's fraternity brothers was there and he was still living on campus doing graduate work.

"Boland, are you the only guy here?" asked Leonard incredulously.

"Yeah," said Boland as his gaze flicked between us and a cartoon on the mounted television. Boland appeared to be in his late twenties. "You drive all the way down from Chicago for this?"

"Yeah," said Leonard. I could tell that he was embarrassed to admit it. "Where is everybody?"

"A couple of the guys, Leyden and Parky, got married recently . . ."

"I know that," said Leonard, "I was at their weddings."

"Oh, yeah, that's right. Rolater got a job and was transferred to New York. Ahern got drafted and Quinlan joined the Navy so he wouldn't be drafted."

"What happened to the other guys?"

"I don't know, they just didn't show." The cartoon ended and Boland now gave us his full attention. "You going to the game this afternoon?"

"No."

"How about the frat party afterwards? I know the brothers would like to see you again."

"I'm heading back to Chicago," said Leonard.

"Let me buy you guys a beer and then we can go to the game. Afterwards, if you still feel like it, you can skip the party and go back to Chicago. After driving all that distance, you should get something out of the day."

"I have," said Leonard as he turned around and began to walk out of the tavern. "Take care of yourself, Boland."

"You, too," said Boland. "Hey, it was nice meeting you," he yelled after me.

"Same here," I said. Leonard hadn't bothered to introduce us.

Leonard and I walked slowly down the street as groups of students glided effortlessly by us on their way to the stadium. "Wanna take a walk before we head back?" asked Leonard.

"Sure, why not," I replied, surprised that Leonard was skipping the football game. He enjoyed watching football.

His father had once told me that whenever he called Leonard on Sunday afternoon down at school, he'd always check the television to make sure it was halftime. Otherwise, Leonard wouldn't answer the phone.

"Feel like talking about the physical yet?"

"Boland was in the army," said Leonard. "He went in after two years of college. He was literally getting on the plane to Vietnam when the CO asked if there was anyone with a college degree and no police record. Boland lied and told the guy he had a degree. He ended up guarding some monument in Washington, D.C., for eighteen months.

"Boland has a very neat mother," Leonard continued. "You know how you're supposed to come home from basic training and your mother looks at you and says, 'You left a boy, but you've come back a man,' or something to that effect? Boland's mother greeted him at the door with, 'Jesus Christ, kid, you look like shit.' "

The last of his words sparked into chuckles that were quickly extinguished by the weight of the ones that followed. "I even found the fact that I had to go for the physical quite repulsive; the idea of me having to be somewhere under the penalty of going to jail. Why me and not you?" Leonard pointed to a girl walking by. "Why me and not her? Why me and not Mrs. Fenns? You don't have to be young and in shape to go to war today. All you need's a finger to pull the trigger. If the physical had been legitimate, that's all they would have had to examine. 'Mr. Cohen, you've been given a deferment. Your index finger is overweight.' "

"Was it a thorough physical?" I asked.

"One of the few things I learned in pre-med," said Leonard, "is that there is no such thing as a 'thorough physical.' I take that back. There is. It's called an autopsy.

"I had to be downtown at the induction center at six in the morning. I couldn't sleep all night so I left the house early and got down there about five A.M. Then I went over to the bus station for some breakfast. They have a twenty-four hour snack bar in the terminal. While I was waiting for my coffee, I dropped my spoon and when I reached down to get it, I ripped open the entire seam of my crotch. I had to walk out of there with my hand between my legs."

"Don't worry about it," I said, "that's the way everybody walks around that bus station."

"True," said Leonard. "When I went to the induction center, the doors were still locked and there was a group of guys standing around. All of us were dressed like slobs except for one guy who was actually wearing a suit. When I asked him why he was so dressed up I discovered that he was Spanish speaking and could hardly speak English. All he did was smile constantly. When I eventually got my question across to him, he told me he was wearing a suit because he wanted to make a good impression with the army. He had no idea what was going on, the poor slob.

"Why do they have to do all of this at six o'clock in the morning?" Leonard asked without expecting an answer. "They'd get you up later than that if they were going to shoot you. We had to walk all over the place in just our shorts and shoes carrying these little brown paper bags they gave us to put our valuables in."

"How did you keep the bag from falling off?" I asked.

Leonard looked at me. "You know, Conroy, sometimes you're a real strange guy."

"Just sometimes?"

"Most of the time."

"Go on," I said.

"Anyway, the first thing they did was they marched about twenty of us into this little room. There was a sergeant sitting at a desk reading the sports section of the *Sun-Times*. Without even looking up, he said, 'Awright yo' guys, pull down yo' shorts and begin jumping up and down.' We were jumping up and down for thirty minutes before the first doctor came and examined us. Not once did that sergeant turn the page. Me, a cum laude graduate, totally naked and jumping up and down all that time with nineteen other guys in front of some weirdo who's pretending to be reading the *Sun-Times* sports section. Jesus, someone ought to check into that guy."

"Maybe they did and that's why he's a sergeant."

"When this old doctor examined me, and I use the word

'doctor' loosely," said Leonard, "I was huffing and puffing like a madman. You know what he says to me? 'That's right. Out with the bad air, in with the good air.' Such dazzling use of medical terminology! Then he ran the stethoscope over my chest a few times and said, 'Hey, kid, I don't think your heart's beating.' Finally, I pointed and said, 'Ah, doctor, my heart's over here.' And he went, 'Oh, yeah.' What a moron. The guy looked like a wino who had just come straight from an AMA banquet."

"Did you stay in that one room for the entire physical?" I asked.

A roar shouted softly from the stadium. Leonard swung his foot. "Kick-off," he explained. I repeated my question.

"No," said Leonard. "We had to go around to these various stations. I overheard a doctor explaining to a new medical examiner that there were thirty-five categories for disqualifying a guy, but it was the last day of the month and in order to make the quota the examiner was to ignore all medical disabilities except bedwetting. You could end up getting killed because you went for your physical on a Wednesday instead of a Thursday. This guy ahead of me in line had a messed-up shoulder. He couldn't raise his arm above his head. A doctor said to the kid, 'Don't worry about it, son, the only thing you won't be able to do in the army is put up both arms to surrender.' "

"Don't you have to do push-ups, climb ropes and do a lot of other things in basic training that require two arms?" I asked.

"Of course, you do," said Leonard. "But the whole physical was a joke. For instance, they hardly checked my eyes. Basically, they just counted them and made sure they were my own. You could have gone all the way through that exam and have been completely blind, have two wooden legs, and had nothing inside but a heart that was barely beating. And if it was on the wrong side of your chest, that would have been okay, too."

"Maybe you should have gone to medical school," I said. "I've been told the army treats doctors a hell of a lot better than it does mere human beings."

"They do," agreed Leonard. "A doctor told one of my pre-med classes that the army has a special basic training program for doctors; six weeks of drinking, card playing and sleeping. And you come out with the rank of Captain."

"If you do go into the army, Leonard, you're certainly going to be doing it the hard way."

"I always do things the hard way," mused Leonard. "Why, I don't know. Most people cross the street to get to the other side. I'd travel around the world."

We didn't say anything as we walked the next few blocks. Leonard stopped just as we were about to cross an intersection. "Speaking of streets," he said as if his previous words had just cleared his mouth, "I think we're lost."

"How could we be lost?" I asked, "this town isn't much bigger than our neighborhood. You must take a compass with you when you go to the bathroom."

"In this town, on the Saturday afternoon of a home game, you don't need a compass," said Leonard. "All I have to do is listen for the stadium and I'll be able to get us back to the car."

We listened. Beyond the sighs of the autumn leaves came the whisper of the crowd's roar from the stadium. "An eight-yard gain for a first down," said Leonard matter-of-factly.

"On an off-tackle run?" I asked.

"Obviously."

We made a left turn and continued our walk.

"So the physical didn't go too well, huh?"

"One part of it did," said Leonard. "We had to spend a lot of time just sitting in line waiting to have something examined. All we had on were our shorts and shoes. Those damn metal chairs were cold and we had to keep moving from one to the other as the line shrank. But I got lucky. There was this big, fat kid in front of me and he got the chair all warmed up. If it hadn't been for him, I would have frozen my ass off. Being in line behind him was the high point of my day."

"Some day," I said.

Leonard nodded his agreement. "By the way," he said, "I met some guy who knew you from Engrim."

"Yeah, who?"

"A guy named Avers."

"I thought he was still sitting in the cafeteria."

"What was that?" asked Leonard.

"Nothing. What did he have to say?"

"The guy's an asshole," said Leonard. "He wasn't down there because he was being drafted. He was actually enlisting. Could hardly wait to get in. You know what he kept talking about? Comradeship. He kept saying that the best thing about the army was the comradeship you felt for your fellow soldier. How the hell did he know? I told him about a picture I had seen in *Time* magazine the week before. It was one where all these body bags, obviously occupied, were stacked under a tree . . ."

"Yeah, I saw that one," I interrupted.

"I said to Avers, 'Under such conditions, it would be quite difficult to swap war stories or throw your arm around your buddy and belly up to the bar.' "

"What did Avers say?"

"He said that somebody had to fight for freedom. I asked him, 'What freedom? I'm not here because I want to be. I'm here because I have to be.' "

"What then?"

"Nothing," said Leonard. "He just kept babbling on like that. I was afraid that if he didn't shut up, I was going to kill him."

"Oh, I see," I said. "It's not that you mind killing people, you just don't want to have to go out of your way to do it. If someone's standing right next to you, however, you'd be glad to do it. You're a convenience killer."

"Certainly," replied Leonard. "I have no objections to getting on a train, going downtown and killing people from nine to five, with an hour off for a leisurely lunch, of course. A killing job that offered periodic promotions, good health and life insurance and a solid retirement program would be quite satisfactory. But to go through six weeks of doing push-ups and all of that garbage, wear a dumb-looking uniform, travel twelve thousand miles and slosh through jungles just to kill somebody is asking a bit much. After all, if American industry can ship rubber from there to here for tires, it can certainly do the same with the natives."

"You know, though," I said, "sometimes, I'll be lying around the house, I mean, I'll be doing absolutely nothing, but not in a relaxed taking-it-easy way. I'll be feeling very restless and dissatisfied because I don't know what to do with myself. And even if I did, I probably wouldn't feel like doing it. Then I think of guys my age, guys I know, fighting in Vietnam and, at least for the moment, I envy them. Not that I think war's a great idea. But at least these guys are doing something they'll remember."

"Provided they're alive to remember it," said Leonard.

"I know that. But at least a guy over there at the end of the day can say, 'Hey, I'm alive.' It's an achievement. There's a struggle. When he gets up in the morning, he knows his goal, going to bed at night in one piece. I'm not saying I'd like to trade places with him. It's just that, sometimes . . ."

"You know who else I saw down there? Donald Fryze. He's been deferred three different times."

"Deferred? That guy looks in great shape to me. I see him jogging by my house every morning."

"He runs five miles a day," said Leonard. "When he goes for his physical, he parks his car five miles away and jogs to the induction center. That way, when the doctor examines him, his blood pressure is sky high. When I saw him, he was in a special line for his blood pressure test. Every other guy in the line was a fat slob. When he got to the front of the line, the doctor gave him a very strange look and Fryze said, 'My family doctor told me that, internally, I'm extremely overweight.'"

"You should do what your brother-in-law did," I said, "have a couple of kids."

"No way," said Leonard. "At least in the army, if you die, you don't have to live with it."

As we approached a corner, another cheer drifted from the stadium. "We go straight," said Leonard.

"I think you're wrong," I said as I began to turn. "We make a left to get back to the car."

"Straight," repeated Leonard, "there's no rush."

"Okay," I agreed as I side-stepped out of my turn and continued walking along next to him.

"I haven't got much use for my brother-in-law," said Leonard. "You know what he said to me? He said, 'The army will do you a lot of good. Having it tough for a change might really shape you up.' The bastard. He should talk. He's never had it tough. He was in the reserves, you know. At least I worked in the store during the summers. You know what he did during the summers when he was in college? He was a lifeguard. Tough job. Trying to convince people not to drown themselves. Now he's working for one of the largest department stores in the country hiring jerks to work for a dollar-fifty a year to sell hosiery. He's certainly had it tough."

"I don't think a lot of people comprehend the reality of the situation, Leonard. You might not come back at all."

"Oh, I'll come back, all right. I can just see my mother getting a letter from the State Department. 'Dear Mrs. Cohen, enclosed in this letter is your son. Please do not sneeze as you will scatter him all over the room.' "

Thinking of a Christmas party I had gone to in freshman year of college. A guy named Tom Ledle had just returned from basic training and was in uniform. I accidentally bumped into him and scuffed his shoes. He really got mad. I apologized but I just couldn't understand why he got so upset over such a small matter. He wasn't drinking or anything like that. A month later, he went over to Vietnam. I heard later that, one afternoon, he and a buddy left camp to take a swim in a nearby lagoon. They never came back.

As Leonard and I walked along, I noticed that the houses were no longer meek, small town bungalows. The occupants of each succeeding block were getting bigger and more impressive.

"Where are we going?" I asked.

"We're walking toward the actual campus," replied Leonard. "It's sad," he said. "One kid at the physical was so retarded that, during a break, he wanted to make a phone call and I had to show him how to use a pay phone. They'll probably make him a general. Another kid, a high school dropout, was telling me he wanted to be a machine gunner. When I asked him why he was enlisting, he told me that the army would teach him a trade. That's a direct quote from a recruiting poster. Some trade. Industry's always looking for qualified machine gunners."

"You think you passed the physical?" I asked.

"Yeah. If I get drafted, I get drafted. But I don't think I'll make a very good soldier. If I was captured by the enemy and they threatened to harm even one hair on my head, I'd give the name of every single American."

"Everyone's name?" I implored.

"I'll skip yours, for a price. Maybe I'll join the Peace Corps."
Sometimes your draft board will defer you for that. At least in the
Peace Corps I'd be doing some good for somebody, I guess. A
guy in my fraternity, who was a year ahead of me in school, did
that. He was sent twelve thousand miles to a village in Thailand
and ended up living across the street from a Chicken Delight."

"Say," I asked, "did Mike Murphy get shipped out yet? You
know, the one who was working at the savings and loan." I had to
be specific. There were at least eight "Mike Murphys" in the
neighborhood.

"Hell, no. After he passed the physical his mother kept telling
all her neighbors, 'My poor Michael is getting drafted while that
Cohen kid plays around in school. Why isn't he being drafted
instead of my poor Michael.' Well, old sob ass Michael went down
to the induction center on the day he was due to get on the bus to
go to basic training and he failed the final physical. You know
what he did then? He called up the savings and loan office and
told them he'd be in there by noon. That's the type of bastard
who should get his head shot off."

"How did he fail the physical?" I asked.

"They discovered a bad case of acne on his back. And for that,
they deferred him."

"I didn't know," I said, "that it was possible to have a terminal
case of acne."

"Sure," replied Leonard. "And in the final stages, they feed
you intravenously with Stridex."

"You realize, Leonard, that if you get drafted, you won't see
any football games on television for two years."

"You're right!" said Leonard, shocked. "Twenty-four months
without an instant replay. Everything else I've thought of, but
never that. I've realized that if I'm drafted, I'll get all my hair
shaved off, put in twenty-hour days, lead the life of a convict and
even stand an excellent chance of getting blown up. But missing
two Super Bowls, that I didn't count on."

"You're a regular Nathan Hale," I said.

"Quite true," agreed Leonard. "I, too, regret that I have one
life to give for my country. God, do I regret it."

Leonard stopped walking and stared across the street at a mammoth, but majestic, old house whose Victorian style betrayed the fact that she had spent her young years in the nineteenth century. On her broad grinning lawn, a few guys were playing touch football with a Frisbee. Two girls had just walked up and were getting into the game. I kept expecting to see Doris Day come out of the front door, engulfed in a hoop dress and seven petticoats, holding her little sister's hand as they walked down the stairs towards the carriage that would take them to the county fair. Across the front of the house hung a large banner with Greek letters.

"My fraternity house," said Leonard. A few minutes of silence passed before I dared to say anything.

"What is this, Leonard? A house or a national shrine?"

"For me, a little of each. See that window on the third floor, the one right above the first 'T' in the banner?"

"Yeah."

"That was my room. I used to see men, especially on football weekends such as this one, standing here on the sidewalk staring up at the building just the way I'm doing now. A few of them were old guys. Some of them weren't so old. Some were like me. I wondered why they felt so compelled to come back to a part of their lives they had already lived. Why couldn't they just enjoy the memories? Why did they have to return and silently sob at the grave? It was over. They had their turn, now it was mine. From that window, it was so obvious those guys just did not belong here."

Driving home, under a cloud clogged sky. No longer buoyed up by sunshine, rows of whitening cornstalks stood like vagrants shivering in the fields. A strong wind cut leaves from their branches. The mild weather of the morning had been devoured by a wave of cold. Birds flew south just ahead of their eviction notice, the first frost of the year. The ground grew hard as it resolved to endure the winter.

FORTY-FOUR

Dear God:

Why do men go to war?

Signed: Conroy

Conroy:

People go to war because they want to be all-powerful. They think that having power makes them god-like. The dopes. I don't have any power at all. None. I don't know how the rumor ever got started that I did.

Because of that rumor, I get blamed for everything. When wars break out, when people get sick and/or die, or when the White Sox are shut out in a three game series, people look up at me and pray, "Oh, forgive us, Lord." For what? A few of the brasher ones observe all the pain in the world and claim it as evidence that I don't exist. And blame me anyway. Can't people understand that some things just happen? There is no reason. Show me, in the contract, where it says that everything has to have a reason.

267

I spend all of my time doing something that people could never begin to do. I create things: the earth, the stars, the universe, a flower, engines. I can take nothing and make it something. People, on the other hand, seem to have a knack for just the opposite.

I make mistakes. I'm the first to admit it. Somewhere along the line, I've made a mistake with you humans. After analyzing the problem, I've discovered that power is a disease that originally ferments in the minds of children because they have nothing better to think about. In the original drawings, I should have moved puberty up to birth.

Signed: God

FORTY-FIVE

A neighborhood woman, who knew I was a friend of Caepan's, stopped by the house on her way home from work to tell me. Only a few minutes earlier, she had seen two attendants carry Cacpan out of the gas station on a stretcher and put him in an ambulance.

"They put the siren on," she said, "so he must have still been alive."

"They always put the siren on," I said, aggravated.

"Oh, do they? I didn't know that."

I didn't either, but that's what I said.

Sitting in the waiting room of the intensive care unit, watching the clock's longer arm stretch for the twelve. On the hour, I would be able to go in and see Caepan for the allotted five minutes.

Friendships formed quickly in that room. An older couple came in and sat down next to a younger woman who was sitting across from me. After the couple talked between themselves for a few minutes, the older woman asked the younger one who it was she was waiting to see in the intensive care unit.

"My son," she replied. "He was in an automobile accident."

"How old is he?" asked the older woman.

"Ten years old."

"That's so young," said the older woman as she sadly shook her head.

"And who are you here for?" asked the younger woman in a voice that reflected more politeness than interest.

The older woman nodded towards her husband. "Bernie's father. We think it's a stroke."

They continued to talk for the next few minutes about where they lived, the prognosis of their respective relatives, what they did for a living. The conversation was interrupted by a doctor who came to the door and asked to speak to the younger woman out in the hall. The friendship was over. She didn't return.

I thought of the first and only time I had to stay overnight in a hospital. I was nine years old. As I lay in my bed at home, waiting to go to sleep, I took a handful of change from a table next to the bed and put it in my mouth, a routine I had done a few times before. What I'd do is jiggle the change in rhythm to a tune that happened to be going through my head. That night, trying to keep up with a fast tune, a nickel slipped past my tongue and lodged in my throat. The old doctor in the emergency room was very understanding. "You're a mental case, kid, you know that? You must think you're a farebox or something."

On my way in to see Caepan, I asked the nurse what had happened to him.

"Are you a relative?" she asked.

"No, I'm a friend."

"Is he married?"

"No."

"Family?"

"None that I know of."

"He had a heart attack," she said brusquely.

"How's he doing?"

"As well as can be expected."

"Is that good or bad?"

"Neither. He's doing as well as can be expected."

"What does that mean?"

"It means," she said in a tone of finality, "that he's doing as well as can be expected."

A heart attack, I thought to myself as I walked towards the intensive care room. What a lousy way for Caepan to die . . . end up in the hospital, I quickly corrected myself. It would have been better if a car had rolled off the rack and had fallen on him or if ten guys had mugged him. But a heart attack was so common, so ordinary. Everyone had heart attacks.

There were five other beds in Caepan's room, all of them occupied. Looking down at Caepan. He appeared to be asleep. The outline of his massive body showed through the contours of the sheet as if the linen was struggling to hold him down. Like all the others, hanging bottles, tubes, and wires shackled Caepan to his bed. Above his bed, a green line repeatedly blimped across a small television monitor.

Although his body lay passively, his head rocked nervously from side to side and his eyes flickered as if he were trying to snap himself awake.

Remembering all the times I had wanted to be sick. When I was a kid, spinning myself around just for the sensation of feeling lousy for a few moments. A cold with good sniffles was worth at least two days home from school and some extra attention. One virus annually struck on the morning of the first game of the World Series. Even as I grew older, I routinely blamed bad days on "not feeling too well."

When I was eleven years old, my body slipped up and I actually got sick during the summer. I only felt lousy for one day. The rest of the time, I was locked up in my room by a low grade temperature. My bedroom was on the second floor. My mother wouldn't allow anyone with a temperature to walk up and down stairs.

I would awaken to waving leaves as they were rustled by the breath of a new summer day. I would watch the grass beneath my window, deep green with dew, lighten and mellow under the growing day's bright haze. And I would be watching in the evening when the lawn grew dim as ribbons of red clouds curtained the sunset.

I prayed for rain, but every day arrived wrapped under a blue sky. I figured that God was just evening up the score. He was probably ticked off with me for staying home so many school days when I wasn't sick.

When other kids went by the house, walking, riding their bikes, talking, I would rush to the window and end up pressing my nose against the screen as my eyes tried to follow them down the street. I would wonder where they were going, what they were talking about, if they knew how lucky they were to be outside, and why me? Why was I stuck inside? And .... I would have to pull back because the screen would begin cutting into my nose.

Finally, one morning, it rained. That day, I had been scheduled to be paroled to the front porch. Instead, I spent most of it sitting in front of the living room window watching a casual summer rain rinse out my world.

That was before I knew Caepan. A few months before his heart attack, on a rainy summer afternoon, I had watched him hoist an engine out of a car and had told him about that summer illness of years ago.

"Two solid weeks of watching days live and die outside my window," I had said. "I think I'd rather be dead. At least then, you don't know what you're missing."

As Caepan worked on the engine, his voice echoed slightly off the overhanging hood. "It was two weeks well spent," said Caepan.

"Why?" I had asked.

"You discovered something that most people never find out. Life's a lousy spectator sport."

No wonder Caepan struggled.

Just then, Caepan's eyes opened and he looked up at me. His words came gruffly as they struggled up through the dry throat.

"Ah, the remains of a child."

FORTY-SIX

How can you show a profit in the fifth grade? On graduation day, Weatherly had told me that he was going to spend half of the rest of his life making money and the other half spending it. But now he was teaching in a West Side grammar school. During the summer after graduation, I had sort of lost contact with Weatherly. Sometimes, you don't want to talk to a person because they seem to be handling life so much better than you. He had always avoided emotional entanglements with women. During his four years at Engrim, the only serious relationship he had developed was with the end bar stool at the Elm Tap, which was a half block away from Engrim. Weatherly and the bar stool were inseparable.

During the first few weeks of the summer, while I was searching for a job, I had talked to Weatherly and he had told me that he had been offered a job that would have him traveling all over the country and, perhaps, even the world.

When I was a kid, every year the family would spend its one-week vacation at some sweaty cabin festering on the edge of a weed-choked lagoon, which the locals, with amazingly straight faces, referred to as a lake. I loved telling my friends that I was going to be "out of town" for a while.

I would have killed for such a job.

During my lunch hours at the Thomas Patterson Public Relations Company, I would often take walks around the downtown area just to get out of the office. One noon hour, I met Adrian Johnson, a girl that both Weatherly and I knew from Engrim. She told me that someone had told her that Weatherly was now teaching grammar school.˙ That night I called him. He was on his way out so he didn't have much time to talk. But he did tell me where his school was located. It was just outside the downtown area. I told Weatherly that I'd stop by and see him during the lunch hour the following day. "My room number is 211," said Weatherly. "It's on the second floor, past the audio-visual room."

"Sounds like a nice school," I said.

"The audio-visual room," said Weatherly, "is where we keep an old record player and the dirty books we confiscate from the students."

"Oh."

The next day, I left for lunch a little early and, because I didn't have much time, took a cab to Weatherly's school. I found it in a neighborhood of four-floor walk-ups, abandoned cars, boarded-up store fronts and vacant lots glittering with bits of broken glass. The municipal green front door was locked. I knocked loudly and then listened to the neighborhood while I waited for an answer: traffic sounds, voices, screen doors slamming on small stores, a dog barking, the clicking on an old lady's shopping cart as the wheels bounced across the creases in the sidewalk. But unlike such sounds that could be heard on my street, these did not make up the notes of a neighborhood melody. Instead, each noise echoed within its own pocket of indifference.

Everything about the neighborhood seemed familiar to me even though I knew I'd never been there before. Then I realized why. It was the same kind of neighborhood I had looked at for four years through the windows of elevated trains.

The front door groaned open. As I went to step inside, a security guard, his hand still on the inside door handle, stepped in front of me. "What do you want?" He spoke with a foreign accent.

"I'm here to see one of your teachers, a Mr. William Weatherly." "Mr." Weatherly would have loved that.

"Is he expecting you?" said the guard as he continued to block my way.

"Yes, he is."

"Follow me," he said as he turned and began climbing a wide-mouthed staircase. When we reached the top, the security guard pointed to a door. "Get a pass from the principal's office and then go up that stairwell directly to your left." I fought the urge to clap my arms to my side and click my heels. He began walking away but suddenly turned around and pointed his finger at me. "Oh, yeah, don't get into any trouble."

"I'll try not to."

He smiled as if I had meant it. " 'Atta' boy."

A few minutes later, walking down the hall, looking for room 211. Students walked by me: Blacks, Spanish kids, White kids, Indians. The ones who walked alone fired sullen glares at me. Those in groups, between their talking and laughter, smiled mockingly. They probably figured I was a teacher. Regardless, I was an adult so I had to be up to no good.

As I passed each classroom, roars of childish noise could be heard. Each roar was followed by a few moments of relative calm before the next wave of shouting and laughter reached its crest and exploded. Until I reached Room 211.

Only a gentle stream of children's chatter flowed through the open doorway. Weatherly was standing outside the door, waiting for me. Arms folded across his chest, he was leaning against the wall with one foot propped up flat against it. He was wearing a dress shirt but it was opened at the neck, the tie was pulled away from it and his sleeves were bunched up to just beyond his elbows. "About time you got here, Conroy, I gotta eat lunch, you know."

I looked at my watch. I was about ten minutes later than I had told him. "Sorry, Weatherly. I had trouble getting past your goon at the front door."

"Oh," said Weatherly, "you mean our Führer?"

"Is that what you call him?"

"Yeah. He was in the German Army during the war. He's always telling me war stories about himself."

"Did he see much action?" I asked.

"He spent the entire war guarding a schoolhouse."

Weatherly pushed himself off the wall and stuck his head into the classroom. "At twelve forty-five, take out your geography books and read chapters three and four."

"This way to the faculty room," Weatherly said to me as he began walking down the hall.

"And to think you could have had a job traveling all over the world," I said to him.

Weatherly began calling off the nationalities of some of the students who were walking by us. "Mexican, Arab, Appalachian, 'hillbilly' in the vernacular, Irish, Polish. Why bother going to see the world if it's willing to come and see you."

A big black kid walked by. "The Near West Side of Chicago," said Weatherly.

"That's not exactly a far away place," I said.

"I've heard kids talk about it," said Weatherly, "and believe me, it's another world altogether."

"So what made you decide to go into teaching?"

"I got another job offer. This one involved traveling too. They were willing to pay all expenses: air fare, housing, rifle . . ."

"The draft," I said.

"The draft," Weatherly echoed. "My draft board canceled my deferment for graduate school but was willing to give me one for teaching."

As we walked past open classroom doors, I occasionally saw a teacher eating lunch at his desk. "Ever do that?" I asked Weatherly.

"Do what?"

"Eat lunch in your classroom."

"Never. Ever have forty-one kids breathing at you at the same time, and all of them with peanut butter on their breath? It's enough to asphyxiate you."

"Gee, it's been years since I've eaten a peanut butter sandwich."

"Don't," said Weatherly. "People our age aren't meant to eat the stuff. Last week, I forgot my lunch and one of my students lent me half of his sandwich. It was like I ate an anvil. It took an entire afternoon of swallowing to get that shit down my throat."

We walked into the faculty room. Weatherly grabbed a brown

bag and two cans of pop out of a small refrigerator. As we sat down at a table, Weatherly slid a can of pop towards me, reached into the brown bag, and did likewise with a sandwich. "Lunch is on me."

"Thanks," I said, "I'll handle the tip."

"Don't thank me," said Weatherly. "Thank Juan Perez."

"Who's he?"

"One of my students. He went home sick this morning and left his sandwich."

"What is it?" I asked. "Peanut butter?"

"Are you serious? You think I'd put a peanut butter sandwich in a bag with my own lunch?"

"How silly of me," I said. Opening the sandwich, I looked under the bread. A brown grainy slab of meat stared back at me. "Now I know why Juan went home sick. He was thinking about his lunch."

"That's Carnitas," said Weatherly. "It's quite good. Try it."

I did. It was. "So how long do you think you'll have to stay in teaching to avoid the draft?" I asked Weatherly.

"I plan on making a career out of it."

"A career! You, who's hated every teacher he's ever had?"

"Maybe that's why," said Weatherly. "I want to see if anybody can do it right."

"Do you enjoy it?"

"Thoroughly. You know, after parents, a teacher's the most important person in a student's life. If a teacher gets up in the morning in a bad mood, when he walks into his classroom, within a few minutes, every student in that room is in a bad mood.

"When you're a teacher," continued Weatherly, "you can make it a real pleasure for them to come to school or you can make it real hell. You can teach them feelings and a sense of purpose that will stay with them the rest of their lives. Or you can give them a lot of busy work and waste your time and theirs. You're the absolute authority in that room. You're God. And I just want to see how good of a god I can be."

"You enjoy it that much?" Weatherly had gone in a completely different direction than the one he had been aiming for in college. Yet he seemed completely happy. How annoying.

"Not all the time," said Weatherly. "There are days when I

have an urge to pass out flu pills. And sometimes, at three o'clock, I have a fear that when the bell rings no one is going to move because they've all died of boredom. That's one commodity I haven't had any of on this job, at least not yet. Pure depression, yes, but boredom, no. One of my kids has cancer. He doesn't have a hell of a lot of time left and he knows it.

"Nice kid. Real pleasant disposition. A few days ago, I caught him with a dirty book. You know what he said to me? 'I just wanted to know what I'd be missing.' " Weatherly crunched his lunch bag between his hands.

"That kind of stuff is hard to take. Very hard to take. Or you have a kid come to class with bruises all over him and you ask him what happened and he tells you he 'fell down the stairs.' You know damn well his parents are beating him up. I have one kid in my room who 'falls down the stairs' at least once a week. I went to my principal and asked him what could be done about it. He said there really wasn't anything I could do and that if I tried I'd be wasting my time."

"So what have you done about it?" I asked.

"Wasting my time. I called all the various city agencies and that was a waste of time. I have a friend who's a cop. Now, whenever this kid comes into class with bruises, I send my cop friend over there to hassle the parents. He tells them the neighbors have complained. I don't want the parents to know that their son's bruises are the source of my cop friend's information. The tactic seems to be doing some good. The kid doesn't seem to be getting beaten up quite as regularly as before."

Weatherly glanced at his watch. "I've got to get back to class."

"Anything else new?" I asked as I got up from the table.

"Getting married during Christmas vacation."

"To who?"

"A girl from my neighborhood. I've known her for years."

"You never mentioned her to me."

"There wasn't anything to mention," said Weatherly. "I knew her from around the neighborhood. We've only gotten serious in the past few months."

"Looking forward to it, huh?" I knew it was a dumb question the moment I said it. At least, a dumb one to ask Weatherly.

Weatherly looked at me strangely as we walked out of the faculty room. "If I wasn't, why would I be doing it?"

I just nodded.

We were standing by the doorway of room 211. Across the hall, a teacher had a student backed up against a wall. Although we couldn't hear what was being said, we could tell by the velocity of the words and by the expression on the student's face that he was being slapped around verbally.

"I've seen that happen a lot," said Weatherly.

"What's that?"

"That kind of stuff. I'm not talking about the tongue-lashing. The kid probably deserves it. That guy's a very fair teacher. But judging from the expression on that kid's face, he probably doesn't understand half of what's being said to him. The problem is if you teach nine year olds long enough, you forget they're nine years old. You start talking to them as if they were the same age as you. Worse yet, you start talking as if you were the same age as them.

"I'm not saying that kids can't be sneaky little bastards, but there are some motivations that are simply beyond them," said Weatherly. "Yesterday, a first-grade boy ran into the girls' washroom. Their teacher, Miss Phillar, who always behaved like a normal human being before, virtually accused the little boy of attempted rape. He probably wanted to see what was in there. Nothing more.

"I found out about it because Miss Phillar wanted to talk to the kid's older brother, who's in my room. I told her she was making too big of a deal out of it. She told me that I was as sick as the first grader was."

"If you don't like such accusations," I said, "you should stay out of the girls' washroom."

"I can't help myself," said Weatherly, as he wrung his hands. "I have a porcelain fetish."

"Ever hit your kids?" I asked.

"No."

"Why not?"

"It's against the law."

"The state says you can."

"It's against my law. If I smack you," said Weatherly, "I could go to jail for assault and battery. Why should it be any different because someone's little. Besides, all you're teaching him is that might makes right. He'll learn that soon enough by himself."

"Someone once said," I began, "that the purpose of education is to teach you how to kick someone's ass around the block. Let me see, now," I said, staring up at the ceiling. "Was that Plato or some raving maniac in the Engrim cafeteria who had been nearly run over by a cab in a pouring rain?"

Weatherly laughed. "But I was right," he said. "Only then I didn't know that the 'someone's ass' you had to learn to kick around the block was your own."

Sitting at my desk that afternoon, trying to figure out how Weatherly had changed so quickly; from a conniving, cynical, sometimes snarling maverick to a candidate for sainthood. Who had waved the magic wand over that nut's head? Of all the people to grow up, Weatherly?

I never saw Weatherly again after that day. Sometimes, you don't want to talk to a person because they seem to be handling life so much better than you.

FORTY-SEVEN

Sitting at my desk, passing papers and going to the washroom to break the monotony. I quickly discovered that the only difference between the Thomas Patterson Public Relations Company and grammar school was that, in grammar school, I got out two hours earlier. And I still had the delusion of playing the outfield.

FORTY-EIGHT

Dear God:

Why do there seem to be so many people around who love to suffer?

Signed: Conroy

Conroy:

Years ago, one of my employees started telling people that the only way they were going to enjoy death was if they didn't enjoy life. Amazingly, they believed him. Ever since, the supply of crosses has never been able to keep up with the demand.

Signed: God

FORTY-NINE

Late Sunday morning. I had just finished dressing to go to the store for some cold tablets. All of Saturday night had been spent sniffling and sneezing. Picking up the phone on the third ring. It was Leonard. He didn't bother returning my hello. "I'm going to kill myself."

"Aim for your ego and you won't miss." While I was mentally congratulating myself for being so witty, Leonard hung up. Immediately, I dialed his number, but there was no answer. Getting scared, I debated whether to call his parents or the police. Deciding to do neither, I grabbed my father's car keys and ran out the front door and down the stairs towards the family car. Thirty minutes and three near accidents later, I pulled up in front of Leonard's apartment building. Jumping up his stairs, three at a time, past the usual revue of winos. Pounding on his door.

"Come in, it's unlocked," Leonard's voice calmly replied.

When I opened the door, I saw Leonard sitting on his mattress, his hands propped up behind his head, staring at a small portable television set that sat cradled between his outstretched legs.

"You asshole," I yelled, "you're supposed to be killing yourself."

"You sound like you've got a hell of a cold," said Leonard. "You ought to see your doctor."

"I've got to get a new one. Our family doctor died about a month ago."

"That's hardly a recommendation of his talents."

I suddenly remember this wasn't exactly a social call. "Fuck you. So why aren't you killing yourself? You jerk."

Leonard pointed to the television set. "I'm waiting for the Cisco Kid to wrap up a case."

I sat down at the card table. "You ever call me like that again and you won't have to kill yourself. I'll do it for you."

"When I got off the phone, I couldn't figure out an easy way to do it." Leonard waved his arm around. "This place isn't exactly a suicider's paradise, you know. The sharpest thing I have in here is a butter knife. I stuck my head in the oven and all I got was an echo. Maybe I could throw myself on my television antenna. I wonder how the A.C. Neilsen people would interpret that."

"Why didn't you go out and get something?" Jesus, was I mad.

"It's raining out," said Leonard. He turned the sound down on the television set to a murmur but continued to stare at the picture. "Last night, I thought I smelled smoke in the apartment. I started to get out of bed but then I figured, why bother? I rolled over and went back to sleep."

"A classic case of 'Fenns disease,' " I said.

Leonard almost smiled. "You're right. You're absolutely right.

"This morning, I really started thinking about things," he said. "Whenever I think about my past, I just get depressed. All those years, I told myself that everything I did and even dreamed about doing was all for the ultimate goal of becoming a doctor. Now I could care less. I'm not any too thrilled about the future, either. Frankly, I just don't know what to do with the rest of my life." Leonard reached out and turned up the level of the sound. Keeping his hand on the dial, he listened to the dialogue for a few moments and then returned the sound to a low indecipherable level. "For twenty-two years I never made a decision. Lately, I've discovered why. I can't. Yesterday, I went into a drugstore to buy some toothpaste. I spent twenty minutes trying to decide whether I should buy the regular or the mint-flavored."

"So which one did you buy, Leonard?"

"Both. Now, I have to decide which one I'm going to use first."
Leonard turned the channel. From the sounds of the new
channel, I presumed he was now watching a football game.

"Who's playing?" I asked.

"Dallas and St. Louis. So now I have a past I hate to look back
on and a future I hate to see coming." He looked around the
apartment. "And this is my present. I think I'm in trouble. You
know, Tim . . ." he said quietly. Leonard rarely referred to me by
name, and when he did, it was always "Conroy." " . . . I don't
think most people need a reason to get up in the morning. They
get up out of force of habit. They get up because the alternative,
being dead, isn't too thrilling either. But I need a reason. Living
just because I happen to be alive isn't enough for me. I know
that's dumb, but that's the way it is."

"Look, Leonard, you've got a lot more going for you than
you're willing to admit. You can do anything you want with your
life. You're a very smart guy. Look at how well you did in
college."

Leonard stood up on his mattress, stepped onto the floor and
began pacing around the room. "Of course, I did well in school. I
had nothing better to do than study. I had no friends, no social
life. All I thought about was getting good grades so I could get
into medical school. A total victim of the Protestant Ethic and I'm
not even Protestant."

"Relax, Leonard," I said, "you're only getting yourself worked
up."

He walked over and stared at the football game on television.
"That's what life's about. Staying within field goal range."
Leonard began pacing around the room even faster than before.

"When I was in college," said Leonard, "one of the few friends
I had, Mike Crowler, was killed in an automobile accident. When
I went to the wake and saw him lying in that casket, the first thing
I thought about was how somebody should notify the school that
he was dead because otherwise he'd get F's in all his courses. I
knew, at the time, it was crazy to think that way but I still had a
compulsion to call the school."

"Do you believe in God?" I asked. A stupid question. The kind
I got enraged at when it was slapped at me.

"Does God believe in me?" countered Leonard.

"If there isn't a God, and you kill yourself, you're all set," I said. "But if there is one, and He doesn't like suiciders, you could be in real trouble. The rumor is it's very difficult to come back."

"Frank Sinatra did."

"Good point."

"I only believe in God when I'm scared or lonely," said Leonard. "So lately I've been believing in Him quite a lot. Actually, I don't think there is a God. Well, there could be. No, I ... I can't even make a decision on that."

"You're your own worst enemy," I said.

"Terrific. Then if I kill myself and there is a God, I can tell Him it was self-defense."

"Your parents are religious, aren't they?" I asked.

"You mean religious in the institutional sense?"

"Yeah."

"That they are," said Leonard, "they still celebrate Passover and Hanukkah in the traditional ways."

"Those are your two major holidays?"

"No," said Leonard, "Good Friday is."

"I suspected as much."

"Actually, we wanted to name it Great Friday, but why get pushy?"

"Hanukkah is about the same time as Christmas, isn't it?" I asked.

"I always thought it was the other way around," said Leonard.

"What does Hanukkah celebrate?"

"In about 165 B.C., we spent three years recapturing our temple from the Hellenistic Syrians. When we make up our minds to foreclose, we foreclose."

"Somebody told me that it lasts eight days."

"Right," agreed Leonard.

"Isn't that rather long?"

"If your won and lost record was the same as ours, you'd celebrate victories for eight days, too."

"What about Passover?"

"Oh, on Passover, we celebrate the freeing of the Israelites from the Egyptians. On Passover night, we ask four traditional questions. 'Why is this night different from all others?' 'Why is Uncle Maury a Gonniff?' And the third question is, 'Why can't we remember the fourth question?' "

"What's a 'gonniff?' "

"Forget it," said Leonard.

I got out of the chair. "I've got to get some cold tablets, Leonard. You want to go to the store with me?"

"Sure." He opened the closet door and slipped on his loafers. "By the way, I've been drafted."

"Aha! So that's why you're in such a carefree mood."

"That's not why," said Leonard. "You really piss me off, Conroy. You haven't been listening to a thing I've been saying."

"I've been listening."

"The draft's just one more thing I have to make a decision about, that's all."

"As I see it," I commented, "your choices are rather limited. You either report for induction, go to jail, or head for Canada."

Leonard tossed open the door. "I wonder if suicide's deferable."

Driving through a tinkering rain, looking for a drugstore. "I really envy you," said Leonard.

"What the hell are you talking about?"

"You've got a job you like, a girl you like. You've even got that vague little dream of becoming a writer. Something to aim at but not die over. You've got it made."

"Bullshit," I said. "How do you know how much I like my job? Or my girl, for that matter?"

He acted as if he didn't hear me. "We'd all like to be immortal in one way or another. Maybe, some day, you'll write a book and become famous. You can use me as one of the characters. A book. Now, that's real immortality."

"Yeah, real immortality," I replied. "Existing on some three-by-five-inch index card in a library, waiting for some pimply-faced kid to look me up so he can fake a footnote."

I thought, people don't forget a home run with two men on. That's what they don't forget.

We drove around for about twenty minutes but couldn't find

anything open. "Why don't you drop me off at my apartment," said Leonard, "and you can go back to the neighborhood and get something at my father's place."

"Okay." I was really beginning to feel lousy.

A few minutes later, as we drove up to Leonard's building, I asked him, "You sure you're not going to kill yourself today?"

"Yeah. I'd never do a thing like that on a rainy day. It's too depressing."

"That makes a lot of sense."

"It does," said Leonard reassuringly. "Today, I've come to realize that the only time I could kill myself is if I was in a completely blah mood. When I feel real good, of course, I have no desire to do myself in. This morning, I discovered that when I'm really depressed I don't have the guts to." He was halfway out of the car now. "And I guess when I'm in a blah mood, I don't have the energy to. Unfortunately, for me, it seems that I'm suicide-proof. Looks like I'm going to be around for a while, doesn't it?"

"It certainly does," I replied.

Leonard got out of the car and turned to slam the door. "Remember the Agnostic's Prayer. May I die in a moment of indifference."

Watching Leonard walking up the stairs of his building and disappearing behind the brown door. He never looked back.

Wondering if I'd ever see him alive again. I wouldn't.

Driving home. Just what I needed, an afternoon of listening to myself.

FIFTY

Saturday night. Driving through a subdivision, trying to follow the street as it curved through a maze of houses. The past twenty minutes had been spent searching for Sarah's girl friend's house. Sarah had met her on a part-time job a few years earlier.

"I think I make a left here," I said as I angled the car around a corner. Sarah, sitting on the other side of the car, didn't bother commenting. She continued to stare impassively out her window.

I drove about half a block before I realized that the street didn't go through.

"Just what I needed, a goddamn dead end."

"It's not a dead end," said Sarah without looking at me. "It's called a cul de sac."

"In my neighborhood, it's called a dead end."

"Did it ever occur to you that everything in your neighborhood is called a dead end?"

At least she was beginning to talk to me. Sarah had not said a word since I had picked her up earlier in the evening. She often used silence to bandage a hurt. Sarcasm was the scab. When that was used, the wound was beginning to heal. The previous Sunday had been Valentine's Day. I hadn't sent her a card. When I apologized to her the next day, Sarah said it was okay but I could tell that she had been very disappointed. So was I. With me. I hadn't wanted to send one.

Turning the wheels sharply, hearing the guts of the car moan with strain as I swerved it around and out of the cul de sac. A few minutes later, we found the right address. Walking up to the front porch in silence and ringing the doorbell.

Sarah and Bonnie Ragolis had met while working part-time jobs at Castle's Discount Store. At the time, both were freshmen in college. One afternoon, Bonnie sold young Edward Lutts a half gallon of mouthwash. His mother believed it was more economical to buy in volume. At the time, Bonnie had a sense of humor. She told him that he certainly must have a large medicine cabinet at home. He didn't get the joke. She had to explain it to him.

Bonnie Ragolis never went back to school. She married Edward Lutts. They both got screwed. She had a baby and he became an insurance man. They bought a house in the suburbs. I had only seen a picture of her that Sarah had once shown me. The woman who answered the door was at least thirty pounds heavier than the girl in the picture. Good Old Eddie. Still dealing in volume.

The earlier part of the evening wasn't too bad. Their kid, Rodney, who was about fifteen months old, crawled around the living room and did a brilliant job of entertaining us. I don't remember exactly what he did but he was very cute. All babies are. I've heard people say that some babies are pretty and some are ugly. That's ridiculous. They're all ugly. They're bowlegged, wobbly, fat, and their heads are too big for their bodies. That's why they make such great clowns. But babies also happen to be big hunks of fresh new life, new hope, which is why they're all so cute, so beautiful.

Rodney crawled over to a corner of the couch, grabbed the top of a cushion and pulled himself up to a standing position. He then slowly started to waddle towards his father who was sitting in a chair a few feet away from him.

Thinking of Leonard's grandmother. She was now in a nursing home and very much like Rodney. She couldn't feed herself or control her bowels. She was unable to talk and could no longer walk. No hope. Not very cute.

Rodney stood by the side of his father's chair as his father told us why the family car was leaking transmission fluid. Rodney began losing his balance. He was just about to topple over. Edward Lutts didn't bother to interrupt his own conversation or even look in his son's direction as he reached out and, with perfect father reflexes, grabbed his son by the front of his shirt and planted him back on his feet.

After she put Rodney to bed, Bonnie Lutts talked twenty minutes about how Rodney had begun crawling three weeks ahead of schedule.

"If he's that good at it," I said, "he'll certainly do well in life."

No one thought it was funny. But at least Bonnie quit talking about it.

The rest of the evening's conversation sounded like a dying man with a harmonica in his mouth. At times, as I heard various voices mope through the conversation, I wasn't sure whether I was talking or listening. Repeatedly, Sarah would ask Bonnie a question and her husband would answer for her. Bonnie constantly referred to herself as "we." Someone turned the television on. Slowly, it extinguished the conversation.

Towards the end of the evening, Edward Lutts tried to sell me insurance. "If nothing else, you should at least have life insurance."

That's not the right name for it, I thought to myself. It's really death insurance. You buy that stuff to enhance your death, not your life.

"No," I said, "I really don't think I need life insurance."

"You're not buying it for you," he countered. "At the time of your death, you have to think of others."

"You can rest assured," I said, "that I'll be in sheer panic and thinking only of myself."

"What if your loved ones don't have enough money to bury you?"

They can lay me on the ground, I thought to myself, marry me, and wait until I "settle down." I thought it, but I didn't have the nerve to say it.

"I can give my body to science," I replied. "My mother always did want me to go to medical school."

He laughed a little. It was a real laugh, not a phony chuckle. He had thrown a few of those around during the night. There was definitely a difference. "That's very funny," he said.

"Thank you." That's when you know it was not. "You're a very original guy," he added.

"Thank you," I muttered again. Original, my ass. Vintage Henny Youngman, 1934. I presumed that he was being nice to me just because he wanted to sell me insurance. Very dumb reasoning, I admit. How do you know if a nice guy decides he wants to sell insurance or some guy decides to sell insurance and so becomes nice? Sarah started talking so it gave me a little time to think about it. I decided there weren't that many nice people around to begin with so I'd better not start questioning the motives of the ones who were.

He repeated the joke to Bonnie. She didn't get it. He had to explain it to her.

Sitting in front of Sarah's house, listening to the engine idle. Neither of us had spoken on the way home. I hadn't even suggested that we park. Never borrow what you're not sure you want to pay back. Throughout the evening, even though we had both done our share of talking, we had not spoken any of our words directly to each other. Now, Sarah sat by her door, staring straight ahead.

I turned on the radio and punched the station to Franklyn MacCormack's show. His rich voice oozed, like maple syrup, through the words of a lover's poem as big band music played softly in the background. I glanced over at Sarah. Her face still bore an expression of stoic indifference.

I imagined a young couple cuddled in a car, listening to the feelings of Franklyn and each other. Saying silly things in silly ways. Realizing that the young couple was Sarah and me not so long ago. I began feeling awkward as I sat there listening to Franklyn, as if I were eavesdropping on a private conversation. Snapping off the radio. When you were high on a relationship, Franklyn was delicious. But that night, being disgustingly sober, I was beginning to find Franklyn mildly asinine.

"Well," I said, "the Lutts certainly are an entertaining couple."

"Too bad they can't say the same thing about us," said Sarah.

"They could if they lied like I'm doing."

"If you didn't want to go, you should have told me," said Sarah. "I would have gone by myself."

"Their family crest must be a yawn."

For the first time that evening, Sarah turned and talked directly at me. "You think you're so superior, so much better than everyone else, so . . ."

"I never said that. I just found tonight depressing, that's all."

"Why?"

"I don't know. I mean, here's Bonnie, the same age as you, and already she's locked into that suburban motherhood scene. There might as well be bars on the window."

"Oh, so now you're against motherhood, too? What's wrong with being a mother?"

"Nothing," I replied. "Mothers are great. Everybody should have one. You know what's really neat about mothers? Sometimes, you'll read in the paper about some guy who's murdered ten people, kidnapped a few kids, and who's burned down four city blocks and when the reporters interview his mother, she says, 'Sammy's really a good boy.' No matter how rotten you are, you can always depend on good old Mom to stick by you. That's nice. Pathetic, but nice. Hitler's mother probably felt that the Allies were picking on her kid."

"Do you think that Bonnie ought to go out and get a job?" asked Sarah.

"No, no. If she wants to get a job, she ought to. But she certainly has the right to stay home and raise her own kid. I imagine that it has its dull moments but what doesn't? Raising a child has to be one of the most creative things a person can do . . ."

"If she went out and got a job, you'd find that depressing, too."

"Yeah, yeah, I guess I would. I don't know. It's probably just the mood I'm in tonight."

"I don't know what your problem is, Tim," said Sarah softly, "I really don't."

"An insurance man," I said, "Jesus Christ, who grows up

dreaming of being an insurance man?"

Sarah simultaneously reached for her purse and the car door. As she pushed open the door, she looked back at me, "At least he grew up."

FIFTY-ONE

Dear God:

Some days, I look forward to having kids sometime during my life. It seems like a terrific idea. But on other days, it seems like a rotten one. No matter which way I go, it seems that I'm going to regret, to a certain degree, that I didn't go the other way. Why are all children non-refundable?

Signed: Conroy

Conroy:

It's not enough that millions of you nag me every day about your problems, now you want me to take back your toys when you get tired of playing with them. So I should have all the headaches?

I should have never given you humans a free will. How did I know you were going to use it to divide your minds? Unfortunately, as you may have already noticed, you can't do the same with your bodies. All of this leads to one of the nastiest diseases I've seen among you people: regret. I've yet to see someone afflicted with it truly enjoy life.

297

Concerning your dilemma with kids, however, I'm working on a solution: inflatable children. On those days when you feel like taking some naive little creature to the zoo, or you feel like having an audience for your life, you just inflate as many kids as you like.

For those other times, when you don't feel like getting up in the middle of the night, when you want to eat a quiet dinner, or you're fed up with going to parent-teacher conferences, you just let the air out of them.

Inflatable children, however, are a new product and are not yet out on the market. Some parents don't realize this. They think they already have them.

Signed: God

FIFTY-TWO

Watching the evening news. The announcer stated that American casualties in Vietnam for the past week were 212. Two hundred and thirteen, I thought to myself. Only an hour earlier, Leonard had called from Canada.

FIFTY-THREE

Leafing through a graduate school catalog as I sat at my desk at the Thomas Patterson Public Relations Company. Mr. Rebe came up from behind me and put his hand on my shoulder. "Ah, Kendall University, excellent school. That's only four blocks from here, you know."

"Yes, sir, I know that."

"You're going to take the business program at night, I presume."

"Yes, sir."

Mr. Rebe began walking away from my desk, but he continued to direct his words at me. "Very good, very good. Always glad to see a young man looking to get ahead."

I would have been very surprised if Mr. Rebe had observed the truth of the situation. "Very good, very good. Always glad to see a young man looking for a place to hide." Graduate school. A few more years of getting ready, for what I didn't know. Two more years to wonder what I'd be when I grew up.

I had already arranged to get off early that afternoon to register for classes. Otherwise, I never would have gotten out of the office.

At least four secretaries were home sick. Executives could be away from the office for weeks and they'd hardly be missed. But if even one key secretary stayed home, the executives would be asking each other where the washrooms were.

At Kendall University later that afternoon, after filling out the usual application forms, I was told that people whose names began with *C* wouldn't be able to actually register for classes until four-thirty, an hour away. The guy behind me in line, Jim Consellca, introduced himself and suggested that the two of us go across the street to a restaurant and have something to eat.

Walking over to the restaurant with Jim Consellca, I felt terrific. After two hours of filling out forms and rereading parts of the catalog a few more times, I was convinced that I had finally found the niche. My life now had a purpose. Unlike earlier that afternoon, I no longer felt like I was using graduate school for a hideout. I was going to get a master's degree in business. Maybe I'd become a tycoon. I wondered how much it would cost to buy a box seat right behind home plate.

I stopped at a newsstand, bought a newspaper and, for the first time in my life, didn't turn immediately to the sports page. Instead, I opened the newspaper to the business section. The stock market report made no sense to me. I turned to the sports section. The White Sox had just traded away their three best players. That made sense. I decided to keep the newspaper. Maybe the stock market would make more sense to me after I registered for classes.

Consellca was a salesman of some kind and not a very good one. For the first half of the conversation, he talked about himself instead of me. He was Catholic, had spent years in a seminary, but had eventually left and was now getting married within a few months.

"Those years I spent in the seminary were among the happiest of my life," he said. "The Most Holy Reverend Conlin, who was in charge of the seminary, was the greatest man I ever knew."

Trying to conceal my rage, I nodded blandly in his direction as I took savage bites out of my hamburger. Even if he was a great guy, how could any man have the nerve to call himself "The Most Holy Reverend?" Not surprising, I thought to myself, that "The Most Holy Reverend" worked for the same company that told everyone the meek would inherit the earth. What a joke. Caepan had once told me that the only way the meek would inherit the earth was if they were willing to kick ass for it.

I thought of "The Most Holy Reverend" I had known as a kid, the pastor of my parish. One afternoon, during Lent, I had served Benediction for him and had messed up something. As punishment, he told me to wear my cassock and walk up and down behind the church until he came out of the rectory and told me to stop.

I walked up and down for five hours. I probably would have still been there except that another parish priest came by and asked me what I was doing. When I told him, he informed me that the pastor had walked into the rectory and dropped dead. I always had a suspicion that, on that afternoon, the monsignor knew he was going to die, but as a parting shot he wanted to make a jerk out of me.

"When I was a kid," said Jim Consellca, "all I dreamed about was being a missionary, traveling to far parts of the earth to help people. I subscribed to all the missionary magazines and whenever a missionary came to my parish, I'd follow him constantly and try to memorize everything he said. In fourth grade, I even took out a subscription to *National Geographic* so I'd know more about the various regions of the world that I might be sent to."

"What about the breasts?" I asked.

"What breasts?"

"The ones in *National Geographic*."

"I never noticed them," said Jim Consellca.

"Now that's what I call true missionary zeal."

"That's all I thought about when I was a kid," said Jim Consellca as he repeatedly shoved a forked French fry across his nearly empty plate.

"So what's stopping you now?" I asked him.

"I told you. I'm getting married. Besides, that was just a child's dream." He laughed. "Marriage changes all of that. We all grow up, you know."

"Take her with you. You could join the Peace Corps or something like that. Or you two could go by yourselves. You don't have to be in an organization to help people."

"No, she wants to have kids in the next few years and . . ."

"So? Missionaries have kids, you know." How the hell did I know? But I was sure they did.

"No," he repeated, "we wouldn't have the money and . . ."

"Why would you need money?" I asked. "You don't have to go to a distant country to be a missionary. There are plenty of poor areas in this country. There are ghettos only a few blocks from here that are a missionary's paradise."

"No, no, no," he said, irritated. "It wouldn't be practical. In today's world, with the cost of everything, it wouldn't be practical."

He was becoming as irrational as I suspected I was. We sat there for a few moments in awkward silence.

It was time to go back across the street to Kendall University and register for classes. As I got up to leave, Jim Consellca told me to go ahead without him because he had to make a phone call. Obviously, he was as anxious to get away from me as I was from him.

I signed up for two courses. I don't even remember what they were. One of them, however, was having its first class meeting that night at eight o'clock. Again, I had time to kill, about three hours. I decided to walk a few blocks to a park that ran alongside the lake.

Walking. Thinking of Jim Consellca and his lost childhood dream. Thinking of me and mine. Had I been a crazy kid or was I now a crazy adult? Wondering, if I was a kid again, would I be disappointed in the man, me.

The edge of the beach that ran out from under the lake was stitched to the land by a wide row of large, jagged rocks. I sat atop one of them and watched as a man slowly shuffled across the sand. The weight of a blue windbreaker sagged against his shoulders. White socks on but he was too late for the hop. His gray streaked crewcut balanced neatly on his head.

Almost suppertime. Rush hour traffic, helicopter reports, don't take Route 45. Everyone had a place to be. He walked on.

A cabin cruiser sailed gallantly by and people waved at him from the deck. He put his head down and pretended not to see. A few seconds later, he looked up and there was nothing left of the boat except a bobbling dot on the distant water. He walked on through the late autumn afternoon that had grown woozy with fog as the sun died an early death in the west.

Wondering where I'd be ten years from now. Eating leftovers and hearing how Jimmy got into a fight after school. Telling her how things were at the office today, how I nearly landed that big deal, and how I deserve more pay. Watching, not listening, to the ten o'clock news. During commercials, giving my views. God, is it eleven o'clock already? I've got to get up early, big meeting tomorrow.

It was nearly eight o'clock. I started walking back towards the downtown area and that class at Kendall University. Sarah had gotten a new part-time job as a receptionist at a medical center. She didn't quit until nine o'clock. I thought about calling her, but decided not to. A few blocks away from the school, I approached the marquee of a pornographic theatre. "HEAVEN'S IN HAZEL."

A choice. Watching a few boobs or listening to one.

Moving down the darkened aisle and making sure the seat was clean before I plopped it down. Dirty movies are so sexless. Within the first ten minutes of that one, everything that could possibly happen to the human anatomy had already been done at least three times. Looking around at the other isolated shadows sitting in the theater. Imagining all of us together on the stage on graduation day, everyone wearing raincoats.

FIFTY-FOUR

Dear God:

Tonight, I met a guy who dreamed of growing up to be a missionary, of helping people, all kinds of people. The coffin who now lives around him says that, in today's world, such ideas are impractical.

Signed: Conroy

Conroy:

A few years ago, could it be two thousand already? A man lived who many people claimed was my son. Whether he was or not isn't important. He made the world look bad so they killed him. Above his head, they put a scroll with four letters on it, "INRI." The true translation is, "Below hangs an impractical man."

Signed: God

FIFTY-FIVE

Five o'clock, quitting time at the Thomas Patterson Public Relations Company. Riding down fourteen floors, shuffling through the crowded lobby and out into the sunshine.

My desk, like those of the other peasants, was in a large open area that was surrounded by the private offices of the big shots. All the windows were in these private offices.

As I walked towards the bus stop, I got very depressed just thinking about it; a totally weatherless existence. If it snowed up to the thirteenth floor, I wouldn't even know about it if it melted before five o'clock.

From what I'd heard around the office, if I worked hard, cut a few throats and got lucky, I might have my own window in seven or eight years. Seven or eight years, just to get what my mother had in every room of the house.

Enjoying a mild afternoon and a mild disposition as I walked to Cohen's store to get a loaf of bread. Mr. and Mrs. Cromwell, who lived midway down the block, were getting into their car. The Cromwells were the kind of people who were constantly taking the frosting off life. I felt like ruining their day so I greeted them.

"Hello, Mr. Cromwell."

"Hello, Tim." He said the words dutifully but didn't bother looking in my direction.

Mrs. Cromwell was already in the car so I stooped down low for her to see me.

"Good afternoon, Mrs. Cromwell."

"Hello, Tim." The words fell like prunes from her mouth.

Enough's enough, I figured. Why torture them by trying to start a conversation.

As I continued walking down the street, I thought about the Cromwells. I had known them literally all of my life, but I had never seen them smile or frown. No one ever came to visit them. They had no friends. And as far as I knew, they had no enemies. Nothing.

Dear God:

Is there a pulse within my neighbors, the Cromwells?

Signed: Conroy

Conroy:

Before I started creating things that reproduced themselves, I wish someone had explained to me the difference between geometric and arithmetic progression. It's getting to be a madhouse around here.

As you know, I put spirits into all sorts of things: spiders, trees, goldfish, bacteria, humans. Of course, the human spirit is my pièce de résistance, whatever that means.

The human spirit is like a delicate prism of glass. It takes the light of life and reflects it into all sorts of emotional shades. Occasionally, I put the wrong spirit into the wrong physical crate. Organization is not my strong suit. I've just checked out the Cromwells and that's exactly what happened. According to my records, they should be frogs.

No wonder they're always so sullen. Since they believe they're human beings, they can't understand why, like other humans, their lives aren't a rainbow of emotional colors such as happiness, serenity, excitement, sadness, you name it. I've given them human lives, but their spirits are simply incapable of handling them.

Unfortunately, somewhere in the world, there happen to be two frogs who have an intense desire to go to Acapulco this winter.

Signed: God

FIFTY-SIX

She's not home."

"Do you know what time she will be, Mrs. Faber?"

"She shouldn't be long. She's just taking a walk."

"Around the neighborhood?"

"Yes. I think she mentioned something about going to the park."

"Thanks, Mrs. Faber. Will you tell her I called?"

"I will do that, Tim."

I was calling from downtown and it was almost quitting time. I had a car with me so I was only about fifteen minutes away from Sarah's house.

When I spotted her, Sarah was walking across the middle of the park's open area, on the part that was diamond seven's deep center field.

Running across the grass to catch up with her, listening to my mind announce another great play. "Conroy is running hard. He may have a play on it. He dives and . . . he's got it. Conroy hangs onto the ball. What a fantastic catch! What an absolutely fantastic catch!"

As I came running up behind her, Sarah turned around to see who it was. I slowed to a walk while I was still a few feet away.

"What are you doing here?" she asked.

Talking between gasps of breath, I said, "I called and your mother said you were taking a walk so I figured you might be over here." I didn't bother mentioning that her mother had virtually told me where Sarah would be. I wanted to give Sarah the impression that I knew her so well that, with just the slightest clue, I'd immediately be able to find her.

She wasn't impressed. Turning around, she continued to walk before I had completely caught up with her.

"I'm sorry I didn't call you yesterday like I said I would, but a friend of mine had a heart attack." A lie, sort of. Caepan had had the heart attack over three weeks ago.

"Anyone I know?" She sounded concerned.

"No, he's an older friend of mine."

"I'll pray for him."

"Terrific."

"Excuse me," said Sarah in an exaggerated tone of voice, "I didn't mean to insult your intelligence."

"You're not insulting my intelligence. I'm sorry I made the remark. Okay, you'll pray for him. Thanks."

We continued walking through the park. Our parking lot was now a few dozen feet adjacent to us. I thought of the night that snowbanks hid us from the world. Neither of us looked in its direction, but I knew it was there.

"I admire your faith, Sarah, I really do." I did.

"Are you sure 'faith's' the word you're looking for, and not 'stupidity' or something?"

"I'm serious. You have a real sense of who you are and where you're going and why. I envy that kind of security. I really do. Maybe you're right in your beliefs. Maybe not. But if they help you get through life, what's the difference?"

"Sometimes," said Sarah, "I do wonder if I'm not just fooling myself. Maybe I am just naive and optimistic."

"Don't tell me that. I don't want to hear it." There's nothing more depressing than to have someone who you're absolutely sure of start being unsure of themselves.

"Where are we walking to?" I asked.

"*I'm* walking home."

"What would you like to do, Saturday night? Presuming you'd like to go out with me," I quickly added.

"I'm busy."

"Another guy again?"

"What I'm doing Saturday night has nothing to do with us," said Sarah.

"Nothing to do with us? As I recall, once upon a time, you and I talked about getting married."

"That's right," she said, "we *talked* about it."

We were now out of the park, walking the streets of her neighborhood. I stepped in front of Sarah and faced her so that she'd have to look at me.

"You know I love you."

"Lately," said Sarah, "you've only told me you love me when you begin to worry that I don't love you."

"I love you."

Sarah stepped around me and began walking again. I turned around and walked beside her.

"I know you love me," said Sarah, "but I also know you're afraid of me."

"What do you mean?"

"You're afraid of me. You're afraid of marriage. You're afraid of growing up."

"That's not true," I said. Every word of it was true.

"You don't know what you want out of life. You've told me that many times. And I don't think you know yourself if you want me in your life. I'm not blaming you. That's just the way it is."

"The important thing is, I love you and, I presume, you love me."

Sarah looked at me, the sternness still in her face, "You know I do."

A good sign. "We don't have to decide right now whether or not we're going to get married."

"In a relationship," said Sarah, her voice straining to remain patient, "there comes a time when it develops into something more or disintegrates into nothing. We're at that point. We're past that point. Besides, it's already been decided."

"I don't follow you."

"I'm moving to Colorado next week," said Sarah. "I have one more year of schooling left and I've decided to finish it there."

"Why?"

"I have friends out there."

"A friend?" I asked.

"All right, a friend."

"Who?"

"You don't know him. He's a young dentist who took over for one of the doctors in my building for a few months. He's from Colorado and he's moving back there. His father's also a dentist and they're opening a new medical building and they've offered me a very good job. But he's not the complete reason."

I didn't bother asking what the "complete reason" was. I was already getting my fill of it.

"What day are you leaving?" I asked.

"Sunday night. I want to spend Saturday night with my family. I won't be home for four or five months."

"Marry me."

"No," she said, "You don't want to and I don't want to."

"Marry me and we'll spend our honeymoon in Tenseed, Wyoming."

She smiled. "I'd forgotten all about that."

"See, I don't forget anything."

Sarah started crying. That kind of stuff kills me. It totally kills me. "What are you crying about?"

She tried stopping, but she only succeeded in turning her soft sobs into gulping tears. "We used to act so silly. What happened?"

"Silly. I think we're acting pretty silly right now, don't you? Marry me."

"No."

"Don't you think we're right for one another?" I asked.

"We are, that's what's so sad. The time isn't."

"Marry me," I demanded.

"No, you don't know what you want. You love me, but you don't know if you want me. You're confused."

"I'm not confused. Marry me."

"Really, Tim, what do you want?"

"You."

"I mean, out of life?"

"I don't know."

"When you were a little boy, didn't you want to be anything in particular?"

"I wanted to be a baseball player."

"Seriously."

"I am serious. I wanted to be a baseball player more than anything in the world. Drifting back across the outfield grass to take in a fly ball. Feeling it smack into my glove. Hitting home runs. Feeling my spikes dig into the dirt as I rounded third base, coming home with the winning run. God, how I wanted to be a baseball player."

"Why didn't you?"

"Are you kidding?" I said, disgusted with her obvious ignorance of the facts of sports. We were standing in front of Sarah's house now. "I have no talent. None ... none. It took me years to develop enough coordination just to wash my hands. What did you dream about when you were young?"

"I dreamed that I'd grow up and meet someone like you."

FIFTY-SEVEN

Going up to see Caepan. He was in a private room now. Standing in the elevator, holding a paperback that I had been reading on the bus. One finger ran along the ridge of the number twenty-six plastic card stuck between the pages.

After Caepan went into the hospital, I had locked up his gas station and had taken Butcher home. My father made me keep him in the garage. Butcher wasn't too crazy about the idea. If it had been a few years earlier, Butcher would have ripped off one of my legs. Despite his advanced years, he had still made a few feeble snaps at my leg, but I could tell that his vicious enthusiasm, along with his strength, had evaporated with age. Earlier this morning, when I went to the garage to check on him, Butcher was dead.

Caepan was sitting up in bed and just looking out the window when I walked into the room.

Standing just inside the doorway. "How are you feeling this afternoon?"

"Okay. Yourself?"

"Okay. I've got some bad news for you, Caepan."

"Butcher died, huh?"

"How did you know?"

Caepan shoved both fists into the bed. "Goddamn . . .Goddamn . . .Goddamn."

"I'm sorry, Caepan, really I am. I took care of him just the way you told me to. As soon as I found him this morning, even though I thought he was already dead, I took him right over to the vet's."

"He's there now?"

"Yeah. Is there anything you want me to do?"

"No. Let the vet handle it. There's a regular procedure, I'm sure. There is for everything else in this world."

Caepan snapped on the television, bracketed high on the wall, with his remote control. A quiz show popped on. "Goddamn," Caepan muttered.

In a louder voice, Caepan asked, "How far do you live from the station?" He already knew that.

"Two, two and a half blocks."

"The walk probably killed him," said Caepan. "Butcher didn't move more than twenty feet at a time in the past five years."

"If you had told me that, Caepan, I would have driven over there and picked him up." A lie. My father would have killed me if I had put that old greasy dog in the family car. But if Caepan had asked me to do it, I would have told him I did.

"Don't worry about it. It happened, that's all."

"I'm sorry, Caepan, I really am. He was just like one of the family, wasn't he?"

Caepan punched up the sound on the television as he said it but I still heard him. "He was the family." He glanced over at me. I was still standing just inside the door. I hadn't moved since I had entered the room.

"Did he try to bite you?" Caepan asked.

"Constantly."

Caepan smiled. "Good."

I walked completely into the room and sat down on the chair next to his bed. Time to change the subject. I was getting tired of talking about Butcher and I could tell that Caepan's eyes were wandering around his mind gathering material for Butcher's eulogy. I didn't feel like listening to a string of stories about how

Butcher had chewed up various people at the gas station. Besides, I had probably heard all of them already unless Caepan was planning on making up some new ones. For such an occasion, I was sure he would. I had much more important things to talk about.

"I'm thinking of getting married."

"This show stinks."

"Did you hear me, Caepan?"

"I heard you. You're thinking of getting married." Caepan emphasized the word "thinking" in such a way as to let me know that he thought it was just the bait at the end of the line designed to hook a discussion on it.

"No, Caepan, I'm seriously considering it. I'm very close to deciding that I'm going to get married." I didn't bother mentioning the fact that Sarah had, by now, refused to marry me at least a couple of hundred times.

"That's like being close to jumping off a building," said Caepan. "Until you take the final step, it's only a nice view."

"Fuck you, if you don't want to take me seriously." He was really beginning to get on my nerves.

Caepan pointed to the paperback that I was holding.

"What's that stuck in the book?" he asked.

"It's a plastic card I use to keep my place."

"Is it a good book?"

"Yeah."

"Is it a great book?" Caepan asked.

"Well, I don't know about that . . ."

"Say it is."

"Yeah, it's a great book." I could tell that Caepan wanted to play one of his little games. Why fight it?

"Is it the best book you've ever read?"

"Yeah," I said emphatically.

"Do you plan on reading it again?"

"I wouldn't mind."

"Is that the only book you ever want to read?"

"Of course not."

"Then why get married?" asked Caepan.

I had to go over the conversation for a moment to realize the analogy he had thrown at me. "You can't compare women and books."

"I just did."

"It doesn't make sense."

"Maybe not," replied Caepan nonchalantly.

"There are an awful lot of people getting married," I said. "They must have some pretty good reasons."

"Some people are like dogs, most dogs, that is. They chase whatever runs away from them. Others get married so there's someone there to hear the door when they open it at night."

Caepan hadn't even bothered to ask me who I was marrying. Not that the name would have meant anything to him. Like my relationship with Caepan, what went on between Sarah and me wasn't fodder for other conversations. Still, I was surprised that Caepan hadn't yet asked anything about the girl I was planning on marrying.

"Don't you even want to know her name?" I asked.

"Her name's Sally Kramer."

"Who's Sally Kramer?"

"Almost every man I've ever known," said Caepan, "has had at least a shadow of a Sally Kramer somewhere in his life."

"Who's Sally Kramer?" I repeated.

Caepan swung his feet out from beneath the sheets and sat on the edge of the bed, facing me. He was wearing one of those hospital gowns. His hair was thinner and the creases in his face were deeper than when he had first entered the hospital. The massive chest seemed smaller. The legs, hanging limply like strands of seaweed, looked like they would crumble if Caepan forced them to go to the floor to support his weight.

"Sally Kramer was a girl I knew so very well when I was about your age, maybe a little younger. I guess I'm far enough away from all that now to say, out loud, I loved her. We had some great times together. Great times. She wanted to get married. I didn't. By then, the relationship was cooling down. At least on my part. We slowly drifted apart. For a while, I debated about calling her up and trying to get back together again but I could never quite make up my mind.

"One day, somebody told me that she was seriously dating

some other guy. That night, I called her, but it was too late. She was already engaged. I tried to get her back, but it was no go. She married him. Since then, every day, every couple of days at least, I think about her."

"That's too bad, Caepan."

"Oh, I don't know. Sometimes, I wonder if I often think about the times I knew her because I loved her that much or because I love the young me."

"Too bad you didn't marry her."

"I'm not so sure. In a lot of ways, I got the best part of Sally Kramer. I have memories of a terrific romance and of a beautiful, luscious woman who was everything a man could want. The sucker who married her got stuck with a wife. You don't marry your Sally Kramer, you think about her for twenty years."

The nurse walked in with Caepan's dinner. He automatically swung his feet back onto the bed and under the sheets.

Looking out Caepan's window I was surprised to see that it was already dark. I got out of my chair and out of the nurse's way. Caepan was pushing a button that raised his bed even higher into a sitting position as the nurse slid his tray, with his dinner on it, up to his chest.

"I've got to get going," I said. "I'll be up in another couple of days."

"Okay," said Caepan as he surveyed the food in front of him.

"Man," I kidded, "dinner in bed. That's really living."

"This is existing," said Caepan passively, "not living, existing."

Walking out of the hospital. God is dead.

FIFTY-EIGHT

Calling Sarah on Saturday night, hoping she'd agree to see me on Sunday. I called on Saturday afternoon with the same request. And on Saturday morning. And four times on Friday.

Her mother answered the phone. "I'm sorry, Tim, she's not here."

Sarah had lied to me. She was out with the bastard.

"Well ... uh, ... thanks Mrs. Faber, I ... ,"

"She did tell me that if you called to give you a message."

"Oh, did she?"

"She said that if she didn't get a chance to talk to you before she left the city that she'd be home on the 26th."

"Of what?" I asked.

Mrs. Faber hesitated. "That's ... funny, her note doesn't say ..."

The possibility suddenly hit me. I got so excited that I hung up the phone without even saying good-bye.

Afraid I might be wrong, I kept the radio off the entire time I was driving there. I didn't want to hear any songs. If I was wrong, for the rest of my life, every time I'd hear one of those songs again, it would flip on the switch and replay the night in my mind. Just what I needed, a life of dodging jukeboxes, radios, and shopping centers with piped in music.

Going down side streets to avoid a few traffic signals. A sprinkling rain continued to fall, causing the asphalt to glisten under the gaze of the street lights. The air was warm and wet with the scent of autumn.

Driving the car slowly, close to the curb, staring at store fronts. The Mod Dress Shop. Atlas Appliances. Stopping in front of a store with a low green awning hanging over its face. Ribbons of rain fell from the awning. I looked but could see no one. The doorway stood at least a dozen feet back from the sidewalk, shouldered by two showcase windows, their nakedness exposed by rows of empty racks.

I opened the car door, stood up on the floor and stared over the car roof into the darkness of the doorway. There was someone there. My God, I thought to myself, someone could have killed her standing there.

I stopped running when I was within a few feet of Sarah. If I had gotten any closer, I wouldn't have been able to see all of her.

"Is this the way to Tenseed, Wyoming?"

FIFTY-NINE

Alone.

Wondering whatever became of Mr. Kearney's niece. Wondering, even more so, what became of Uncle Elmer.

"Who's in there?"

Light from the lobby of Collier's Funeral Home pours through the crack in the opening door of Parlor Number Three.

"It's me, Mr. Collier, Tim Conroy. I called you last Tuesday afternoon."

He swings open both doors. "What are you doing in here all alone?" There is suspicion in his voice.

Very annoying. What can I steal? A few folding chairs? "Waiting for you, Mr. Collier. We have an appointment for eight o'clock." I pretend to look at my watch. "It's about that now."

"Well, what can I do for you?"

"I'd like to make arrangements for a funeral."

SIXTY

Caepan never returned to his gas station. Today, it stands boarded up.

The Prudential Building is no longer Chicago's tallest. At least four other buildings look down on it. For the past two years, a sign has stood in front of the elevator that formerly ran straight to the top: "Observation Deck—Temporarily Closed."

People still drive the Dan Ryan Expressway and students continue to ride the trains to Engrim University. Weatherly is still teaching and people still stand in line on Saturday mornings at Betterman's Bakery.

But a watch shop is now within the walls that once held Cohen's Food Store. Two blocks away is a supermarket where you cannot walk in and simply buy a bottle of pop and a banana. The store doesn't have any cold pop and bananas are sold by the bunch, not one at a time. Checkers check, they don't discuss how things are going.

Franklyn MacCormack went the way of the big bands.

There is a vast empty field where Riverview once stood. Though the one-legged duck doesn't bother anymore, summers still come to

Chicago. But they're sadder ones, now that those acres of Riverview have been replaced by the world's largest graveyard of laughter.

Across the alley from where Conroy lived, there is the backside of a Methodist church and nothing more.

Somewhere there is a woman on the worn edge of youth who knows that, someday, she'll be there when the Kolton Building is torn down. And she'll remember.

Timothy Conroy died at the age of twenty-six from cancer. At the time of his death, according to Caepan, he had lived four years.

Dr. Leonard Cohen